LUNARNI[illegible]E
PES[illegible]A

CW01582512

Book 1

CAGED WITH THE SPRITS

by
Sally-Anne and Jovan Matthews

MAPLE
PUBLISHERS

Lunarnise Pestra – Caged With The Sprits Book 1

Author: Sally-Anne and Jovan Matthews

Copyright © Sally-Anne and Jovan Matthews (2023)

The right of Sally-Anne and Jovan Matthews to be identified as author of this work has been asserted by the author in accordance with section 77 and 78 of the Copyright, Designs and Patents Act 1988.

First Published in 2024

ISBN 978-1-83538-323-0 (Paperback)
978-1-83538-324-7 (E-Book)

Book layout by:
White Magic Studios
www.whitemagicstudios.co.uk

Published by:
Maple Publishers
Fairbourne Drive, Atterbury,
Milton Keynes,
MK10 9RG, UK
www.maplepublishers.com

A CIP catalogue record for this title is available from the British Library.

All rights reserved. No part of this book may be reproduced or translated by any form or by any means, electronic or mechanical, including photocopying, recording or by any information storage and retrieval system without written permission from the author.

The views expressed in this work are solely those of the author and do not necessarily reflect the views of the publisher, and the publisher hereby disclaims any responsibility for them.

CONTENTS

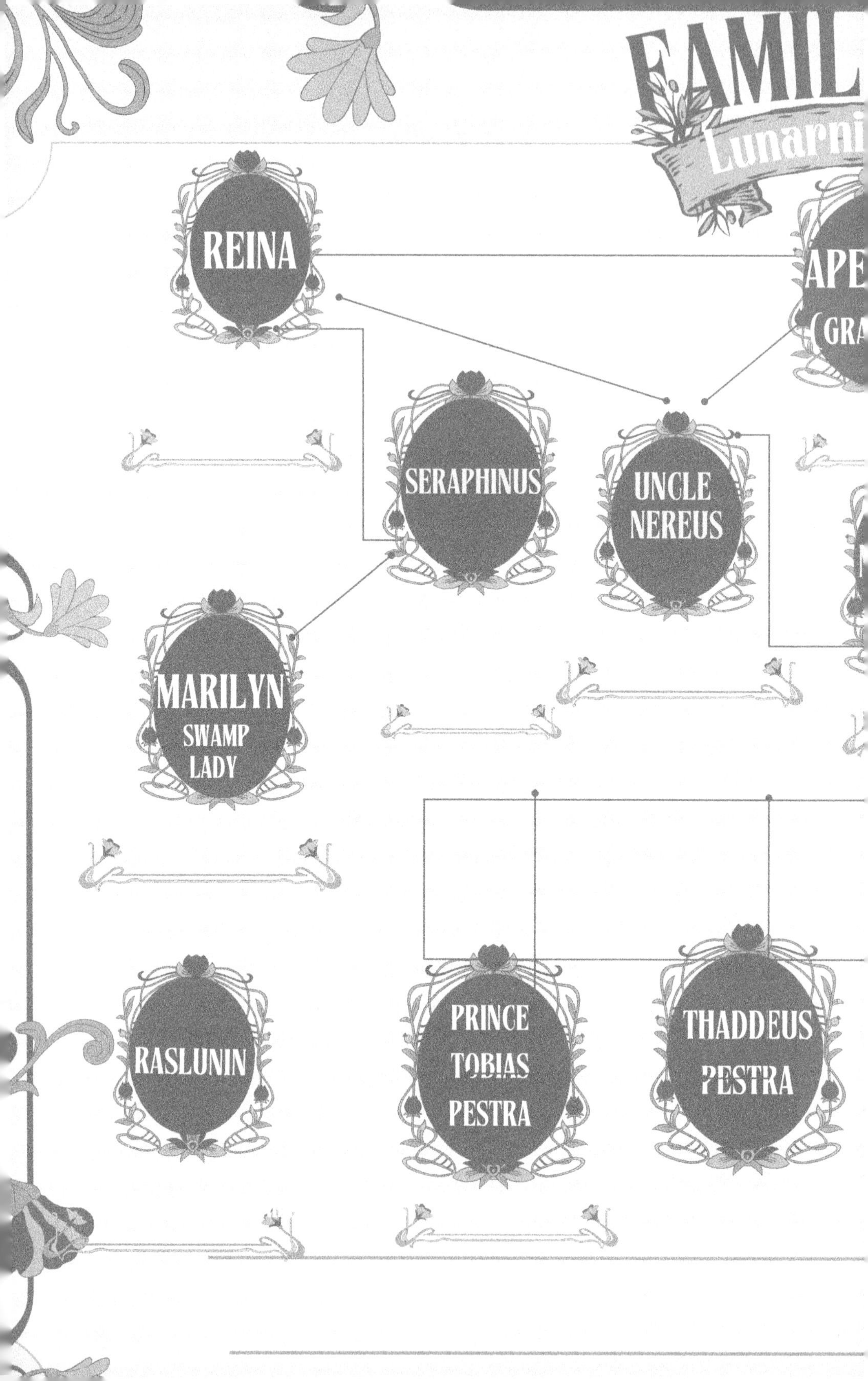
FAMIL
Lunarni
REINA
APE
(GRA
SERAPHINUS
UNCLE NEREUS
MARILYN SWAMP LADY
RASLUNIN
PRINCE TOBIAS PESTRA
THADDEUS PESTRA

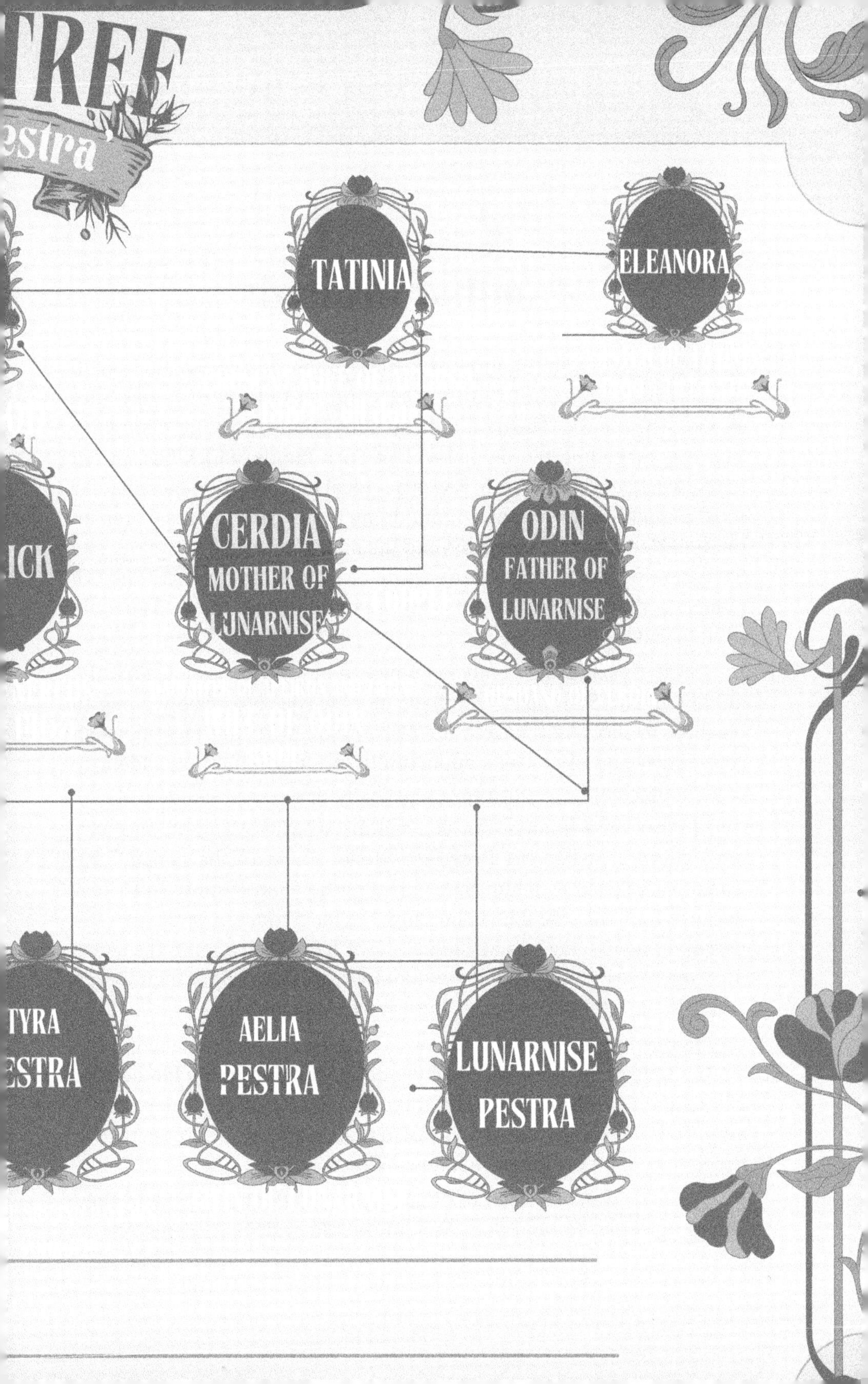
TREE
estra
TATINIA
ELEANORA
ICK
CERDIA MOTHER OF LUNARNISE
ODIN FATHER OF LUNARNISE
TYRA
ESTRA
AELIA PESTRA
LUNARNISE PESTRA

Chapter 1

Familiar Ground!

It was a vivid and luminous day back in the beginning, along with the frosty breeze of the flowing wind and clear azure sky that looks to die for. This is a fantasy story about a young pixie fairy that was picked up by the malevolent Sprit family, which has settled in the world of Tiger Wrath. It was a typical and common morning for most people, as they went around doing their usual chores. Later, an unidentified object from far beyond the mist would make a sound. The Sprit family liked taking out the waste or picking up the dirt from the plates, so they could hang out with the middle-class nerds, as people used to call them in those days.

Well, this specific family is known to be very critical against the unknown. For example, if you have money, you're probably going to be their friend. They have a lot in common with the local devilish community and use it as an opportunity to capture their own identity to go higher until one day they got a challenge.

("Hold on a minute, can you tell me what is going on and why am I talking?" asked the Designer. "Hello, you with the pencil?" the Narrator took a look at him and said his name, "Sam, I know you." "Just because I am the one who is holding the pencil doesn't make you the person to advise me." As he looked down from the room in the skies, "And one more thing, how do you know who I am?" Sam then took a closer look, "Oh hello, Jake," so both started to catch up.)

Just as there was a sudden wave of dark mist that formed in the air, the wife of Sir John, Marilyn, would be cooking in the kitchen for her husband whilst he would be at the local bar trying to gain people's attention. He would take them back to their marriage bedroom to give them a good gift or that's what he would think.

Well, he was married but didn't seem to care about his wife, they would fight like cat and dog. Back in the olden days it seemed to be fine. (Narrator, "Is that what I'm supposed to say?") Sir John Sprit says to his wife, "Why are you not doing as I ask of you?" as he stood up tall holding a pipe. "What would that be?" his wife Marilyn replies, repulsively.

If you wonder why she is mentioning about the cooking and cleaning process, well this is happening all around us, and it's what the Sprit family does a lot.

One day Sir John wasn't happy about his wife Marilyn, as he spoke of their relationship. "You're not doing enough for me." Marilyn, "What do you mean I'm not doing nothing for you, I thought it was a civil marriage that we share? Anyway, Sir John I don't feel too good at the moment," (Narrator, "Oh no Marilyn, don't tell him that you are pregnant.") As she stood still in the kitchen for a moment. She was wearing a long, flowery dress that went past her knees so her husband wouldn't accuse her of anything.

Just as the Narrator thought Sir John shouldn't hear what he says, he heard it clearly.

(Narrator, "Oh no, he didn't, is this aloud?) Sir John then turned round from the other room and there was anger in his eyes as he said something under his breath. "Hold on, is it true, again? Say, is it true?" asks Sir John. Marilyn smiles, with happiness in her eyes. (Narrator says, "Unlucky for her, what a butcher! He can hear me too.") "What?" then Sir John punches Marilyn in the face and she falls from the top to bottom of the stairs. A big bruise to her head as she looks pale and frazzled. There are stars flying above her. (Narrator, "Oh no, that's not good, I didn't see that coming. What have I done?") While Marilyn was struggling with pain she is left to suffer from the injuries after tumbling down step by step. Sir John looked down and just smiled after opening the front door to walk away. (Narrator, "Could you imagine him getting up to go out? He has got a nerve. Coward!")

Marilyn says to herself, 'Now what should I do? He's evil to me like he understands my thoughts and feelings but uses it against me.' (Narrator interrupts, telling her, "You should defend yourself and use his power against him.") Marilyn asks, "How do you expect me to do that? He is too powerful. After all he has a way with words so nobody will notice anything." (Narrator, "Well now, now, don't get yourself in a pickle, do you want my pencil to help with the needs of your situation at the time?" Just then the Designer draws a pencil and gives it to Marilyn. Narrator says, "Whatever you do, keep it in a safe place. This should protect you from harm but use it wisely.")

Lunarnise is an unusual girl for many people that don't know her. The family she grew in, did not like anyone, let alone her. Lunarnise, always having a smile, is a pixie fairy with wings, and will yet discover a third eye after growing a little. She has long sage hair, brown eyes, strongly built body. Ever since the family had noticed her on the porch of their house the Sprit family has always been invading her private affairs, though growing up all she ever wanted was to be accepted in their family. She hoped to get appreciated amongst all around her, but little did she know that evil was coming from far and wide.

One day an explosion drifted through the skies and Lunarnise was holding out for her life. Looking around, she says nothing out of fear. (The Narrator cries out, "Wait a minute you seemed to have forgotten that this story will become a movie." Designer, "No way, I'm drawing you people from above. Though it will be interesting to keep an eye on." He then mutters, "Jake, Jake. Where has that boy gone?" They both speak quietly hoping no one would hear them.)

Lunarnise, "I can hear you from down here, you know," even as she continues being scared. Just as she is only starting to know the feet of her ancestors, from out of the blue there were footsteps coming towards her. Don't forget Lunarnise is a young fairy, yet to learn how to talk, walk and how to defend herself. Lunarnise growing up was just one big joke, but her neighbours around had her back and she began the journey in the worst places possible. Well, she had a passion for music and liked to pray in the local Church of Saints. O Destiny, little did she know that it changed the way how the Sprits handled things. Just then out of nowhere Lunarnise gets out a pencil and draws a round circle. To her surprise a small creature comes out. (Designer, "Hey you down there, only I draw the next scenes but that's unusual! Where did she get the pencil from? Oh, I get it, she secretly took it from Marilyn. I have to keep an eye on that." Narrator, "Okay tell me what just happened there." As both Narrator and the Designer of the book were talking, the creature decided to say something.) Creature, "Oh no, oh no, oh no." (Narrator, "I beg your pardon. The small creature that has been summoned up by Lunarnise was cute, orange like a Pokémon ball, when afraid just like a little baby teddy bear.") "Oh, yay oh," Lunarnise to the creature, "I'm going to call you S.J." She spins the creature around, it flops to the ground. Lunarnise, "Oh no," rushes over, but S.J. gets up. Lunarnise, worrying, "You are cute, but I'll have to hide you from the rest of the family."

(Narrator, "Well, seems like you got your hands full, it's like teaching your child, ha ha ha." Designer, "Oh, come on now Jake, oh just to let you know quick, Sir John is looking angry and he is about." Narrator, "Was that you Designer?") Lunarnise, "Wait, anybody there? What can I do for you?" A voice from out of nowhere responds, "You need to be patient, my child." Lunarnise, "Who's that? Are you for real or am I hallucinating?" Lunarnise was sitting on her bed, nervously.

Just then there was a loud noise from outside the house. Was it a shotgun fire or something else, that's not recognisable. "I wonder what is happening out there?" cried Lunarnise. Enters Roland, "Someone is shouting." S.J. "Yes indeed." Back up in the room where Lunarnise is, S.J. was lying on the bottom of her bed. Suddenly stumbles over to her and they still have to learn who Roland is. He is the world's keeper. S.J. "I'm sure in time all those people past, present and future will get to know his talents." He is now with Lunarnise, muttering, "Nem en, nem em." Lunarnise says, "Dooo you want to be friends?" S.J. looks at her up and down, Roland's eyes are sparkling. (Narrator, "Are you sure you understand what he said?") Lunarnise, "Kind of," as she looks to where he was standing. (Narrator, "Hold on, how do we know if he's good or bad?") Lunarnise, "In this world we have to try and understand and trust others." (Did the narrator understand what was going on?)

"Lun," says S.J. (Narrator, "Aww, look our little friend's starting to grow with words. Lunarnise, did you hear that?") "Oh yeah, I did. It was lovely, S.J." "Love. Lun loves." (Narrator, "See guys, what I mean." Lunarnise has tears rolling down her cheeks. Designer, "Lunarnise, are you crying? Here's a tissue, girl." He passes a box to her but he couldn't reach so he drew it next to her.)

Again, they heard noises from outside and it sounded like someone was trying to sing and just then knocked over the bin. Dogs begin barking and cats meowing loudly. Lunarnise became a nervous wreck, "Oh no, he's back from the locals." (Narrator, "Who's back?") Lunarnise paced around her bed several times, panicking. "Oh, you don't know Sir John? Please everybody, please hide. He'll come to my room to shout at me, he's drunk." As she looked around the others had already hidden in different places of the room. Lunarnise, said under her breath, "My goodness, that was quick."

Back outside, Sir John was on his way to the house stumbling over everything in his path. Sir John, "Look at me I am gorgeous, the beautiful woman followed me but now I'm lonely, where'd she go? (Narrator, "He isn't speaking about another woman is he, what about his wife?" Designer, "Which one you talking about?") By then Lunarnise is looking scared, "What do I do?" (Narrator, "Please calm down. Sir John is making his way into the house and up the stairs, we're all here for you.") She panics and hides under her quilt. (Narrator, "We've got your back.") She is walking backwards and forwards in her room. Again, others are waiting patiently to get him away from poor Lunarnise. Who will help her out when she's under attack from that horrible situation she has been through the last few years? (Narrator, "Wait I've got a plan for Lunarnise to disappear from here but I need a clear path to throw it when he's standing in front of her." Just then there were footsteps approaching towards her. Narrator, "Quick, girl, do you know what you're going to do? I got it.") Sir John shouted out, "Lunarnise where are you, are you in your room? Come out just a moment." "I need to get something on." Sir John was tapping on her door from the outside. Lunarnise, "I said, I will be with you in a minute," as she gathers up the courage to say this to him.

As conversations were going on, it had become night time with the wind gushing heavily, blowing the trees, outside hissing sounds start up. (Narrator, "Hold on a moment, you with the pencil. Are you supposed to hold the pencil and draw something?" Designer, "Oh yeah, that's right, oops, that is why they say they need a good Narrator for this book." You can hear him laughing from above. Narrator, "Now you're just showing off here or you're making me blush.") Lunarnise, "Guys, guys, he is about to enter the room and explode, oh I see what you're doing." (Both, "What?" as they look from above and behind the wardrobe. Jake, "He's just behind the door, are you ready?" Sir John, "Well, I'm going to enter the room whether you're going to let me or not." Lunarnise, "Oh no, don't please, I'm nearly there. Two seconds, okay? I'm decent." Little known to the others, she has a plan of her own after being encouraged. Sir John smashed the door down and entered, it fell to the ground with a loud noise and dust flew everywhere.

(Narrator, "Oh no! what's that sound?") Lunarnise takes out the emergency pencil and draws. "I think I'm going to draw a Thanatos." (Designer, "Well you do know that what you're about to draw is the world's keeper and protector?") As it was not long ago when Lunarnise was able to walk, talk, run and learn she looked so much confused when drawing a creature like a dragon. (Narrator then gave his verdict on what name to give him. "I shall call you, Roland Bankelete, the world's protector and you shall have the powers of a hundred men.") Lunarnise looked and smiled, "This shall be fun, even though I drew him he's known to all." When the drawing was done, he was just a baby standing, shaking and scared, in the bedroom with Lunarnise. She stretched her arms out to pick Roland up. He gave such a cry, looking at her, and then curled up on her lap as he was small. As all this was happening Sir John was in a trance like he was frozen. From what, no one has any clue what went on behind them.

(Narrator, "It's believed he tried to kill you, Lunarnise, but to your good fortune, someone or something came to your rescue. All these years I have learned never to trust nobody and nobody is your friend.") Lunarnise, "Jake, thank you so much I shall never forget you, join us on an adventure."

(Narrator, "Umm, it seems to me that you have lost the ability to trust people just because of your past experience.") Jake looked up straight at Lunarnise into her eyes and he felt warmth of a new family, then nodded his head to agree. (Narrator, "Nobody should ever need to go through this in life. When you see something like that you have to report it to the authorities. Let them deal with it, you can even overcome any fortress that could be holding you back, give your prayers to the Lord and he will guide you through. Designer tells Narrator to be careful as Sir John is starting to wake up. Narrator, "Right away! I was playing with Roland." "Oh okay, I suppose you could say it.")

Suddenly, a goblin appeared from nowhere. It was only a few hours away from dawn. He came rolling into the room and raced towards Lunarnise, and spoke in such a good manner to everyone in the room that they looked up to hear him. "Well," as he was coughing, "I am delighted to be here as you called me, your honour."

They all looked shocked. "Well, I do apologise for being rude, let me introduce myself, my name is Tobias Pestra. I'll tell you a little secret not even my own sister knows. Well, your honour please explain to these lovely people." (Narrator, "Well, first of all stop calling me 'your honour'. It all began when he was young, long time ago when Tobias was just a kid. You see his family didn't want to know him because of the horrible situation that was going on, one bad marriage after another. I was able to get him out of there and protect him." "So, you see as we are explaining how we came about all of this, it's slowly getting light," the Designer explained. Narrator, "Oh no, you don't, that is my role in this story. I am very much delighted to explore this and you have taken it away from me. What are you going to do now?" Just then the Narrator brought down his arm to point at the camera, "I'm sure I'm pointing up at the skies." Designer, "Who's pointing at me? I find it to be rude and disrespectful." He turned his pencil upside down to then use his rubber and rubbed out the Narrator's arm. Narrator, "Oh, so you want to play that game, do you?" Then gets his pencil from his pocket and draws his arm back.)

Tobias, "Oh, come on, stop playing around and focus on the book. Well, for your own information I think you both would be required, don't you agree?" As he says that, as he is walking towards Lunarnise, "She is my sister." To everyone's surprise, "That is something we have learnt today." Lunarnise looks shocked when she hears the news. Tobias, "Oh come on, so you didn't know it was me, pickles." Lunarnise, "Oh but somehow something seems wrong, you look different." "It's because I have picked up powers on the way from a wise old man." Everyone smiled, to Tobias's surprise. Right there in front of them Sir John had completely unfrozen before their eyes, "Don't worry I will deal with it," replied Tobias. He spun around and they both vanished into thin air. At this minute there was a gush of silence and dust through the room and everything cleared. (Designer, "Oh, here we go what has happened?" Narrator, "Well, this is a first. I've never seen this before, what just came across. Just as both Narrator and Designer were talking about the goblin Lunarnise had left the room. Narrator, "Well, do you know that she doesn't know Tobias is her brother?" as they both look at one another. "How do we know it's real?" Designer listens and tries to tell him that she is returning to the room, by coughing a few times. Narrator, "Oh, I can assure you he wouldn't do anything wrong, I know.") Lunarnise says, "Who's my brother? Do I have a brother? How come? I was an only child." She looks confused as she walks through the door.

Chapter 2

Welcome to the secrets of the Unknown!

The sun is about to shine for the first time in the morning, it's nice and warm outside as it is inside. But some things don't always seem to be what they are, there's always unexpected surprises that come our way. Lunarnise, "I've never had a roomie before." (Narrator, "Why haven't you told me until now?"), as Lunarnise started to look frazzled, then stood up and gazed out of the window.

As they were talking there's soft drums being played, and suddenly, there is singing from far away.

"Look at me now, Lunarnise, please let us share our gift to you as it will only get bigger," Roland runs around the house in excitement. "Oh, look at you now, my baby you're growing up so fast." As she was saying that Roland growled so loud that there was a sound no one could hear but Tobias. ("As were talking," says Narrator, "I know somebody heard that disruption. Well, Lunarnise, look out for your brother, he will hear what you can't." Designer tells her, "You will have met him and you are not going to understand but shall meet several times throughout your journey. Try to pay attention to the small details, you'll only then understand what is being told to you by these wise words.") Lunarnise, "Umm, I wonder what all this means I hope and pray to the Lord that he will give me strength and wisdom." (Narrator, "You'll only then become great by doing these 3 things - address your fears, embrace challenges, and use your strengths. Learn how to use them all together and collect knowledge.")

Roland shouts out, "Lunarnise, where are you hiding? Come, I have something for you." As he said this someone else appears in the room down stairs with a magical voice as soft as the wind. Lunarnise, "Who is this, may I ask?" To herself, 'I wonder what he wants.' As she stood firm, Boy from the bubble answered, "Oh, don't mind me, I just got here and I am not sure where I am. I think I'm lost. My name is Kulumbush." Lunarnise, "Well Kulumbush, first of all nice to meet you, you're not dangerous, are you?" Lunarnise starts walking down the stairs. (Narrator, "Oh my, look at you, girl, you are all grown up. Remember the three things.")

Kulumbush, "By the way, have you seen my cat? She has been missing since yesterday, could you please help me find her!" (Narrator, interrupting, "Isn't he lovely? He has such good manners." As he was talking Designer was drawing a pipe. "A pipe?" Narrator says, "Why would anyone want that?" "Well I guess I could give him a flat cap, lol.") Kulumbush, "Kilimanjaro I can see, I can taste the smell of fresh air beneath the clouds of the sun." (Narrator, "What does that mean? Never heard of it before. Now, where has Lunarnise gone?") Roland comes running to them. "Oh no, that's it." Stops. "No, no, no don't say it at all." He slobbers all over each of them and then smirks when he sees everybody.

(Designer, "Oh, come on boy you got to be kidding me, even from up here I'm soaking wet." A stick was drawn.) Lunarnise decided to make an amazing appearance from what it looked like an unknown place. Narrator shouting out from nowhere. Lunarnise was playing with Roland on the floor when he jumped up at such high speed as he was shocked by an unknown object. Everyone started to laugh and talk amongst themselves about what's happening. As everyone else was laughing and talking, Lunarnise spotted the stick on the ground, reached down and picked it up. I wonder what this is! She looks around but no one seems to have noticed. 'Umm, this may come in handy later, I'm going to put it in my backpack.' (Narrator seems to have seen what she was doing but not quite sure if it should be told to others, but then decided to keep quiet.) Tobias who just jumped on to the top of the stairs was about to walk through the door when he saw Lunarnise in front of him.

As a big gush of wind flew by, Tobias was calling for her attention when she was spun around, and she disappeared in daylight. ("Okay," cries out Narrator, "can someone please tell me what is going on here?" Designer, "Umm, seriously, you got to be kidding me, I guess we are needed for this job.") Tobias, "And what would that be? That's my sister, she's been taken with them." ("Oh, you haven't," replies Narrator, "you have not told her then.") Tobias, "You see man, it's like this." (Narrator, "Guys please, we have to go now.") Tobias, "Oh yeah, Fronk, let's do this." (Narrator, Fronk is Tobias bestie.)

In a moment, all of the crew are ready for this adventure to save their beloved Lunarise who has been blown away in the gust to an unknown world. (Designer, "Ha, Jake, did you just make that up?") Tobias, "Let's go before it gets dark, this way through the back of the house, nobody will suspect us there."

(Narrator, "Oh, looks like you have been here before, Tobias," as he begins to walk out of the house.) Tobias, "Well, you wouldn't know where you have been if you're going from place to place." He manages to close the door behind them. "I hope that we don't have to come here again, after all it looks familiar." (Designer, "Okay but we need to look at this, there's two paths - one is a chain of events and the other is an adventure awaiting us, what shall it be?" as he stood at the back of the house through the secret gate and speaks boldly with the weather forecast as calm as the sea.)

Kulumbush, "Has anyone seen Jake?" when he tries to call out to his cat. (Narrator, "Who in the world is Jake? And by the way it's a nice name," as he stands in front of the many paths, shouting out to Kulumbush.) Roland, "Let me tell you something about Jake, he is a puppy that is so squidgy and just round like a ball." They heard playing and bouncing coming out of one of the paths. Its hairs were brown with the mist in the skies, as the sky filled up quickly. Tobias cried out, "Look, you see what can happen, instead of talking let's be moving towards the light through the tunnel."

(Narrator, "Right, you heard the young boy go, go, go.") Jake, "Yep, nep nee poo." Tobias, "Okay, who's talking?" when he noticed a fluffy ball rolling around them. Kulumbush, "I think that was Jake," remembering that it's his cat that he had lost. (Narrator, "Okay here we go everyone inside now.") Tobias, "Kulumbush, what's wrong why are you shaking, and frightened?" when he came over towards him before entering the building Narrator had mentioned. But Kulumbush only shook his head as it was clear he had no idea. There was a passion which came over him to kick out and punch. As he was kicking, he began screaming out loud. Tobias, "Does anyone know what is happening with Kulumbush?"

(Designer, looking on helplessly, "I believe that there could have been a meltdown. I have unfortunately seen this kind of thing before, many years back." There was a sudden jingle, a touch, and a square box appeared on the floor from nowhere.) Tobias, "Narrator did you just say something? Was this you up there, sir?"

Now everyone seemed to be getting hungry and tired. Tobias, "Okay you're giving me the creeps now bro." (Narrator, "Well that wasn't me, man, you got to believe me.") Tobias, "I think Narrator could be right, my friends." After Kulumbush kicked out he began smirking as he was looking outside from inside. There was a sudden silence within the dark scary path of the unknown.

As it was peaceful Narrator took on his role and picked up the strain. Tobias leant forward to grab the box, held it in his arms, and danced around with everyone smiling. There was a song being sung in the far distance,

"Here we are, walking through the Unknown Garden,

we going to as we wanna walk with you with all around!

With temptation as we go at the side of the house!

And leave all the worries behind! Lunarnise gets sucked in a hole, animals shouting, "Oh Jesus." So were heading up the road to see the fight and win. I love this adventure I wish it could be over!"

It was sung by all until they started to laugh then the more Narrator wanted to say something, the louder it got. Narrator, "You are going to find your sister, Tobias, it's just a matter of time." A voice calls out, but no one dares to respond. "Oh well," it speaks anyway, "there's a web in the corner and use the skills you all have been given by somebody wise enough to give you this advice." Just then there is lost communication between Narrator and Tobias. Everyone, "Tobias, Tobias, where are you?" Kulumbush, "I think we have lost him." As he says to all that can hear, they go deeper and deeper into the hole big enough for a rabbit to get through. Out of the blue Tobias shouts out from ahead, "Did you call for me? Well I am here." He is up in front of everyone as he thinks it's his job to protect all from danger.

Before their very eyes a handsome young man who appeared tall, slim and brown eyed fighter dressed in a brown warrior suit with pink, purple and blue hair tied at the back.

(Narrator, "I think that is his true form, I think I'll try and keep my eyes on you, Tobias.") As they were going down deeper Tobias lit up the lamp. A magical voice, "Remember each and everyone's strengths," shouts out. "There is only one thing to do - practise upholding your gifts." Then it fades away. Roland appeared, "Rest assured, my young, I the Lord keeper will be attending you throughout your journey as there's dangers ahead. Your first quest is finding the fun pipe from the unexpected, trust in no one but believe in one another's capabilities." As they were continuing their mighty quest an old man in a long cloak and a feather hat appeared. "My name is Stimpultonnes, but you may call me Harold Impul Sprintuls," he said, "I also will be protecting what I can, as I Stimpultonnes, a friendly wizard, have many abilities so if you require anything don't hesitate to find me."

To their surprise a great white cat appears out of thin air, with a big sack on his back, that may hold up to four people. Stimpultonnes, "Tobias, take three but pick wisely, only the right people will succeed." "Pick me, pick me, here we know you can do it, look at the bright side. What can go wrong?" the persons assembled cry. Tobias, "Right here goes nothing, then I suppose first person chosen is Fronk, second person Kulumbush. Harold, "Just a moment," as he interrupts, "give them a test to find the remaining party that will go with you on this adventure."

Tobias notices that there's extra people that start to prove themselves. "What do I do, they all have proven to be good, is it possible to take all six? Narrator Jake, Helena, Poppals you are also in, congratulations." (Narrator, "I have one question, do I need to fight as well?") Then they all get inside of the ride. "Well, that will all depend on how Jake shall stand out in the coming events, prove us proud boy, as long as you don't fall over." ("Right, it looks like Designer may have to pop down to give you some moral support." Designer, "Okay just a moment I'm about hopping through, and I will be at your service.") Just as he was talking, he was holding Jake's head to climb down. "Oops just a bit to the left, Jake, that's it, nearly there." (Narrator, "That will be fine," while the Designer finished climbing down. Designer, "Hi, pleased to make your acquaintance, my name is Sam. Yes, I know who you are, Jake.") Just for you readers to understand we have borrowed the name from the new fluffy friend for the Narrator. As both Jake and Sam were talking, there was action happening at the other side where Lunarnise was captured, with her pet. It wasn't a pleasant sight as there were village people running around.

They had pets whose backs they would ride upon. A lot of shouting was going on. Lunarnise was in a cage within the walls of the big old shoe warehouse. Lunarnise, tears streaming down her face, "What is going on out there?" She sounded sad and hopeless, then wondered, 'Is this my life?' It was a cloudy and dark place with each being the other's enemy, people that used wild dogs as ways of travelling and speaking in a different language. Everyone here speaks *Frahini.* Unknown person, "Nat Not Ah Am Me Orm," meaning we don't accept visitors. (Narrator, this must be justified as he whispers to Lunarnise, "Dont worry, help is on its way.")

Just as the tribe are roaming around their village, there was a sudden sound, then light takes the story back to the good guys who are out on the path looking for Lunarnise. (Designer, "Okay, let the games begin." As they were discussing, Narrator was getting ready for the test of a lifetime. Narrator, "Sam, you may have to take it from here as we are going through this.")

Stimpultonnes, "Right then, all of you, you may choose three weapons, pick." Roland, "Okay, I choose rope, bow & arrows, and a stick." To himself, 'I can hear people talking about this from behind me, I wonder what they are thinking?' While others were talking about his weapon taking, Roland was walking down the hill. They saw a village from far away. Tobias, "Oh yes, it is just perfect for us to mingle with them," grinning in shock. He was standing taller than the rest of the crowd. Sam, "I'm joining in too." Jake, "This game will be interesting and inspiring for the whole team to play." Then he turned to Fronk and Kulumbush, "Are you guys going in to play too?" Fronk and Kulumbush just looked and nodded their heads as they approached the entrance. The pair started talking and making jokes whether they should have a go. Both said together, "Well what have we got to lose? Let's get justified."

Stimpultonnes, "Okay, then I'm ready to help you out with the skills that we have for winning the entire tournament." Jake, "Did you know that? At least give it your best on the playing field, everyone good luck." They had reached the end of the road where the village is located. It was a calm and quiet place - well at least until one of them speaks out loud. Unknown voice, "Well, I think the game should begin now. Oh wait, I just heard that the village princess is going to be here to announce our arrival. Who is Lunarnise?" (Narrator, "Well, hello, they're my friends. How are you doing today and are you hungry and tired? Follow me. Tobias, is that you again?") Tobias, "Who me? No I'm over here." Something or someone is lurking around that they don't know about. (Narrator, "Oh, I am truly and utterly sorry for that inconvenience.") Tobias, "Oh no, you don't need to apologise, let's follow this young lady, sorry we didn't get your name." Young lady, "Oh, I'm sorry my friends, my name is Helena, I'm a mighty warrior." Jake, "Pleased to make your acquaintance, now let's follow this young and beautiful woman, this way all."

Helena, "Our village has been home to our people for thousands of years, and will be there forever if it is kept as a secret from the underground world." Even as she was educating the newfound people, there was a strange feeling that she was getting.

Someone rushed over to her and said, "I'm so sorry to interrupt, my lady, but you are needed for a tournament, I will send someone else in replacement to welcome all here. Please be patient and bear with us." In the meantime, there has been movement in the underground, dogs running around, and people crimping their heads in the battle of the witches. People shouting, "Ah ah ah ah, they are coming for you, you're mine now, just as how I collected your mother." Lunarnise, "No, you can't do that and I know that she is alive." Underground man, "Nat am em eva norsorba isambi." Meaning 'Not true, we are looking for her, but in exchange we will accept a soul instead of you as long as you make us your ally.' Lunarnise accepted the offer and it was agreed that she would return to the group after the tournament and when they got their prize.

It's dark and cold in the big underground with lots of different sounds and smells. On the surface of the world there were tournaments starting, as the sun was shining bright and magic emerged from people's hands.

Song:

All people singing.

"Hooray who me,

Hooray who me, we are all singing together,

Keep your love and keep your faith,

Were ready for the mountains that are coming from above!

We have so much love to offer you,

And keep you safe from the dark!"

Something unusual happened. Lots of people came out of the shadows from above and showed themselves to the villagers below. (Narrator: "Guys, sing it out louder than before." "Here we go," says Designer.)

"Hooray who me, hooray who me,

We are all singing together,

Keep your love and keep your faith,

Were ready for the mountains that are coming from above!

We have so much love to offer you,

And keep you safe from the dark!"

X2.

Tobias starts rapping,

When I eat an Orange, it tastes like porridge. From These Bars you'll start whinge, take a syringe, Your Acne won't take no Blasphemy!

(Narrator, "Wow that sounds amazing, did Tobias just rap like? Sorry, I'm lost for words. Well it's time to get wise and get a contract for him,") as Jake sits down on a rock watching him sing. Then all the mountain people started climbing down on the back of lions. Kulumbush, "What the heck, they're real life lions. Run!" He ran like a rabbit far away from the lions, all he could think is that he would become their snack. Stimpultonnes, “Wait patiently until you hear the sound of an unknown creature, momentarily speaking from the mistress. We seem to have lost Tobias.” Whilst everyone had taken eyes off him, he has changed appearance and now he’s a muscular guy with a bow and arrow. Tobias, “Guys it’s me only because I’m a shape shifting person, doesn’t make me look bad. I’m ready to fight. I met Puss in Boots and he taught me a trick or two.” (Narrator, “That sounds really good, now we have entered a new era and in the middle of the camp.” Designer coughs, “Yes, let the games begin,” and as he’s talking he accidentally picks up a duck instead of a gun. He doesn’t know and fires it, the duck screams. Quack. Then magic is shot in the skies with a trampoline course above the village just like a circus.) Roland, “Well I’m sure this will be a challenge for the whole world to see and learn how magical things can be when you work together to make it through.” Kulumbush, “How do you suppose we do this? It’s too high in the sky for me.” Fronk, “We will have a go and help with jumping on each other’s back.” He looked over at Kulumbush and said, “Chicken.” (Narrator, “Use what materials we have and make from scratch.”) Stimpultonnes, “It’s okay to be shy about your teammates, you shall be chosen which group you will work with throughout the competition. And you shall meet the team members who will also be in the school. The school is yet another stage of development for the students within Tiger Warth,” as he stood up in front of the whole crowd with a microphone in one hand and a spoon in the other.

Chapter 3

Let the Games Begin!

"We believe that good people should be in one team, the unknown individuals shall be in another and the last group shall choose their destiny. The rules of the game are, there are no rules, fair play shall prevail in the game," Lord of the Fegenitar College of Power announced. "Tobias shall do the honours by introducing the head of class."

Tobias "Welcome to the club, a sensational woman and a great leader who is known to the people - Miss Clariot Humberton." At this everyone whistles, claps, and screams. "She is a Headmistress from far beyond that you would never know, good luck with your new project and we look forward to working with you."

Miss Clariot Humberton: "Well, I do say you all seem to be very supportive of my arrival. I hope that I can support you in your journey, and thank you Tobias for giving me the opportunity to be here today." She stood straight with a microphone so all could hear, "Roland."

Roland, "Pleased to announce my arrival as I am the world's keeper, and I come of peace, my lady. This country is not in any shape for me to declare it being safe, oh no. Listen to what I'm about to tell each and everyone around me."

Stimpultonnes, "A war is about to begin yet you don't look afraid, there's amongst you, peace which will help you from falling, but have you got strength of a thousand men? I have been to the mountains and seen what is never to be seen again, killing people like cattle slaughtered by frolicking kind people with wild dogs. As they can see from above the village it will make you actually achieve your highest level so like a good king once said boldly, your level can be a great way of getting to know your enemy, knowing their next move."

(Narrator, "Also Stimpultonnes will be looking out for you but he also knows that you will be reaching for the forest by the end of the tournament. If the dogs get you, you wouldn't be able to make it alive, so be careful with the decision you take, wisely. It's like a menthol, you don't know what to expect when all falls." Then he goes towards the tournament to help with the needs of anything possible, small or big.)

Tobias, "I'm up for it, is anyone interested to know what the outcome should look like? Let's go, Fronk you look enthusiastic with head between knees."

As everyone else gathers around from far beyond their homes, it's calmer weather than usual to the point where you might be tempted. Tall buildings that look far in the distance to little trees that shine through the sky it's dry enough to make your heart beat with the wind. Softly played music like Scottish pipes and drums that make your mind wander through the clouds.

Miss Clariot, "Raise your eyes, roll back your teeth, swing with all the power and begin the process. Well you heard it all clearly." Stimpultonnes, "Gggg Go," then quacks, then ducks again. "You can see all the people are getting involved with this. And you might imagine how ridiculous it's going to look - legs on top of people, arms in places like you cannot even know, hold on, there's a few groups of people who are actually involved in this."

Stimpultonnes, "We shall name the groups that are responsible for the most common attitudes towards progress," as he walked over to the judges on the other table, "you may also consider that we will name them as we continue." There are many people that are higher than others, and there's whooshing and screaming from all sides, cheering from the rooftops and the mountains.

Jake, "You know something? I can hear a call from the mountains." Stimpultonnes decides to call it Mountainterus. "Okay so will use that for far away people. As we look a second from the huts, I'm going with Villgarious. I have a name for a third group, how about Gruwpertorious?" Stimpultonnes, "Jake, you have delivered a splendid announcement, thank you, sounds good to me."

Roland, "At the end of the votes we have got, Mountainterus as group 1, Villgarious as 2 and finally we have Gruwpertorious - this is beginning to be interesting."

At the end of the first round there is a very close match among the teams.

Miss Clariot: "We have an announcement for the teams. Gruwpertorious just made first place, with Mountainterus following in second place. Well done, it was hard for second place as it was difficult to tell."

Just as the announcement was made there is news coming that the underground are on their way to invade. Oh, it should be noted that they have been training from day one to challenge their opponents. There is upbeat music and drumming in their songs, "De am or a tii, De am or a tii," which means 'till you may die.' All the way to the battle fields there's no way out for us now, they are known to be powerful creatures." Crowd, "Harold, aren't you going to do something with your stick?" Stimpultonnes, "And what is that supposed to mean? You all have powers within yourselves, now is the time to shut them down and now is the better time to learn." (Narrator, "I'm going to enjoy this one, the time is here, the time is right now.") Tobias, "Let's charge for freedom," and runs in for the kill as he picks out the tallest among them. There are dogs barking, crying children, noises coming from all directions, singing and screaming music playing. Guns being fired, arrows going through the air, swordsmen are stabbing people from left to right.

The leader of the underground called Atchon comes forward to the queen of the hills. Atchon, "Mu hime ni Chichimec hignis." I am looking for a lady, Your Majesty. Queen,"Is this how you came to ruin my town, and you didn't come to me?" Atchon, "Nep be oh, bold meh bor." Everyone stops what they are doing and draw back to the dogs with them as their heads went down.

The sky was full of clouds of smoke, legs are everywhere, but whose they were supposed to be, one can't see. "In this mysterious passing I think that we have done well, most of our men are standing up," Tobias is pleased with himself as well as the rest of the groups, then out of the blue Tobias runs over to Atchon, "Where's my sister what have you done to her?"

As Tobias is holding a double sword to his neck, Atchon looks down. He is a little taller and relaxed in front of the queen. Atchon coughs, "I have not and won't hurt her, but she has agreed to give me another soul in her place, she seemed to have it all planned out." Atchon's assistant, "And from little of what we knew she's a special child, it's nobody here, I can say that your honour." Fronk, "If that's the case why did you come here to fight?"

At that point Fronk coughs up a bit of blood. Stimpultonnes, "Everyone move to a side, I know what to do." He lifts his hand that's holding his stick. "I'm going to move quickly to make sure any hurt is healed. Fhistlebum," he shouts, "there that should have done it. Can you please cough for me and come forward, Fronk?" Fronk tries to convince him that he cannot do such a task but he feels better afterwards.

Atchon, "You are a true wizard of the world, and you didn't even say anything all these years. I honour you," as Atchon was amazed with how he handled the whole situation. "From now on I honour you and respect you."

It has been kept secret for years that the underground may have cheated death, while others suffered by torture from the unknown. Their price has been a big factor for their success, but how longer will it remain a mystery from the world's eyes? Until recently there was one of a young generation who has been a tremendous threat and she lives within who dares to make it glow.

(Narrator, "This is usually the kind of disturbance that happens when you hear a sweet voice from the past.") A glance at the camera reflects a young woman shining so bright as she blushes. "Oh, my lord, what have you done that's amazing in my life, knowing you, this is the first." (Designer, "Who is that, bro, is she an old flame that you have forgotten about?" then starts laughing as he stood next to him.) A wind blows through the sky inside where they are, with the light shining down. It looks amazing from over here. (Narrator, "Oh so how did you follow my lead? You were far, busy, thought you might have never wanted to see me again." You can never predict the twist of life as these two love birds are among us as strangers and rekindle their relationship.)

Jake, "Hey Claudia, this is my field of work, what just happened?" He talks with his wife who also happens to be a Narrator, "How did you know where I was?" "You left your pacemaker at home so I thought I'd return it to you." Tobias started to shake his bum as he worked on a new video for all to watch. All of a sudden, he was dancing as if there were no tomorrow, with the crowd cheering, "Go Tobias, go Tobias!" It was a great moment for all to see.

Fronk and Kulumbush were able to get together and play a trick on him and accidentally hit Tobias to the ground. "Oh, dear goodness, we are so sorry," they said. Tobias just smiled, "It was only to get my attention, alright gang, lets clean up the mess. We haven't beaten them but stalled the underground bad ass team. What happened, why are all running away quickly?" (Narrator, "Oh, my friends there's a new problem heading our direction, prepare yourselves for the next level of horizon. This is the next generation of intelligence that will allow us to grow stronger within our communities and take responsibilities.") Claudia, "As my dear friend has written before each of you, let us take this opportunity to stand firm against bad." The minute Claudia spoke, something amazing happens, and it is better than a meteorite.

As the skies are blue and the sun is shining bright over the horizon, and a little creature seemed to be flying in the background, Roland turned to Tobias, "Well, you know what we have to do, what was causing confusion among the rest of the group." (Okay well, Tobias and the Narrator had got into this together when they had a similar situation before but we will leave that aside for now because we are concerned with what is in front of us.) The sun sparkles in delight, the crowd gets up and starts singing and dancing to show off their amazing skills. (Designer, "I'm going to place tables on both sides of the road leading up the hill in front of the buildings." Narrator, "I don't like this as I know we will be heading towards a new city." Sounds like Narrator is struggling with the fact he's been living with his secret wife for a while now and he doesn't realise who or where she is from. He looks with a frowning face and a smile that makes him look so sad, even though he is standing up tall. Oh, then the Designer looks appalled and draws stilettos underneath him, oh my God this is so cute.) Everyone laughed, tears rolling down their faces.

The three teams get ready to compete in the next round and line up for the race of their lives. They get the last preparations done as they drink water, stretch and crouch down. "On your marks get set go, quack," they all start to run out on the road. In the background crowds cheering them on:

Everybody sings the song, *Go on marching to the warth of the wall, then we can see what will achieve* x2.

Kulumbush, "I'm running, I'm running where is Fronk?" Fronk shouts out his name, "Where are you?" "I think I must be near the end of the line." He sees a powered bike with a rocket on the back of it, goes to the side to collect it and then starts pedalling off. Before he knew it, he was going fast through towards the finishing line, but before he could reach it he flew up into the sky. Oh, hold on, there's another herd of animals in the area galloping down the hill towards the contestants already racing. He sees this and starts a conversation with himself, 'I need to let someone know about this. It looks like they want to join us in the big race. Tobias, isn't far off as I can see a horse is gone to the side pulling at the lady with the green hat trying to claim it's his. Oh no, Narrator is laughing until he gets tears down his face.' Someone shouts from the crowd, "It's just another day in Tiger Warth." 'Oh, what am I seeing now? Claudia has hopped on to the back of the horse that did cause some trouble and she's galloping to the finish oh my!' Kulumbush is telling the story at the moment as he flies through the air, looking scared as a clown.

'There's Tobias in the front three and there's evidence of playing football because they are ahead of the others. What an incredible performance from Narrator and Designer!' Kulumbush has just made an entrance. But didn't he fall off the bike earlier today? Fronk, "Pleased to see you, yeah," as he's gasping for breath. 'Looks like the front four have scrapped the football and are now hopping over each other's backs as they are running. Hold on, I'm just receiving information on the whereabouts of Sir John Sprit. His partner in crime has found him in an outside world that is -10°. He has frozen over. But seems to be stable and breathing slowly so I'm sure he will be looking for Lunarnise again. It's getting late so we should think about camping out for the night, I suppose no one has got any camping gear.'

Sam, "Why does it feel like I have to do everything around here?" Jake, "I'm shouting out, Sam. Where are you? We need your attention. Even he is lost in the wilderness, oh well what will go wrong?"

Claudia starts rubbing her hands together and in a circle at the same time, it's an old tradition that sees them gain temporary powers. Roland, "What are you doing with your hands? Just ask Sam!" Claudia, "Who's Sam?" as she stood up, puzzled. Then says, "I'm guessing it could be Designer, am I right?" Roland nodded his head, smiling at her. Claudia, "Oh thank God, I got something right for once."

(Just like that, the race was over, who won it we don't know for sure because there's a huge building in front. It looked lovely like a camping place built like an army base with different activities. Narrator, "Well, it looks like we know where we're going to be tonight. At least we can have fun with all the different objects, obstacles, there is to do.") As everyone reaches the camp it gets dark, then from nowhere tall lamps start falling down to the ground and lighting up so bright. (Narrator, "Right, let's go this way, now we can see the path. Oh my God, look at those beautiful ponds over there and it has a mermaid sitting on top of the water bed.")

Tobias, "That's so cool, can I touch it too?" as he was walking to the door of the building. To his surprise the eyes were following him. Right until he reached out and grabbed the door handle, opened, and walked inside. Kulumbush, "Dddd...did you see that? That is one spooky object. I want to go home. Oh, I'm still looking for my cat anyway." Fronk, "I'm glad we have reached the indoors now, what else can go wrong? I don't believe in any ghost." Anonymous voice, "That guy has been annoying," says one of the pictures. The other picture, "I'm sure they won't spend the night here with all that happens in his house. They will run away halfway through the night with their heads between their asses, ha ha ha ha ha." "Look at this place it's built for a queen to live in, it's so beautiful and clean, no dust anywhere yet no one is here." "But little do they know it's an abandoned place, well, so people think colours are clean and warm beige and yellow plus orange." A good-looking woman comes towards them, and speaks in a calm and beautiful voice, "Dinner is served by 20.00 hours so find your room with your names on it and put on the clothes that are in the tallest wardrobe and I will see you then." Before anyone could say anything, the hostess was gone. "We better go and find our rooms and get cleaned up, and dress, too," says Tobias.

Kulumbush, "Wait how do they know all of our names?" Roland, "I'm guessing it's the trend these days, people know a lot about anybody." As they were all running around trying to look for their rooms, Tobias, "There's a long corridor with a lot of doors all the way down on both sides, all with different colours with two messages written on the front of all doors saying,

Open me if you dare to retrieve your gift now

Good luck with your findings!

(Narrator, "Why does this look so familiar? Have I been here before?") While Jake is talking he notices Tobias changing form to an animal. ("Oh, come on, what, again?")

Chapter 4
Hotel of Surprises!

Kulumbush, "Howdy partner, where are we going?" as he looks all around the corridor, "Oh, I see now. Are we going to try a door?" Roland, "Let's keep walking, it's a long way off so we can pick a door that way." They hear a squawking noise coming from inside the room they all are in. As they walk closer to where the noise is coming from, Kulumbush looks pale. Kulumbush, "Please, can we go back?" as he stands shaking. (Narrator, "I wouldn't worry too much, after all you have one another's back, and my friends, if you take a closer look its only Tobias.")

Everyone, "How do you know this could be the famous Tobias?" Stimpultonnes, "Well I suppose I can see, so I will explain it to you. He has a black mole on the back of his neck which distinguishes him from anyone else." A bird squarks and flies. As he's making those sounds he hits the shiniest door in the corridor. Kulumbush, "How do you know, anyone can have that mark or could be imposing as him?" Kulumbush notices a facial expression that Tobias pulls, and says, "Tobias, squark three times, so we know it's you." The bird squarks as he's been asked, and everyone looks puzzled, but happy because they knew that they would now be safe in the hands of Tobias.

(As Roland is the world's keeper we think he should have the opportunity of opening the door.) He walks over to the shiniest one and looks at all the people who are just standing there. Roland goes, "Nothing, one, two, three." As he turns the handle of the door he is interrupted by Stimpultonnes who shouts, "Don't open!" looking worried.

[Crowd scuffs in surprise]

In a quick response Roland released the door not knowing it didn't click properly. An unexpected consequence would happen later but all the immediate attention was directed on Stimpultonnes as he led the way for everyone to see. "This way, I know the door we should be going into." He stood next to the green door. Roland went to the door and pulled down on the handle and opened it.

As he walked through the door he heard a voice that he recognised from the past. It was a beautiful forest, full of greenery, tall trees and animal sounds coming from everywhere. Everyone started to follow through with joy in their hearts, [singing and laughing]. "You know this is nice when you're feeling good." Each and every person had gone into the forest of dreams. "It looks amazing," cried out Kulumbush.

[Crowd talking, animals singing and music playing]

Tobias was the only one who got to the top of the tree quickly and changed form to a man. We believe it could be his original body ("Wait, didn't he have powers too? Never seen before, he's holding something that has lit up the world, look at that, it is amazing." Narrator, "Come on guys let's go, follow me this way.") They all start to sing as they make their way through crowd. *Follow me, follow you, look before you.* When they were just about to get into a rhythm, they get distracted by a bunch of sexy girls who are half dressed.

[With a whisper of laughter from the audience behind the trees]

Fronk, "Tobias get down from there, let's get going as we have to find shelter before it gets dark," as he starts blushing at the half naked girls.

[That was it, he then climbed down to reach the ground]

The girls came up to the crowd and started talking in a different language, and everyone went, "Wow! I have never seen anything like this before," and they look lost. "I wonder if they could help us," someone from the crowd said remotely. "It looks like we have reached a temporary point where we can get a shower and eat something and rest. And then we can move on to the next location where the third activity will start. With it looking to be getting darker we will follow the light and focus on getting everybody inside."

Back at the hotel it seems like a lot is going on here. Lots of people are coming to visit and they are shouting and talking, drinking and having fun. Until from the door that wasn't locked properly behind by Roland, out popping his head, is Sir John Sprit. "How can it be? He was banished to an outcast land." Sir John Sprit, "I just heard what you said, and how come I'm ending up in a prison that looks like a hotel?"

Hotel Hostess, "Oh no Sir it's not like that, how may we help you?" His ally, Ponsternose walks out next, all smiles.

Hotel Hostess, "Oh hello, professor, I didn't see you there, how has your day been?" as she stood up straight behind the counter, ready to let the other staff know by a touch of a button. Ponsternose, "Very well thank you, young lady. Now could you be so kind to help us out with the directions to the party, please?" The professor tried to smile at her. Hotel Hostess, "Very well, follow me gentlemen." She knew what she had to do get rid of the other group fast. She is in for a shock when her attention turns into a disaster. That they both are planning a plot to destroy Lunarnise. (Narrator, "Will the Hotel assistant give in to their conniving ways? Let's wait to find out. She is whispering, 'I need to be a better woman to fulfil my responsibilities and not to make mistakes.' Claudia "I wonder what she is talking about. Does that mean she knows one of them and understands their responsibilities, how they deal with people? Umm, I need to find Sam quickly and tell him what is going on here I need to tell him that I miss him.") Just when Claudia was about to leave to find him, she was hit from behind by a bolt and she fell to the floor.

Ponsternose, "Ha ha ha that'll teach you, you're going to the pit with everyone else," picking up Claudia. She tried to scream but he held her mouth closed with tape. (Will anyone save her, or will she be stuck just like Lunarnise?) A sudden change in weather, there was a dark cloud that covered everywhere just out of the blue. Atchon appeared on the back of a werewolf to collect her. "Master, I will see to it that she is in the cage next to Lunarnise." Sir John looked surprised, and said, "You have Lunarnise and you didn't tell me." Atchon, "Oh yeah master, I forgot to mention that to you, I thought you were told," as he got off his dog and stood in front of Sir John.

Sir John, as he hits him over the face, "What have I told you before? Don't hide anything from me. I'm warning you don't do this again." So off he goes in the mist of the dawn and vanishes in thin air as the clouds disappear into calm, dark skies at night. The Hotel Hostess looks appalled, seeing what happened to the poor woman. There was nothing she could have done to prevent it, but she had to do something about it.

Back at the jungle house there were a lot of people who wanted to drink and have fun [Music upbeat, playing]. Two female warriors were standing on the side walk watching all goings on. First warrior, Helena, "Well girl, are you ready for the next fight? There's one coming up, we have been tipped by our friend." Second warrior, Poppals, "Who is this guy that you are talking of?" Helena, "You're telling me you don't know? Well it's Tobias, a great ninja warrior who's capable of being a king." Poppals, "I didn't even knew that he was a ninja. Well, that's nice we learn something new every day. That makes sense now, even if you don't know what qualities we can carry on our journey in life." As it's a calm and peaceful night out in the woods with just the singing of the birds, crickets making noises. (And never jump into conclusions about what you think, I strongly encourage people not to judge a book by its cover.)

Both warriors started to scream when they saw their idol, who is also their protector. Helena, "Oh my God, look at him he's in front of me, wow!" She smiles and walks over to him and then freezes in the middle of the room. (Poppals tries to say, 'kiss him already'. (Wait, Tobias looks over at them and moves his head to one side, then brushes his hair with a comb while he sits on the couch with the lamp on his other side. There in the corner of the couch and looking at her is Roland, the world's keeper. I think he wants to say something to Tobias about what the girls might be doing.) Roland, "Tobias, please don't buy anything that you don't think is right." Tobias looks over at Roland and nods his head and then gets up out of the chair to greet the ladies as they approach him. Both warriors, "Well hello there, Tobias, thank you so much, you have been an inspiration for both of us, so we're here to help you out and, with your kindness, to join the team."

Tobias just looks at both of them first, from head to toe. Tobias, "Okay, please follow me this way, we have an activity just about to start. If you participate, then we can see your qualities." So, both warriors look at him and agree to take part. Little do others know that these ladies have been abandoned and their village destroyed. Right then there are a few different types of games that are going to be included. Tobias, "I hope that you all are enjoying the experience. And finish the games that are already available, for the new one that is coming up soon. Well, ladies and gentlemen, boys and girls, we are waiting for instructions for the first game to commence, shortly we will begin with archery. It may seem to be a little bit of a challenge with the sun light gone down, and the only option is the moon lighting."

[Designer drew a few archery poles at the side of each other]

First up is Jake, he comes up picking up the bow and arrow, pulls back and fires the arrow at the board and it's a strike. Tobias has a go at taking a shot, oh it goes straight through the first arrow down the middle. "Right," says Helena, "I'll go next, and I'll show you how it's done." She takes it upon herself to take the shot. (Narrator, "Okay but that's not how you hold the arrow, at least point it straight with your arms high.") Before he could even begin to tell the woman, she had released the arrow that confused the crowd. Meantime, back underground there's a lot of chanting and screaming as the dark cloud thickens.

Lunarnise is reunited with her pet who is jumping up and down, so happy, dancing around, to see her friend. She wakes up in the next cage to Lunarnise. Lunarnise whispers to her, 'We will be okay, don't worry. I have a plan to set us free.'

Lunarnise's little furry friend is now looking scared as he covers his eyes and is shaking. Lunarnise takes a look at him and says, "What is wrong, why are you scared?" That minute there's a big sound coming from behind them and shouting. Someone else shouts, "What is going on, you're not going to eat us alive?" Lunarnise looks all around in fear. "What do we do? I'm sure if we trick him he will become confused what he's supposed to do." As they were talking a big giant was walking towards the cages which are in a room hanging from the ceiling with pink slime larvae. With the approach of the giant, he's trying to get closer to the people trapped in the cages. The darkness of the waters rises, there is no light in sight! But the breeze of light wind beneath our toes.

Claudia, "Wait, there's no wind inside here, what's happening, why people are looking worried?"

But for the moment there is hope, winter's darkest waters, given how cold it may get, we believe that this will rise!

"We are still waiting for the vain to glorify the Lord and make peace with all!" Lunarnise hears the words, "You need to be kind to all, be happy and humble. Remember that the essence of life is to love yourself and not to lose your mind over others who want your downfall." "That seems like a good thing," Lunarnise says as she's scratching the stick that she doesn't remember being passed to her. A light shines on the end of the stick. She looks at it in shock and as she's about to throw it in the slime larvae, simmering shimmers, lightning sparkles and fires off to the wall opposite. "Now what do I do and how do I work it out?" As Lunarnise tries several times to get it to work, there's much happening at the other end, back at the camp site. Helena had thrown the arrow into the air and it landed in front of the fire. With a message reading, 'I am alive, wait for me to rise up and take the next step.'

Fronk, "Oh, oh look, I know what this means, it's a good thing for us, at least we know that Lunarnise is safe. I'm sure Tobias will be very happy to see her again soon, it is coming from within." As for Tobias, he isn't the only person waiting for her, the young and gifted woman. He takes a different form as he transforms into a bird face, Gryphon, and becomes a spirit guardian. (Narrator, "You are confusing us, my dear friend who are you now?")

Tobias, "I'm not different to who you have known me to be. I'm taking this form from now on and I will be a guardian. And will be notified when I need to leave to protect the innocent lives of those in need, then return home to my people." Everyone looks at Tobias and gasps, "We have never heard you speak in such a way before. Is there anything we could do to help?" As Tobias stood straight, wings appear. Fluttering wings, Tobias starts practising to fly around the campus. But every time he does, he falls down to the ground, sounds of silence in the sky, and screams of Tobias whilst he runs along the water, and falls inside and gets wet. Roland, "That's good Tobias, I could do with the help of a very special friend, now that you have courage." There's a big roar in the air as Tobias lifts his head, with a pig grunt to finish off, then looks up at the stars. Now that Tobias has taken over the fold of a Gryphon he has to take on the role that protects the egg from being destroyed.

Back underground where loud voices were heard in anger, there are two giants – one, a bouncing boy and the other, a quiet girl who has a good heart. The boy was like a bully who would crush his prey in seconds. And people would believe that he would also attack and eat them alive. With the exception of the girl giant. At this point she was just trying to be nice, so technically was helping to try and free everyone from the cages. She picked up a piece of wire from the floor and started to twist it into the lock. The lock snapped off and the door opened up the other doors of all the cages. Everyone was happy and nervous about getting out of the cages and making a run for it.

Lunarnise, "Team, please could you stay close to me and follow me and my pet, but first we need to go round the side staying clear of the larvae." S.J, "wasi waa."

Chapter 5

Lunarnise Finally Meets Tobias!

The next stage of this book is where Lunarnise and her new friends have escaped from the shadows of the Sprits. But little is known about Sir John, who has found his way into the world again and on his way to becoming the king of kings. Literally every single person will get him caught, without prejudice or even consent from the world's keeper. S.J, "wugi wuwu." Lunarnise, "Yes, boy we are going to climb down and walk out the building and then start our journey to the jungle," as Lunarnise and her new friends finally find a way to get out of the cages. And climb down. Someone watches them and runs off to find Sir John to explain what's happened. (Narrator, "It's nice to see you again, ma'am, how are you feeling today? Have you eaten anything yet?")

Lunarnise, "No Sir, but Im looking for some fresh fruit to eat on the way, is it possible that you could have a wife who is pregnant? And was thrown into the cage where I was." That's how they met one another.

Jake, "Hold on, she was next to me, then I fell asleep. When I awoke, she was gone." "That sounds strange but we need to find out where she is." Claudia, "Jake are you there?" Lunarnise, "We need to be very careful about the dogs." They stood outside, waiting for the instructions to arrive, so they would know where they were going. It was another day in the woods and birds were chirping, monkeys, screaming and lions, growling.

(Designer, "Just to give you some notice that Sir John is still hanging around, and yes you think that he is gone, but he's not." He turns round to see what has happened to everyone that was caught. Narrator, "But he was taken away by the one and only Tobias, wasn't he?")

Lunarnise, "Tobias, who is he and where did he come from? Do I know him personally?" (Narrator, "Well, Lunarnise looks puzzled, at least someone could tell her.") "Tell me, tell me what?" she cried, "and I think there's something I don't understand. S.J "wuga wugu wa wa." Lunarnise, "Yes let's go." That might've made S.J happy with everything running smoothly and people starting to go their own directions. But then someone rolls themselves to the front and says, "If you need our assistance just call us and we will be happy to help." Lunarnise, "How do I do that?" The person handed her a whistle, "Just blow it three times and it will send a message." She picked up the whistle from dropping to the ground. "This place looks quite mysterious and familiar like something I have seen before." A soft cry through the woods, music with a relaxing theme, but like a music of persecution.

Lunarnise, "I wonder what kind of sounds are coming from the woods and I hope that we can find the cry, S.J. And be able to help them with their needs." Unknown voice, "Help me, lift me up, Lord help me through my weakness. All my life I have been faithful." S.J, "raw, raw." At least Lunarnise is gathering the attention of some people who are just willing to follow her lead. And what it looks like, to fight back against the threat that's been coming from the underworld. Hold on, we got some information about the release of Claudia, Narrator's wife who is running towards Lunarnise and shouting, "Come on everyone follow us."

From nowhere as if it was quite before there were birds flying, monkeys were singing the unknown song that was sung. Claudia, "Hey, young lady, wait for me I believe we can help each other out!" as she rushes over to Lunarnise. Lunarnise, "What do you say, boy, shall we let her join us?"

As she was addressing her friend he began to nod his head and run around the spot. "Well, consider yourself part of our team," Lunarnise replied with a smile to Claudia. "Come on over, let's go, I think it's this way." Half a metre along the path, they came to a maze. A talking monkey stood next to the entrance. Monkey, "Hello ladies, how may I help you? Look, I have three paths I can present to you and one of them is the key you're looking for."

Both women look at each other and say, "Well, what have we got to lose?" so they both decide to walk through the entrance. S.J. moans, looks where Lunarnise is and comes towards her quickly. Monkey "Oh, one more thing, I forgot to mention. Before you leave, you should carry your stick at all times." Lunarnise to herself, 'how did he know about my stick? It's been passed down a copy from Designer.'

(Designer, "Yes ma'am, you called for my attention, how may I help you? Oh, umm, hello Claudia, shall I tell your husband?") Claudia,"Oh yes, I didn't think of that, may I ask you not to mention anything to him at this point? Let us ladies catch up a little more, let him worry about us a while longer." ("May I ask the reason for this, is it because he got lost in the woods trying to find you both?")

"Oh yes, with how it is getting dark really quickly I am sure we can pursue on our journey, tonight is nice and warm." Lunarnise and her pet are looking very sceptical. Claudia, "Well, what do you think of trying out the path on the right?" Lunarnise, "Okay, I can see how you are looking at me. Let S.J. go, I'm sure he will choose a good one for us to begin our journey." Just as they were discussing whether to go into one of the three paths, S.J. started to hop up and down and dance around both Lunarnise and Claudio's feet. He was doing it that fast he ran off into one of the paths. Claudia, "Right, looks like we have a job to do. He's run off on one of these and we will have to find him." "That would make a lovely gift for us to get a clue where he has gone, listen to his cry."

In the meantime, back where the rest of the team is staying, they had no idea what was happening or if Lunarnise was still alive. Tobias, "Well, my fellow people let's continue our activity together as it's the last one. Now has Poppals done her shot?" Roland, "I'm sure that you will have a turn as Helena has completed her first round." They were talking about the final round of the first activities before they start harder training to become protectors of the world who will act behind Roland, when they heard in the distance some people screaming and chanting. There were screams and sounds of galloping coming from far beyond, just like a boom, a herd of dogs was running towards them out of nowhere, 'what do we do about this one?' The herd of strays was very loud and getting closer, they weren't barking, they were snarling.

Roland, "Atchon, pleased to make your acquaintance, how may I assist you?" He walked towards where Atchon was. Atchon speaks in his own language, "ath aw wuw huu0," then translates it to English, tells his dogs to be quiet and sit. Atchon,"Okay, let me explain, I have travelled far and wide to search for your team, we believe that there's something special out here that could help people like me and my group." Stimpultonnes, "Please Atchon, I dont know where you have been but I assure you that we know nothing of this, and you have the nerve to come here. My people have told me everything." Kulumbush, "Yes that's true, but I can say, walking through these woods, I have heard whispers coming from the bushes, people calling out. 'Do you know that I have this special egg?' " Stimpultonnes turns to look at Kulumbush, "How did you manage to escape Tobias's friend?"

Everyone smiles, and looks at Kulumbush at amazement. Now that it is dark, birds are chirping, owls are singing. "How do you expect us to trust or believe you?" Then someone laughs from the back of the crowd, "Were just teasing you, look - you look scared." Atchon, "Oh thank you, my son, you weren't supposed to have told me that, I'm sure, and this egg is going to make you mental." Stimpultonnes, "Atchon, no one has been able to find the whereabouts of such a thing, it has been a myth for many years." Atchon, "Anyway, you old man, enough of this talk, we will see who's the strongest when the right one is in control."

Atchon laughs as he prepares his army to vacate without a battle, then he shouts in the distance, "Till the next time we meet. My team will be ready for you, good day, my young fellow citizens." Kulumbush, "Oh, fleckaltons, what did I just do? I'm sorry sir," then kneels down on one knee with his head bowed, ('I shall take my punishment now').

Stimpultonnes, "It's okay, my young child, you weren't to know if you can be quite cunning to trick people, don't worry, there is a battle coming." And says under his breath, 'I know about you, I have to keep an eye on you.' Tobias, "This just means, my dear friends, that we have our hands full as we need to prepare for the fight against our enemies." Looks and says as he has one eye on Kulumbush, "If you know any information on the egg please refer back to me or Roland." Stimpultonnes, "I'm right here, I can see everything so don't be afraid of the Klang."

It is a dark and miserable night for the rest of the people, as they look for somewhere to sleep. Do not disturb others as there's still a lot of light and sounds coming from the outside of the house. "Well done to all of you, we start different activities and training for our students, this will help us rise above all,"

As she (the unknown voice) begins singing, animals began dancing and making noises.

"See the way how life gets you down!

Well even if you are single or in love, come to think of it!...."

Tobias, "I'm starting to feel like there's something else more to me than I think, I wonder what that could be?" He was trying to think about it when the first female warrior, Helena, approached him and said, "Well, hello my dear prince, how are you today, do you have a minute? I want to talk with you." She was checking out Tobias from head to toe, as she is gasping, to herself, 'Wow, what could I ask for if he was by my side?'

Tobias notices her checking him out but pretends not to look. "I'm sure that I have made your acquaintance before but I don't know where." Helena, "Maybe. There's something about you and I would love to get to know you better," as she looks at him with a smile on her face then tumbles over a rock.

What a relief as both of them walk into the night, staring into each other's eyes. Just then there was a loud noise and Tobias says, "I got to go." As he was about to fly off he shouts, "Let's meet at first light." Helena was talking about how she couldn't wait for their little meeting and how she was excited. She walked back to the place where they were staying. Poppals said, "There is something strange going on."

As they reached the entrance, a short distance away, and the women were talking about how special they were, inside there was a show that was happening when they went through the main door, and it looked so familiar. There were bright lights and singing that sounded like a dream come true beats, that weren't even heard before. (Narrator, "A band stood before them as it was common for the Tiger Warth world, full of different creatures. It was as if they all came to tell their stories.") Just as they were enjoying the band there was unexpected shouting from down the road. Oh no, it looks like from a distance, no, Sir John Sprit it can't be, wasn't he banished from this world? Wait he has crewmen, he's still after Lunarnise, where is she?

In the meantime, Tobias was flying over the clouds to the north of Tiger Warth, to visit an elderly member. He has gone for extra training to become better at being a night guard and a helper of the land as he is learning how to be a ninja. As music came from nowhere, Tobias, "Well I wonder what this will accomplish?" The Wise old lady, "Welcome back, Tobias, you look great. Are you ready for the next challenge? Don't worry I have got your back."

Right then Tobias is approached by a highly skilled agent who has been investigating a suspicious criminal named Peter Han. Tobias is persuaded to attend an intense martial arts tournament in Han's hometown. That would mean gathering the images of Han's involvement with Sir John Sprit, shortly before his arrival. Tobias learns that Sir John is responsible for Lunarnise's capture. But as he continues his quest into becoming a spy ninja, he finds out that Lunarnise is his own secret sister.

At the mansion where Tobias had come, the Wise old lady lives all alone with her butler and her cook. Inside, there is a large room at the end of the hall; a nasty, dirty wet looking room filled with cactuses and an oozy smell. Not even dry, barely warm, with nothing inside but all covered in white and a table on one side of the room. It had a nice round rabbit hole for the door that took the room underneath the mansion to another dimension. When entering, the hole seemed to be going on and on for a while, as it wasn't fairly straight but was like a tunnel. The Wise old lady appeared from behind the steep slope and she looked up at Tobias and said, "Are you ready for the next chapter of transformation and have you levelled up?" as she prepared the training of life. Tobias, "I am ready for the next level to begin with my training. Just let me know what to do next."

Within minutes of the Wise old lady being introduced there was a small group of rabbits in black, walking towards Tobias, to greet him. They were rabbits that walk like humans, slightly taller than the people, who also have long beards. There is no evidence of any magic about them but what they do know is ninja as they're black belts and trainers. And they are the ordinary everyday warriors who help you to disappear quietly and quickly when evil comes around. They have eyes like eagles and can hear folks talking, for miles, plus being slim, and skin being orange and green, helps them.

Note that the Wise old lady had taken over adventures from her father who built the mansion from scratch for his only daughter. And luxurious rooms under the sea as hotel suites. With knowledge and experience, she has learnt and is able to pass along to others especially Tobias. He is raring to go and get back on track to become the world's best as he prepares to train harder than ever.

Meditating music was put on to help Tobias relax. As Tobias put in his effort to begin with the training, one of the rabbits tells him to start again. He wonders why he is doing this over and over again. To his surprise he notices he puts his left foot in when he shouldn't.

Over at the camp where Narrator and Designer plus all the villagers and friends are as they are, suggesting that Lunarnise is missing, they are also getting ready for a fight against evil to save her from being made into a machine. It is a cold and lonely night here in Tiger Warth. As the night starts thickening and the storm passes through, the louder it gets and Sir John is lost in the woods. Fronk goes, "I am extremely worried about Lunarnise, where could she be?" Kulumbush gets agitated. He begins to walk up and down, turns and looks around every time the door opens, stares at his watch constantly.

(Narrator, "Oh no, he's starting to behave like he's in love, oh wait a minute, with? No way, oh that's so cute.") Kulumbush, 'Oh my, you are right is that what it looks like, Sam? Could we just keep it a secret for a while?" In an instant, there was a gush of wind, a flash of light and then came a marvel ball that goes by the name, Sterito, he is a little ball with hands and feet.

On the other side of the path there was Lunarnise and Claudia who seemed to be struggling with the maze. A tree moved out of the ground and started to chase them away. They managed to escape and hide. Just then Sterito made an appearance as he came to rescue both Lunarnise and Claudia from the ground tree, "Please stand clear." He raised up his hands and a ball of light shined. He moved his right arm quickly to the tree and it froze enough for them to move past. Just as that was happening there was music playing and Lunarnise had managed to take the hand of Sterito to greet him. Sterito turned to her and said, "Yes, master Pestra, I have come to warn you that Sir John is looking for you so be careful. There's also a rumour going around that there is a brother looking for his sister and it's closer than you think, and I will be there for you throughout."

Lunarnise, "Whoever that is, I'm sure they would be delighted to finally have met each other." By now Lunarnise is starting to wonder, I hope it will be a surprise for that person. Still what she doesn't understand is that it is her. (This is being told quietly so Lunarnise doesn't hear). With it being a calm and quiet night as they enter a cottage in the middle of the maze, and they were walking through the door there was an old man standing inside and looking at them with a smirk on his face. Lunarnise mentioned to Claudia that he seemed to be friendly but creepy. Claudia wondered how would they sleep tonight, as he would be watching them and by the look of it not many people come by here. Lunarnise, "I hear footsteps from the outside of the cottage, what are we supposed to do now? Oh, I have a pen, I had forgotten."

Lunarnise takes out the pen and draws a big hole in the floor in front of the cottage. She manages to capture the likes of Sir John and his team on a temporary basis as they fight to make a sharp exit.

In the meantime, at the main camp war is starting out again as they fight for the egg of light. The underworld makes a breakthrough, they capture it and make their way back under. As soon as it happens Roland and the two women warriors rise up and put their hoodies on and they all make their way to the fields at a slow pace. Tobias is aware of the dangers that lie ahead and is ready and complete with the training and bows forward to the rabbits. At the cottage, Lunarnise has managed to sleep but is woken by a strange and mysterious creature that stands over her body and pulls out her heart. She starts crying and her body is being dragged into the sea; just as this is happening she forces herself to wake up to realise, thankfully, it was only a nightmare.

"Cottage protector, basically she's not going to make it through the night," says the broken man from the door, "if you don't hurry and get the one and true sibling." "This is happening too quickly but honestly how do you know that?" "Find the missing link that opens up the whole new story and then unfolds the original school. I hope no one can hear me but there's a sibling who's in hiding." "That's what I'm saying about the fact. I don't think it's going to go easy for you and your team but it is achievable as long as you trust in one another's abilities," replies the cottage protector.

Claudia, "Well, we have a lot of work ahead of us. Lunarnise, please stay by my side, you are vulnerable you can be captured anytime. With the dream you have told me, girl, it's because you have a powerful spirit and you're a sibling of a powerful prince."

Lunarnise, "What's this you are talking about? It's not true. All that time I have been wondering about it and not told anyone else how I felt inside." Wind picks up and moves towards the hole where Sir John is inside. "Quick you need to move before he gets out of the hole and moves to us, I can see his face. Quickly let's go through here." As they climb up the hill they see him in the distance but they don't look back. Their hair is blowing in the air.

Beating of the drums begins, both Lunarnise and Claudia were running into the light, their hair looked blossomed and shining like flowers. Sir John shouted out to Lunarnise, "Hey girl, please come over and let me out of this mess, I will look after you." Claudia said to Lunarnise, "Don't mind him, it's a trick. Continue with your journey and never stop or look back." Lunarnise was in a dangerous position as she felt herself drawn towards him. "Oh no," Lunarnise cries out. Claudia, "Please stop and think about what you are going to do."

Lunarnise draws a ladder to help him out of the pit. "Ah hah hah, yes you are mine now," Sir John grabs her and pushes her into his carriage that seemed to have come from nowhere. As dark as the night is, it seems that Sir John has cunning ways of luring people into doing things that they don't want to do. With the night at a smooth breeze Lunarnise was unable to stop him from trapping her. Luckily for Claudia she had hidden beneath the ground. Sterito appeared out of nowhere but he was too late, Lunarnise was taken for the second time. Sterito, "Why did I get here so late? I know you can hear me, Claudia my dear, Jake is going out of his mind with worry."

"Oh, my goodness I love the fact that he has been thinking of me all the days we've parted ways." That thought has given her encouragement to continue with her journey to helping others and rescue Lunarnise from her father. "This is my turn to shine in this world and turn to friends who can also help on the path of success," says Claudia. As Claudia walks into the night she starts singing, "*Into the Night I begin, the world can be in a spin. You won't get me, you won't find me, do do doh do doh.*"

High in the sky there was something hanging over in the distance. Claudia said, "I think I know who that is. Could it possibly be Tobias? Ho wee ho, I'm over here." He noticed her and went straight up to her. Tobias then looked at her with surprise, "What are you doing here? I've just come back from my training, everyone has been worried about you, especially Jake." Claudia, "Tobias, do you know what is happening to you right now? You're turning invisible, how do you do that?" Tobias, "Isn't it amazing? I learnt that with many other things. Oh, by the way, where is Roland?" Claudia, "Oh don't worry he's not far from us, in a house somewhere, but let's not focus on him because Lunarnise is captured once again. This time her father has taken her in a carriage."

By the look on Tobias's face, he was already getting furious, plus he doesn't know what truth lies behind. Tobias was ready to fly, with Claudia about to jump on his back, when Sterito came over to Tobias. Sterito, "And where do you think you are going? My master is locked up in a strange house. Oh, and there's a puzzle you need to figure out and a key to unlock the magical school. We have to figure out how to get Lunarnise as it's getting late." Tobias, "I know a shortcut, come, hop on but get ready for a bumpy ride." As Claudia was climbing up on his back there is a big explosion in the distance. They both look and wonder what that could be. Tobias says, "We need to go and warn the others." Tobias starts flying over to the camp where the others were staying. That might surprise Sam as he was seen pacing through the corridors.

"Hey guys, welcome back, and Tobias, you have found my partner? Well enough of the small talk, look at you. Where have you been? I thought I'd lost you. Thanks for your help once again, pal. I heard about your training, how did it go?" With the chilled air and the heat just waking up, everything seemed fine and the people were all happy to see them both back together. "Hold on there's one more person that you should know about, Tobias." "I think I know what you're trying to say," repeating in a soft voice. Well at least a few of them stood up and were able to speak about their experiences in the last couple of days and everyone was talking and smiling. Tobias, "Right, what is the key, that I have been told about? A secret passage of unknown premises and something I don't understand what it means."

"Well, Tobias, it's good to know that you are safe, pal." "Sam," Tobias replied in an anxious tone, "yes I'm still here and I'm not far behind you. "All those things are a riddle and a quest for you, my dear friend. As I have seen you are only behind the very last one into solving the problem that will open up another passage in connection to the school and the egg of light." Tobias, "Oh so it's a metaphor in theory." Sterito looked confused. Sterito,"Young master brother, you have to go through the forbidden path to save Lunarnise." Tobias, "Okay, I genuinely get that but you called me something back then." 'Oh, my dear Claudia, I hope he didn't get it back there,' Sam was trying to whisper. "I'm not sure if he got any of that. I'm pretty sure he will want us to get an army ready to go and break free Lunarnise from the enemy."

Tobias, "Right then everyone, I am going to require a group to come with me to free a very important person. Who's willing to risk their lives?" Calm music begins to play in the background, the song starts beating at a good pace, and the first person who agrees to go is Helena and her associate. Tobias looks overwhelmed by her appearance and winks at her, (Oh no Tobias has to be careful not to attract attention from her. Well how do we know that she's not a spy and only wants to capture him, let us keep an eye out on her and her friend). Stimpultonnes, "Well, when I was younger the ladies would always be around me like a swarm of bees." Sam then looks over and says, "I can remember it very well, Sir." Kulumbush, "This doesn't make it better than it was before and it's left her all out there alone," as he looks around first to see if anyone is looking at him to pretend to show his concern.

Tobias, "Have I missed something important here and is there anything important I need to know before we start to look for Lunarnise?" Everyone just looks at each other and thinks - does he already know? As Tobias thinks of a way to save his friend and walking through the passage of the place a secret room appears in bright sunlit colours. It's as if the room is filled up by sand dust with the tallest of ladders that you have ever seen before. With the cutest of all animals of all time but there's also something about this that's unique. "Right, I think it's up to Roland to decide whether he or someone else should take the challenge that awaits them." Tobias and most of the others come over to the room to play a part in resolving the situation and the rescue involved. Chiming music bells in the background. Helena, "Hey Tobias, there you are. I've been expecting you but here you go. I'm with you all the way, I look forward to what's ahead."

Roland, "Well, you guys may have time to catch up with each other after we complete these mysterious quests and save a sister from a Danzel in distress." "She looks fine," Tobias says as he is ready to climb up the ladder. He shouts out, "I won't fly up as it would be cheating." As he climbs over and stands up straight with his head up to the sky, everyone looks in despair. Roland shouts out, "I will be with you all the way and you get to choose one person to set Lunarnise free." Tobias turns to Kulumbush to take care of her and release her from the prison of her own father. He nods his head and accepts. (Narrator, "Do you know what you are doing, as you do realise that Kulumbush likes Lunarnise?") People start to sing, *everyone in the world, getting ready to fight! Literally boys and girls are getting hitched, be careful our teams will challenge! Everyone in the world, getting ready for a fight!*

Tobias continues to make his way into the light of the darkness universe, with Roland and Kulumbush behind him. Just then there was a shadow in the sky that nobody could explain, everyone down starts screaming at the unknown and to the three lads going. But there were no responses from any of them so all the people remaining started marching towards the unknown path. They were told never to go down unless there was an emergency, but in this case, they decided to go ahead and look for Lunarnise anyway. Stimpultonnes, "You know what to do now, go." The weather, all nice and calm, everyone got on their way and started singing, *Lunarnise, Lunarnise, we are coming to release you from your misery so get ready, girl.*

That very moment there was an unknown object floating in the air and it looked like it was moving towards them. With all their energy it seemed to have disappeared from the sky but how did it happen?

There was a huge, wicked laugh. ("Oh, look, it's getting closer above, no way," shouts Narrator.) "It can't be, what is it?" cries out Sterito, "It is Valoie."

Stimpultonnes, "She is a very knowledgeable woman who had a down to earth temperament until one day evil took over her life. I'm sure with enough love from people around her evil shall be broken from her." Valoie, "Oh, so you have met my accomplice. Yet you still stand alone and you refuse to help me conquer what belongs to us." Stimpultonnes, "Yet, I will never stand with you or for you ever again and you lie, as my heart has been broken by you. Now you have everything as you're supposed to be married to the devil in disguise."

As a relief from the past Stimpultonnes had broken free of Valoie but the witch stumbles on and tries to get others involved. She believes that Sir John is an accomplished man who is able to help her needy mind though he is unaware that he will be eaten alive. Valoie stated in her message to Stimpultonnes, "Just before you leave I want something from you, like your stick." "Never," shouted Stimpultonnes and blinded her eyes as he ran out. He managed to escape from the evil witch so he decides to head back to help the crowd and conquer the evil, and to deliver Lunarnise. A smooth voice shouts out, "Help! I'm in trouble, please come to my aid."

Ahead of him, there's a huge gap that he needs to cross, it's all covered in bushes so Stimpultonnes gets out his stick and then says, "Move aside and release this creature," as he swings it backwards and forwards. Just as he was swinging it a head appears and squeaks, then it hobbles over towards him and is scared until he shows a picture of Lunarnise. He then jumps up. Barks with joy as his head moves sideways, face changes. Surprisingly, he jumps and then looks back, squeaks. S.J. starts running in the direction where Lunarnise is held. It's bright morning and the weather is calm as everyone else is off to go to the farthest side of the world to the north where they should locate Lunarnise.

They stay in the light so that the day creatures wouldn't get too close, then S.J. starts making some strange noises. As they all start climbing up towards the top of the mountain they see a huge explosion ahead in front of a mall. Just as all three groups get closer to the mall they see troops in separate lines waiting to attack in front, on horses with sloth heads and their hair slicked up like gel. "Oh my, I haven't seen anything like this before," says Stimpultonnes. "Groups are you ready for this? Charge to it and give them your best." There was a person who was coming forward on their own, her stick held up high. "Hold up, Stimpultonnes, don't you recognise who they are?" "I see the resemblance it's your long-lost daughter look at her, and how she has grown into a beautiful woman." Stimpultonnes, "Oh yes Sam, I am grateful, my daughter. I am at your service, how may I help you?"

In the meantime, back at the sandy room, Tobias holds his head up against the wind that's blowing through to prevent them from getting into the hole while retrieving the egg and the secret key to the unknown. "Roland, are you seeing this right now from down here? It looks like you got something heading towards you from above." "Kulumbush, I see it. From what it looks, it seems to be a train coming out of the tunnel from the clouds, is that possible?" "Well, anything goes here." Roland, "Prepare yourselves everyone, everyone's life is in jeopardy, who are on the train." Kulumbush, "What? Tobias, use whatever you have been taught by your sensei." Tobias, "Yes, sir." Tobias prepares to slow down time to get the train back down safely. He rubs his hands together backwards and forwards as he starts speaking in French. That makes the sound of a very loud voice in the process of the train starting to slow down time with a big clear ball around it. So, it protects everyone that is inside the train. As Tobias is starting to slow down time Kulumbush says, "I didn't know that you could do this." The whole world freezes along with it. "Roland," Tobias says, but there's no answer so he turns to see he is frozen halfway up the ladder.

By this time the world has come to a halt. Tobias, "This is very interesting to see how you all have managed to keep still by my holding time. It's scary to think who's going to be telling the story whilst I get them all down safely.

"Well boy, I hope that you haven't forgotten about me," a soft and gentle voice speaks from beneath. "I'm sorry I haven't introduced myself yet but give me five and I'll tell you what you need to know. Sorry what's your name please?"

"My name is Tobias and I am a second lead to Roland, the world's keeper of this place, and if you can see he is beneath me." "Oh no that's one thing that I cannot do I'm only a Narrator, I jump from book to book to read through peoples' stories. I've been brought in here to assist. For example, you've frozen the whole world and I heard that it's amazing. So, I pushed open the gate that allowed me access, it's said that Tobias is looking comfortable as he is slowly moving the train towards the ground. Oh my gosh, look at everyone's faces as they got frozen. It's a calm but cloudy day here in Tiger Warth. My friend it's about time you should know who I am, I have been with you ever since you were little and abandoned." Tobias, "Oh so I do remember that you were the first to teach me how to talk, walk and how to define myself when in need. I am totally in need, FATHER, yes, but why don't you show yourself?"

Father, (otherwise known as Noah), "I was waiting for you to recognise me first, young child, now I show my true self." The unknown man comes clean about who he really is. "I am a Centaur that has become a great man for my friends and family, I'm the only one who can help amongst my tribe. My son, you've been trained really well. Let me help to complete your job and turn the train in the correct direction. Because it's going to need both of us to move it to a train line." Tobias looks overwhelmed and turns to his adoptive father. Tobias, "Yes please, Father." Noah, "Right, are you ready? When I count to three we're going to pull it down together as a team, that means all hands on deck."

The count-down begins as they both look ready and eager to go. Three, two, one, go - they both start pulling the train and carriages back to land as hard as they possibly can. As soon as they are about to finish one of them accidentally falls off, so they grab it one more time and this one is a success. With the luck of Noah he gives extra strength that comes from his own strength as lightning strikes from him. Tobias sees Father with this power, "How did you know that I have been training for years to reach this level?" "It is something I have been working on and I have passed it on to you also, but where I have got my friends to help you with this power."

"Oh, so that was all you but how did you know where I was, have you always known? I hear the town say something about a sister, do you know anything? I recall hearing something like this and I need to help that person look for her after I find the key and egg of light."

(Designer, "Ah ah oh, I can talk but I can't move, oh my friend, Tobias, what's happening to me? Hey I didn't recognise the train for a minute. And I see that you have met a famous and popular man, how extraordinary?") Tobias, "Yes, this is my father he found me and brought me up since I was at a young age. Oh, hold on, how come you are able to communicate with me, I'm just shocked." Noah, "Sorry boys we have to go now and deliver the train and the carriages. We will find you soon, come on son." Thunder crashes as the train is removed from the clouds, there's a tall dark slim figure leaning down from above and he doesn't look happy with Tobias. Roland speaks with the unknown person, "Who has sent you here and where do you come from?"

Unknown person, "I know what you are looking for and where you can find the key that unlocks the school from underneath for it to be released to the top service. Only one can access the secret code with the key, he is young and bright, second to Roland." In seconds Tobias claps his hands together with a mighty swing and then the world is released, everyone can hear and move around again. "Regardless what happens next we shall be ready for the worst." Tobias, "Roland please continue with our journey to get the key and to claim back the egg of light."

"Okay," replies Roland, let me take the lead. "But you need to come back and find me to finish when I retrieve it, as it needs to be done by my second sidekick." The minute Roland is released he climbs up the ladder. As he reaches the top an angry unknown person walks towards him but then crashes to the ground. "Oh my gosh I need to see if everything is fine with the person who is trying so hard to get back up, what could have happened?" Now the weather has changed so quickly and it seems to be getting colder by the second, "Oh wait, now it's getting warmer."

Woman, "Well to be honest I think it would look like it could be me, but I'm still trying to figure out how to understand what power I have." Tobias and Noah start to make their way through the obstacles after delivering the train and carriages. It seems that someone else has found them both, but with the characteristics they have between the pair it's known that nothing can stop this team. In the far distance there was a huge light sparkling in the sky and they see which way it was coming from. Tobias, Noah and Kulumbush make the same observation that started their journey together, hoping that they will find the key or the egg.

Someone sings, *Shall we bay tonight, shall we bay to you, shall we bay, tonight we lead the way*. There in the distance go Tobias, Noah heading towards the river that holds the shining light. What is that supposed to be? I can hear Roland singing and shouting in the background, he's running and holding up what looks to be like a key.

Roland, "Tobias, I did it. I thought the giant's one hit to the head was all I needed after several attempts. Now I cannot finish it off, it's been told that the second has to complete it, so I am passing it over to you, Tobias." Roland passes over the key to Tobias and he sees a sign on the floor of the shape of a key. As it's passed through to Tobias he notices that there is a new twist in the key hole, it appears to have three sticks from the ground. "Oh, I know this one we all need to grab each lever and pull them all up at the same time, I'll pick red," says Roland. "You take the black one, Noah," and finally that leaves Tobias to grab the white one. "Are you all ready? We go together on my count. The weather is good here but if you look all around there's fields as far as you can see." Three, two, one - they all pull up at the same spot.

A key hole appears from nowhere in front of them, as they all prepare to assist Tobias. Roland, "Right then, you know what you need to do, we are here to help you out if you want." (Designer, "Hold on, what about me? I can justify my assistance.") "That would be a great idea," as a chair is drawn. Tobias, "I wouldn't think I need this as it's a pleasant distraction just in case it is needed. With the air being so nice and warm it would probably look great in what's about to come."

Tobias then reaches down with the key and turns it around. As that's about to happen a big dust storm is brewing. He is pulled out by Roland and Noah. I think something is happening to the ground as there's music playing in the background and the floor disappears. Flags are flying high from underneath, on poles, a building is coming up and it's looking like a giant castle. With it presenting in the middle of a huge field, what a great sight! Just as it finishes, a senior woman walks out from the building.

Headmistress Clariot, "Hello, my dear citizens, my name is Clariot and I'm the headmistress of this school. I'm pleased to meet you."

Chapter 6

The forbidden school!

"Now Tobias, have you sent out the troops to help look for Lunarnise?" "Yes, all of the groups who are in the school are going to bring her with them." Clariot, "I'm holding an opening day for all the students that are involved this year, so come along when you're ready. And Tobias, please come down, don't fly around the top of the castle too close, it could come to life."

The wind blows strong. As trees get weaker, voices from far seem closer than what you would think, then there was silence as Tobias spoke. Tobias, "Thank you for your kind comment Miss, I'm going to find and bring back the famous one, see you soon. I can see that within the school people are walking around inside and around the building. Plus, people who are left behind are going to get involved with signing different individuals' tops that they are wearing. Oh, my goodness, what are they doing? Paint flying around red, green and blue, I'm guessing they're going with those colours for the groups."

The three groups are on their way to the far end of the world, to get Lunarnise but for people to know that they are getting closer, there's a dark and slippery path they are walking through. There are big walking sunflowers heading towards them. Fronk is at the front and decides to draw his sword, at that stage the smallest sunflower cries. "Please don't swipe your sword at me for the sake of my friend who is lost in the forest, but I will never forget this moment and neither will I ever you all." They got up and walked towards them, they didn't know what to expect from them but to get ready and strike. Then they started to walk away and one whispered to Roland, "Call us anytime and we will be at your side and help you."

There's shaking of the world as something was about to happen, but nobody knew it was the school that was doing it as it just wanted to be released. Kulumbush, "Oh no what is that, did you hear it? Plus, it was so loud." Stimpultonnes, "That will do it, with a little bit of luck my power should have worked. Oh my, you are looking beautiful, my lady."

With the power of looking through the ball, Stimpultonnes saw something amazing then recoiled in shock. Sam, "Sir, are you okay? Do you need to sit down for a minute?" Stimpultonnes, "Indeed Sir, thank you very much, you are kind." Tobias, "You made it, we are absolutely delighted with your service and the troops have been given their orders to go inside and take out the young lady." Tobias gathers up his courage and stands on the nearest rock, lets out the loudest roar. Immediately, something magical happens as it turns into a song. Song being sung! By an unknown voice again, "I wonder who that could be," says Kulumbush "and where's Tobias I can't see him anywhere." Everyone laughs at him.

On the other side of this mountain there's a fight between the three groups and the unknown people in the battle for Lunarnise. There are heads being sundered from their bodies and blood flowing everywhere. All kinds of weapons are being thrown around. People shouting, "Release the prisoners, especially Lunarnise, bring her to me or have your brothers' and sisters' lives taken."

Someone from the crowd shouts out, "Halt, bring her to me, my child of the unknown." As he is talking Kulumbush walks out of the cave carrying Lunarnise in his arms. Noah puts his hoodie down and everyone looks around in surprise. "Kulumbush," says Noah, "bring her to me. I know where the loud bang came from earlier. It was this young princess." Noah puts his hand upon her head and says, "From today I take you in as my own and help you." Lunarnise, "Thank you so much Father, and everyone who helped with my release. This spell has been broken with the great loss of Marilyn." As Lunarnise began to look sad for her loss, Noah turned to her and said, "Look on the bright side, my child, sometimes we need to make tricky decisions that will hurt but it's the will that keeps us pushing forward."

Noah, "I would like to introduce you to a very special person in your life but you both know each other and never realised. It is believed you have a sibling now that Stimpultonnes has already agreed for me to provide for and protect you both. Tobias, come meet your sister." Tobias turns to both Lunarnise and Noah then comes running towards them. Tobias, "Well, hello madam, I have been waiting for this moment since our father found me out there in the open all alone and abandoned. My family was killed by land people." Lunarnise, "Come here, big brother I need to get used to this one. Give me a hug."

Both Lunarnise and Tobias hug it out for a few minutes, speechless, as they looked at one another and both whispered, 'I'm not going to lose you again.' Stimpultonnes comes over running fast and hoovering in a floating skateboard. He looks funny as he floats over the water. Stimpultonnes, "You need to come quickly the school is under attack by Sir John and his team."

Stimpultonnes rushes back towards the school and takes out his stick in preparation, "This time you will pay." Roland, "Right, you have heard him everyone, get ready to challenge him and save our state from the evil." So off everyone goes to the back of the mountain to get to the castle known as the school. ("Hold up," shouts out Designer, "where have you been, Jake, we've all missed you. Noah had to take care of things for you." Narrator, also known as Jake, "Well, let's say I had to take care of a few things but thank you, Sam, for asking, I'm here now.") Sam stands in front of the crowd just before he helps out with the mess at the castle, still dressed smart.

Roland takes the lead with everyone else following him and Tobias seconds behind them all so he can watch out for anything unexpected. As they reach the fortress Tobias couldn't help but say, "How have we got ourselves into this mess now? Everybody charge." "Well it looks like someone has just frozen everything out, oh no why am I still talking then? Oh, I see. Tobias where did you come from?" "As he's got his paw on my shoulder I wanted you to look." "Sam, I've been trained by the three ninja rabbits." (Narrator, "What do we do now, how do we make this stop?") Tobias,"I've got an idea. How about we share the castle with them and then challenge them to different levels of difficult activities? Trust me I have a plan to get rid of the unwanted people." (Narrator, "That sounds a great way of getting them out in the future, so is it a bit like Harry Potter?") Tobias, "Oh no, sorry it's not quite like that. It has its own twists, and monsters with the unknown consequences." Tobias closes his hands and pulls them apart to unlock time and eventually everyone moves again, as Kulumbush shouts from the crowd, "Could you please repeat it again?" Tobias just looks at Kulumbush's face and says, "Never mind."

Stimpultonnes, "Right, I give this entire yard of people three groups to challenge for the first year's cup, now I shall hand over to the Headmistress of the school." Clariot, "Thank you Stimpultonnes, right then, ladies and gentlemen, boys and girls are you ready to find out who is your team?" Everybody screams as they wait to hear where they would be going and who would be their team mate. Clariot, "So the three groups - first we have Mountainterus as they are bad, then we have got Villgarious as average and finally Gruwpertorious and they seem to be good." "I hear people call the school, The Enchanted School of the Forest, is that right?" says Stimpultonnes.

Fluffy comes to run up to Lunarnise licking her face and jumping around. He is a baby dragon with bat wings. Sir John, "May I say something about some individuals that are here?" He starts looking with a smirk on his face, a look that he is planning something behind their backs when they are not looking. Clariot, "No you shouldn't, wait until you find out who is in your group so you can get your chance at winning the cup. Right, I have Sir John for one group, I need two people for the other teams. Sir John, your group shall be called Mountainterus." Sir John, "Thank you, oh and you look beautiful tonight," as people start to look at him they know what he's up to. Clariot tries not to look and starts blushing, "The second group should be given to Ponsternose and your group shall be Villgarious."

Ponsternose, "You are welcome, we will win this battle." Sir John looks over at him in disgust. Clariot, "I think the last one should be given to Noah. Can you handle the pressure?" Noah, "Yes madam, you can count me in, I'm ready to go out for gold." Miss Clariot looks over at Noah and smiles and Noah notices her reaction, "And maybe one day I can come back here to see her," he whispers. Just then she catches his eye and quickly nods before anyone could see. At that sight everyone looks over at the gentleman who was walking down the corridor swinging his hair sideways.

Head of school walks out of the office from the back of the castle. He is a bit plump and short, with a beard and dressed in black suit. Head of school, "Well hello, how is everyone doing today? I am proud to announce I will call out your name and give you a number from 1 to 3. One being Mountainterus: two being Villgarious: and three is Gruwpertorious." Everyone looks. "Is that the same guy from the corridor? Oh my, we feel embarrassed." Then he speaks. "Head of School Group 1, Atchon and crew, Group 2, Helena and Poppals and the village people, and finally group 3, Tobias, Kulumbush, Fronk, Lunarnise, Jake, Sam, and Nixo-Stain-Dexun will be amongst them. He's smaller than others so please be careful, Sterito." Clariot, "Right, teams have been chosen so I'm going to need you all to find your rooms and get some sleep and be ready at dawn. Group one over to the end of the castle, group two to the left of the castle and group three up on the second floor now let's go." Lunarnise, "I'm going to enjoy it here, what do you think, Fluffy?" Fluffy responds with 'wow bow'. Just as she was saying this to Fluffy and walking around to their side looking for the room, Lunarnise came across someone who seemed to be a professor, Professor Pickalford.

"Well, hello my child, it's an honour to finally meet you, your mother was a great teacher. I hope she is well. Lunarnise, "My mother, oh yeah, she is no longer with us, Sir, she risked her life to save me from evil. And he has found me here." As she stood at the door wondering which room she was in, Professor Pickalford, "Yes, we have been informed of this and he cannot do anything. Besides you have Noah to protect you. Anyway, it's time for you to go to bed, here's your room, good night and sweet dreams." "That makes sense," says Lunarnise as she walks through her room and washes, and flops in her bed. Fluffy looks up and jumps beside her and they both fall asleep. As everyone is in their rooms and sleeping, Noah is patrolling to check out if his team is okay. By doing this it meant that he could go to his room. As he was going into his room the whole floor started to rock and jingle, Noah turned around and there was nothing. Noah sighed and looked outside, went back in and slept.

In the meantime, on the other side of the castle Sir John's team had different plans, to confuse the situation between the two other teams. They planted a tree in the middle of their garden, little to their knowledge that it is able to talk about others but not in a pleasant manner. Ponsternose tells him that this isn't good and what if the Head of School finds out. Ponsternose, "I have just realised that you are taking this seriously and it will also make our friendship suffer." Sir John looks up at Ponsternose and grins. Ponsternose, "Oh so it's like that, is it? We will see who's the better person to guide our team into victory," whispering, so as not to wake up anybody. (Designer, "Jake, Jake, where are you? Can you tell me what is going on? We have to let Noah know." Jake, "No, let us observe this situation during the recess and remember our place. We have been assigned to Lunarnise, we're devoted to her presence.")

The microphone speaks, "This is Miss Clariot. It is not tolerated of any person to be up and out of their rooms, you never know what to expect when you're dealing with these groups in a conspiracy to challenge for the championship and cup. There's a whole bunch of fairies that have been caught in the crossfire of Atchon and I don't think they are Lunarnise's family. Because they were carrying a box and they decided to hide it in the bushes just outside of the school and a location sent to the direct people. So, they took off and went back towards their home as well as throwing kisses to those who see them and shout out, 'work as a team to survive'."

Stimpultonnes walks around the corridors, to make sure that everyone is sound asleep in their rooms, and to be prepared for any villains. Sterito, 'I need to tell Lunarnise that there is a package outside of the school left for her notice. Could this be a trick?' he wondered. Stimpultonnes, "There was an unexpected delivery that had been sent to the school playground for attention to, with the land gulls flying overhead ready to pounce. Hold up ladies and gentlemen I think someone is on the ground what do you think? Is there a chance that they will be able to get up? Hold up whatever it is, it's just gone underneath the sand pit, has it self-destructed before anyone could reach the box?"

As this is happening the castle bricks are coming off not knowing they were running out of their spaces and they seem much alive. (Narrator, "You were told from the beginning that this castle is much alive and listening and understanding what you require. And at the same time, it doesn't respect the disliked people." Sam, "This is news to me because this castle has unknown secrets.") And the floor is going up and down, drums are being played, Noah shouts out, "What is happening outside? It woke me up," as he stumbled to his feet.

On the other hand, downstairs and outside in the courtyard there was something else about to happen. Two humans with crocodile faces were walking around and laughing at the activities they got ready for the groups. What people don't understand is that they plan to upset all groups with the upcoming events. Stimpultonnes, "Jake and Claudia, what's going on here, what is happening with the building, is it magic or could it be a coincidence?" Jake, "Well, it's something like that, you wouldn't believe it until you see it for yourself." "Well then my dear, let's enjoy this moment together whilst it lasts." Out of the blue the door swings open and off its hinges to run out on the playing field. Claudia and Jake look in surprise but then suddenly something happens. A boy is lost in the woods and shouts out. The door skids to him and grabs his arm. Drags him to safety and his dragon that is covered to his neck and then takes them back to the castle. It is believed that the boy is called Dillon.

(Narrator is surprised by the fact that this was known to the school, now you have met with secrets of the unknown who has the ability to make a difference. Is there a nurse who can assist with this boy and dragon as they lay on the ground, but conscious and breathing?) Stimpultonnes, "I'm so glad to see that there are people who are willing to help you, just wait until Tobias gets wind about it. He is a good friend of his from younger years, and I think that they were somewhat of brothers." (Narrator, "Well my fellow humans and Americans, it is about to be dawn, look at the skies with the stars going to sleep and the sunrise approaching.") As the sun is coming out to shine on the horizon, everybody goes to the windows to check this out.

The castle is rising up and awakening from its shadow of the night. Roland says, "What a wonderful and beautiful day!" Animals start to call out, it being 5am, people realising, 'is it that early'? Then a voice announces, "Training begins today, get up everyone come stand in a line." All three teams slowly get up and start to wash, clean their teeth and have breakfast, then make their way to the front. Drums play in the background with winds that start to race through. Everyone starts coming together outside, looking at each other's faces and saying, "Is this what you're favouring to do in the relation between butter figures?" Head of school walks into the courtyard from the top of the castle. 'Quick,' people whisper, 'he is coming.'

'Silence in the Shadows of the House' song begins to play in the distance, *Ehh bil ell ehh bil ehh, whenever you walk, you know I smile, I want to be on your shoulder forever and lie next to your heart!* Head of school, "Right then, ladies and gentlemen, boys and girls we are here to welcome you to the school of the unknown, yet to acquire a name."

Clariot, "That's it. Some good moves that Tobias is showing us or is showing off." Jake, "You know that is not true, now you and Fronk get up there." Miss Clariot had just walked upto everyone and passed the Headmaster in the corridor, she said, "Oh I'm sorry, sir, I didn't notice you there."

Roland was standing at the front and said, "I need the head of all three groups to get up to the front where the table is and pick a few from your team. Later I would like to see if you know your team and see who would challenge later." Within seconds of being given instructions it looks like the whole of these people have already made it clear they had forgotten what was going on. Sir John looks happy that he has made the announcement, he is convinced a team will fail.

All three groups have been given instructions to go to the forest and find the first stranger who sticks their head up. They head out into the forest to find the three wise people who no one knows will help. One of the groups goes off to the left to see what they may find, group two goes straight through the middle and finally three, heads down to the right. Everyone shouts out, "Good luck." Noah heads to his own path with group three, "We will find out what happens next so that we can choose right."

Wind is blowing higher than expected, Noah looks up and says, "Hold on to your hats, the weather doesn't look good here." Tobias, "We should find something unusual." There was a little bit of confusion about what they were supposed to be doing and an unexplained person was standing in front of them. Roland, "A person half my size built a bridge unto my level." They stood still and looked at each other.

Next minute the under sized person came closer and Roland asked him, "Where did you come from?" He replied, "I belong to this plant." It was okay as it was the only beautiful one that shines like a star, "You should see it at night," says Fronk, "I have walked through here many times before. You will like it, I didn't know that you were a son of plant, I have heard many such stories." Noah looking up, high and mighty, and his hair blowing around in the wind, "Wait, where has this unusual weather come from?" "Stand up straight, soldier," says Sterito. As he tells him he flops down to the ground. "Oh, look at that," says Kulumbush, "what have you found here, boy?"

Wind blows faster and breaks the ice cubes, all three teams have arrived back at the fortress. (Narrator, "The Empire has spoken hastily, it looks like we have taken in three members of the public, so Head of school do you accept?") The Head of School walks from where he was sitting, down, takes a stroll across the courtyard. He looks at his three freshmen who are clueless about their positions. Head of School, "There is no call we don't answer, there's no faith that we betray. (Narrator, "The Empire asks to bring peace to our nation, to all groups.") Stimpultonnes, "House of representatives or trainees accept, group one we never forget, we have never forgotten group two, we shall conclude, but (alarm bells) and group three Noah, - Noah, Roland and Tobias." Head of School lights up three different papers with a message that groups will read one each, then disappear after 5 minutes. First one reads, 'you will learn about how your pupils are affected or fail the test'. Second tells a tale about the unknown. Third, 'enough, you have a mission to find the truth about what exists'.

Head of School, "Well let's see who each group has found and who they are before continuing." Sir John, "Well my team has been working on the project and we have found a solution to this by picking up an old lady." Ponsternose, "Say hello to my new little friend, meet Woofers, a fluffy dog or that's what I think." Woofers looks familiar, Jake notices and is quiet. Head of school, "Okay, that's interesting but what do you know about them, and Noah what do you have for me?" Noah, "An amazingly talented actor who made her own movie via the new platform, meet Princess Isabeline."

Tobias, "This sounds really cool but I'm just curious what kind of stuff is going on." Roland, "That, my brother, is Sir John, he has been up to something since he got here and we need to beat his team." Tobias, Kulumbush and Fronk plus Lunarnise all look over at Roland and Noah, and smile. (Narrator, "This is the point where Fluffy comes to run around us and then he sneaks into Sir John's group and ties up the whole team with string.")

As Jake was saying that, Fluffy had already done something to the team that was meant to confuse them. "Oh, my goodness, is that what she has done look over there, it's funny." Everyone laughs and looks over to see what was happening in the other group, and then is disturbed by the Head of school. Head of school, "I'm sending each group on a task to see who can carry out their assignments in a timely manner." That is what they were told but the moment two groups took the lead and went on through the school where they weren't allowed to go, was when the whole school started to spin around. There's something about this school as it's not the first time something has gone wrong or unusual movements occurred. It is like a fair ride. Claudia, "Amazing!" Jake, "I've never seen or heard anything like this before. What are we supposed to do about it?" Tobias,"We should all get together and prepare for the next biggest challenge of our lives. I'll fly in around it to try and distract it whilst others involved can help slow it down."

Roland gets an idea of what to do with the way how it is going round, which will take some work but 'I wonder if it is worth doing?' Roland, "Roughly, the size of the space is limited so let's just hope we can grab its attention in getting the ball following the school." Lunarnise gets up and goes to her backpack and takes a skipping rope, and throws it to Kulumbush. "Now slow it down." That is the point where Kulumbush and Fronk have to go head to head to attempt to stop the spinning. Kulumbush, "Right, Fronk, are you going to catch the rope when I throw it over to you? One, two, three, here goes nothing."

They both grab the rope and then stand back to hold it and with a mighty force the castle collapses from its feet. "Hooray," everyone shouts, "We did it, we did it, this is the way we go to bed and pull it from your head." "You never know what to expect from the unknown - is anyone ever going to rename the school? Any ideas, guys?" The school sits down in the same place, the castle moves its stones to a wider angle to look like it's got its arm thinking about something and looks so funny. The two teams who were in the castle are still stuck on the ground, after being thrown around. Can you imagine their faces when it was spinning? The weather is so calm at the moment with echoes that could be heard for miles. There was a lion growling, wait, isn't that Tobias? Jake, "It looks like we are going to need medical attention over here, someone has severely banged his head." Just like that Sir John grabbed his arm and pulled him over closer, then said, "I don't know who you are but I have my eyes on you." With all his power he threw Jake down in the basement. "Ha ha ha, this will teach him." Lunarnise heard of what happened from Claudia and rushed into the castle and followed the lower stairs. With others in her team not far behind these stairs seemed like they were going on forever. As they got closer to the end of the tunnel of stairs, heads appeared to be moving away and it looked to be Sir John and his team. He looked like he is up to something, throwing balls of fire to destroy the main structure. Someone else needs to take control of the whole situation.

Lunarnise picks up a staff and runs towards Sir John. Roland, "Watch out he has turned around and now he's behind you, girl. You concentrate and focus on attack." Magical music playing in the background, as different types of pictures that are on the wall all around the staircase are coming alive. Tobias, "This will come in handy when he goes to challenge us." Helena, "Right, teams we're going to be up for grabs by anybody so let's be ready." Tobias, "Oh yeah that's right what Helena said." Tobias pauses as he looks over to her then says, "Did she say that correctly or not?"

Stimpultonnes, "Tobias, stop checking the young woman out, what's coming over you now?" ('Is there something that I don't know,' he says in his mind. Lunarnise, "He seems to be in a trance. We need to help him so he doesn't hurt himself, quick someone help." Kulumbush, "I see where it's coming from, over there someone has got his hand up with electricity that is guiding them." Fluffy jumps up and down, running around making noises. Roland, "Stay still, my friend, what is the matter? Oh yeah, I can see. Let's help our dear friends."

In the blink of an eye they both touch Tobias's tail and vanish as it has been said they are close by with the regular season starting, when part of the castle starts coming to life. Helena and Tobias find themselves in a situation where they are inside of an old picture. Holding onto each other and then start kissing romantically, (oh my gosh everyone has noticed the difference in the photo). Stimpultonnes, "Is that not master Tobias and who's the lucky lady? Oh yes, it's the warrior. Oh, my boy, how's he going to get out?" Noah, "Oh my goodness how was that possible, how is he going to get out of there with a member of team two?" Roland, "Sir, I do say that the picture on the wall does look like, oh my what a pleasant surprise!"

As Roland was saying, Tobias and his acquaintance jumped out of the picture, and made a clear jump back into reaction. Tobias looks at everyone around as they seemed shocked, what just happened? Stimpultonnes, "Welcome back." Tobias, "It's good to be back, isn't it my dear?" Helena, "Nnnooo!"

Helena is kept in the same picture with time running out to save her from the fire ropes around her neck. Stimpultonnes, "Hold back, children, I got this. I've seen this somewhere before, here goes 'ricopop'." The fire disappeared from the rope, beating of the magic drums. Lunarnise is overwhelmed with what is happening, she begins to wonder if there will ever be light at the other end of the tunnel. She starts taking a swing at Sir John but then he moves to avoid the danger, how did he do that? As Lunarnise struggled to get him, Sir John, "You cannot do that to me as I am watching you all and making sure what plan you have." "You can never be too sure of what you're going to accomplish with what you are going through." There's a huge fight going on among all the groups. Tobias is trying to make sure that everyone stays healthy. Lunarnise is jumping on and off the rocks sticking out of the castle, as she's running around everyone's heads to try and attack Atchon and Sir John. Just as Lunarnise thought she would trap them in an abandoned world they both set confusions between themselves. And when they thought nothing would happen, there was a hand that came out of nowhere and used a spear that shrunk Sir John and Atchon.

Roland, "I've been waiting for this moment," grabbed a jar with a lid to put Sir John into it, picking him up and screwing the lid up tightly. A shadow goes past really quickly with the spear. I guess we will never know who that was. Tobias, "We have to thank the unknown person." "Hurry," everyone says, "we can party now." Fronk, "Hold on, guys please turn around, quick question, where has Atchon gone? He is missing." (Narrator, 'So, I am not sure if I'm captured anymore I need to get up and go quickly before I see anyone').

The fight is over here, everybody's going crazy to get up the stairs. (Designer, 'Well done, to you all for completing this amazing quest and we look forward to the future projects. We have a supervision that will arise, learn from what you believe in. Oh why, oh why, guys like you have done well but need to team up to get successful'). Stimpultonnes, "What we are trying to say is that you all need to start working together as team and trust in each other's abilities. It's believed to be the first in history that there is an active source inside of the brain of the castle which is how it communicates, but it's unknown whether there is something else inside that remains mysterious. Will anyone ever discover the truth about this secret passage?"

Everyone just looked through and motioned, 'let's go'. The castle starts playing a tune peacefully as they slowly leave, all except the teachers. Noah, "Teams, are you ready for the next quest?" All three teams are finally in the courtyard and are practising their own style of games ready for what will come. Head of school makes his way to the field for a discussion on coaching within, ('or should I be concerned about the teaching?') Head of school, "I would like to announce that we are down to two group leaders, something unexpected has happened to the third leader so who will like to lead it?" Poppals, "Why don't I step in till you accommodate someone?"

Stimpultonnes, "I don't see why not. Step right into the flames, girl, I hope that this won't hurt your friendship with Helena." As all the teams are back with their leaders they don't realise that there's a bigger problem than they have ever experienced. Ready for the next stage they are walking out of the courtyard and through to the next level. That's when they walk into the forest and through to the jungle where they will encounter a new enemy.

Chapter 7

Dark and slippery Jungle!

Sterito, "Master, are you ready for the toughest challenge of your entire lives? There's a lot of preparation to become champions. Well what are you waiting for? Let's go."

"Welcome fellow students, unknown teachers, associates I hope you are well prepared to take on the league," an unexpected voice proclaims. Who it may be is not known to the eye of man as Stimpultonnes tries to look around. Stimpultonnes, "This way through, but be careful not to step off the trail as we have no idea what happens, it's looking like a vegetable trail with different colours." (Music) Tobias, "I'm guessing that this is to take away any potential pressure from you."

Lunarnise, "Hey girl, where are you hiding? Come out, come out, wherever you're gone, you know that I can find you."

"That sounds really cool, though where is the little fluffiest cute thing gone? Show yourself," calls Aviana. Lunarnise, "Hey girl, you found us, how? How long have you been tracking me?" Aviana, "Well you see it's like this, I was one of those who helped you escape from the prison, I didn't want you to see me." Fluffy, Lunarnise's friend came running through, full of joy. Lunarnise tells her to stop. Fluffy was going too fast to the gravel where they weren't supposed to be. "Hey girl, where were you going? Oh, I see you're racing to mummy," says Lunarnise. It's getting dark on a cold Wednesday afternoon. And Fluffy was lying on the ground with a rope around her leg. "How are we supposed to get her out of there? Once again, we're all going to spend time together in the woods, in the creepiest of all places. You choose where we lay our heads," replies Tobias. "At least there's going to be a campfire with a few people accepting that quest to find firewood. Roland is part of those so please be gentle with him." Lunarnise, "I love you guys around me, it makes me feel good and I want to sing and dance but first I have to rescue my little friend."

Everybody laughs, "How do we help you, my dear princess? Wait, is that possible? In fairness to all of you we need to prepare ourselves for the night, let's eat some food together and be merry." Claudia, "I agree with you but firstly can you see that where Fluffy is, it's sinking sand so we need to make it fast?" Tobias gets to her side and lift hers up. Flying up, he grabs her with all his strength. He then begins to fall down a slippery slope. He tries again harder and manages to save both himself and Fluffy. "Hoorray," all clapping, saying, "Well done."

An unexpected surprise is coming from the skies, looking at Tobias. 'Who could that be?' he whispers. Tobias, "Nixo-Stain-Dexun, oh my goodness, I wondered where he had gone to, now I see him closer. He's my friend who looked out for me and we have been friends ever since." Nixo-Stain-Dexun crash lands on the ground around the side of the camp and looks like he is hurt. "In fairness, my child, what happened to you? I will call amongst my friends to make sure that you get medical care. And bring you straight back as soon as you recover, as you know my son," says Noah. Tobias just smiled as his dad galloped into the woods with his friend on his back. Noah, "I can see my son happy."

Kulumbush, "Hang on a minute! I think I can see a bat in the background. Is he just walking through, can he do that? Hey buster, get out of here." The bat turns to him, pulls out a gun and aims it straight towards him and says, "Are you ready for me, punk?" then continues to walk through the screen. Stimpultonnes, "Now you are being sarcastic or just being plain stupid," and walks away, smiling to himself. (Narrator, "Well, you know anything is possible here in the wild, don't you think?" Designer "Come on, Jake you're making me laugh, it's not even in my schedule. Stop playing with me.") Bat, "Don't mind me, guys, I'm just lost." His wings are a shield of steel as he is a grey bat in a yellow jumpsuit and wings. Bat, "Bye all. Oh, is that the exit door?" He walks through and disappears.

Everyone is shocked and shouts out, "Who was that guy? and he has the nerve to walk through here." Chill-out music plays smoothly throughout the whole passing. Lunarnise, "I'm just trying to get my head around it and wondering what it would be like if I'd lost a friend, not knowing there's more happening out here." There's galloping sound. Tobias, "Dad, you are back so soon, how are you and what's the situation with Nixo?" Noah, "Well my son, he is stable and healthy, recovering from an arrow." Tobias, "What happened to him, hope he is well, when can I go and see him?" And starts pacing up and down. "Where is he, what happened? I wish I could have been there too." Noah, "First slow down, I'll take you to him in the morning, he should be well enough by then."

One group starts putting up the tents as dark clouds are closing in. Everyone chipped in to get it done faster. Supper's ready - soup and bread, plus drinks for all. Sam, "I'm going to play a little trick on some of these kids." Jake says, "What a good idea! I shall hide an arrow in the middle of the ground for the next game."

Stimpultonnes started to play the guitar in the middle of the camp. He starts getting attention from all of the forest. Fronk then went into the darkness of the forest to see if he could find a small group of people who had gone into the woods earlier. He didn't notice a small muddy-like pit and slipped into it. He was unable to get out so he yelled for help. A strange and terrifying sound came out of nowhere and there was a shadow looking at him as he looked terrified and helpless. It made him feel like he lost control, the shadow came closer and closer. "Please don't hurt me," Fronk cried. As the figure grew closer it appeared to be a dirty woman who was completely covered by the swamp. "Don't worry my son, I'm not going to hurt you," she whispered. "Why are you whispering?" asked Fronk. "Well you see," says the woman, "it's like this. It goes back to when I was young and married. My husband was a player around other women and he was a narcissist in many different ways." The whole story was told to Fronk and he was amazed by the way it turned out. "You don't seem to be able to hurt a fly, why are you looking the way you do?" said Fronk. "I have had to disguise myself because of Sir John, have you heard of him?" "So, you're Lunarnise's mother! No way." "Please you have to calm down, I don't want people hearing you. Oh, by the way young man, my name is Marilyn," she says quietly. "If I know my daughter, she will work two and two and put them together. I do hope she is fine." Marilyn graciously looks up to the sky and wonders as she says it. She then leans back to lift the young man out of the swamp. "I think I need to get you cleaned up, come with me, boy. Let's go back to my house to clean you up, boy, have lunch and you can go back to the camp." Fronk,"Hold on a second, how do you know about the camp area around the corner?" Marilyn,"The animals let me know my daughter was near, but I have to be careful because there are eyes everywhere watching us." They both reached the house and Marilyn cleaned him up and let him eat. She walked Fronk back to the campsite and as he mixed in with marshmallows, Marilyn returned to the swamp.

Lunarnise looked up at the unexpected arrival of Fronk and the lady, and gets excited that she knows her but doesn't know exactly from where. She goes back to sleep without Fronk realising she knows anything about the situation. Tobias is flying around low doing a local patrol around the area, to see if everything is alright. "So far so good," he says. Roland looks up at Tobias as he checks all is clear, he then figures out how the jungle is not what it seems and gives Tobias a signal to come down.

Tobias sees Roland's sign and comes back to land, while a piano is played. Everyone else is sleeping. It is nearly dawn, everything looking so calm and peaceful. Roland is up alongside Stimpultonnes. Unknown to everyone, Marilyn comes and she starts preparing breakfast. 'I want to remain as close as I possibly can to make sure that Lunarnise and her friends stay safe,' says Marilyn to herself, softly. Before her very own eyes there is something that has fallen to the ground, it turns out to be a sphinx cat covered in sand, with wings. Just then there's a big bang in the sky and trumpet sounds starting off quietly but getting louder as it gets closer. Marilyn uses her own instruments to grab the cat faster than anything to help and hide it away from plain sight. Suddenly, there is a huge explosion just outside of the campsite, and a group of riders were heading towards them.

With the horizon so bright in the distance and the horses in Egyptian style plus the gold shining so much, spears pointing out like they can kill, this is where people need to pull together to fight back against these forces of evil. A short knight comes out to speak up for his army, "I'm prepared to fight for what belongs to me but if you hand over my precious treasure I won't let that happen." Roland, "I'm the world's first soldier," as he steps forward. "I believe my team and if they say that what you're saying isn't true or even seen anything then I stand with my people, my Lord." The knight of the school stood close, as he spoke, "Right, I have to take your word for it and totally understand where you are coming from. Okay, lads and ladies, let's go home." "Roll out," he replies with tense music playing in the background, then out of nowhere he starts some dance moves and says, "I don't care if I look ridiculous."

They all start to leave their positions as they were getting ready to battle for the rights, and try to claim their prized possession. The moment they started going one of the best women fighters dropped out and little did they know she was close with the cat. Fronk had been watching what happened and he was looking at her, as he took a shine to her eyes. He walked over to her. As soon as he got close enough he looked over at the young woman and said, "Salaam aleikum." The Egyptian woman was surprised by what Fronk said. She smiled and said, "You are welcome, to hear someone else say that makes me happy. It means 'May peace be with you'." She walked away from Fronk, swinging her hair from left to right, which caught the attention of Fronk, as he fell down in front of Tobias.

Tobias, "Oh my, I remember this from when I would get them to notice you." Egyptian woman, "Hey boys, are you coming or not?" She looks back at them and flashes her eyes. Marilyn, "I'm guessing that someone is flirting here and poor Fronk doesn't know that." Quietly, to herself, 'Looks like I'm going to have to be here for as long as I can to watch out for these kids and mother them.'

"Kids, come and get your breakfast now," says Marilyn, smiling first time in a long while. Least. Then the cat comes to her and meows. Marilyn looks at the cat and says, "I'm going to call you Cleo." (Editor: This episode of the knight, Egyptian woman etc. can be cut off)

Cleo looks up and starts purring. "I guess you like that, girl," as Cleo looks at what Marilyn said and she continues purring. Kulumbush looks at the other side of the room and finds a control panel and a song. *Owner of a lonely heart* starts playing, of course yes, then everyone looks over at him. The Egyptian woman walks up to him and says, "If you really love her then why don't you prove to her that you can protect her, no matter what?"

Kulumbush stands up straight, slightly embarrassed, and clueless about the situation. The Egyptian woman then goes over to Lunarnise and tells her, "I think he's in love, girlfriend," and whispers, 'but I believe he may be a spy so be careful,' and walks away.

Lunarnise, "What was that supposed to mean? Was that meant for me or was it you teasing me again, my dearest brother?" Tobias turned to look at her, "Sis, I think someone is falling for you." Laughs, as he goes in front of her. (Narrator, "Stop teasing the poor child bro, look man it's not funny anymore. Dude, do you remember when Helena had a crush on you? Now that was hilarious.") Helena, "Yes darling, I'm still here and I've not forgotten about you," and comes over to kiss Tobias on his lips. He steps back in shock at what just happened. Sam, "Dame, guys, what have I missed out on, why are we all standing out here?" Song plays, *Let's get it on,* then fades away slowly.

Noah comes back from his morning run to see both Helena and Tobias kissing. "Oh, my goodness, I've never seen anything like this before, wow!" He proceeds to his checks and says, "I'm proud of my son." Lunarnise teases Tobias for being a little romantic, "Oh Tobias, hope you're not using your tongue," as she steps back, laughs. "See who's teasing who now!" A voice speaks from behind, "You can never predict what life will bring but in exchange you have to be there for one another, no matter what." Fronk,"I'm guessing that could be Marilyn," as he walks over towards everyone. Marilyn laughs as she came from the trees in the distance, "I'm happy to help where I can." People are laughing and screaming and dancing around to drumming music being played in the background. Everyone is busy talking to each other, and do not notice the sand pits just ahead where a beetle crawled and fell inside. Tobias looked around to see what was happening, a small group had gathered in the pit so someone would attempt to rescue them.

Stimpultonnes, "I have an idea, why don't you grab the plank of wood from behind them, to help pull them out to safety?" (Narrator just got there as they were going down but lost the little furry friend, "Who has seen the cute one?") All the other people who were around watching, pointed downwards, someone shouts, "Does it mean we need to go beneath the floor we're standing on?" ("Okay, I guess I should follow," replies Narrator. "Please, someone explain this to my wife." He dives into the pit, head first. Designer, "Oh, I do hope that

Jake will be okay and able to return home after." He looks puzzled and confused as he walks up to the pit, with the weather picking up speed as the wind blows through.)

Roland, "Sam, my dear friend, I'm sure he will be fine," as he comes charging over from where he was sitting. Cleo came out of hiding to show Lunarnise where there's an outside opening to the pit that nobody else had seen. "Wow, well thank you girl," as Lunarnise rubbed the back of her left ear and Cleo gave out such a big meow. With everyone gazing up to the skies and the lush of leaves that made the forest sounds, shaking off the desire of a chocolate river flowing through the steamy waters. And the beating of the rain falling down so quickly making it a mucky surface for all to see clicking through the tiny cracks on the trees. (Editor: Isn't everyone looking down the pit?)

The sleeping orchestra awakens as soft music becomes louder! Noah comes trotting down to where the door is and tries to get it open and calls the group of people who were in his team to find the rest of them and get them out.

Tobias, Roland went running through the door with Kulumbush, and Dillon followed shortly afterwards. "Right let's go," says Dillon. Looking at the stars as he walks and stumbles to the floor and rolls down a pit. Tobias looks over and says, "What just happened here?" Within seconds there was a gush of smoke coming out from the distance.

Roland and Tobias decided to be careful about the possibility of unexpected events, as stories were being told about a two-headed land shark. "I believe it could just be a misunderstanding between a rock and a snail," as they both saw the same thing over in the light, that looked to be the mystery. Roland rollercoasters over the edge, and Tobias looks in shock. A voice says out of nowhere, "Rescue me, bro." Tobias opens his wings and flies down from above. Like people have been saying there's something hidden inside the world and moving around, it's likely that they might be true. As there's movement within the walls of the cave but not sure what it may be, "Keep an eye on what the shadow looks like, Kulumbush," says Stimpultonnes.

(Designer, "Well do you know that this is a serious problem? It's a second time something like this has occurred. First of all, who's calling me by that name?" As he looks down, "Oh, I'm sorry my dear." Voice, "Well, what do we need to do about this situation? Wait let's bomb them up, we will never know who they are but we'll catch whoever is responsible, he, he.")

Claudia looks at Lunarnise and says, "That's disgusting, how would they feel if it was you?" Cleo then walks up and makes a big wind spiral to help those falling down the hole. A few moments later she has Tobias and Roland secure in a secret room belonging to an elf. Roland says to Tobias, "Hey man, you need to duck your head, there's not enough room for anything in here, let's find another way out of here." At the sounds of thunder there is screaming from beneath, as well as thumping on the walls all around. "Brace yourselves." "Noah please help me," shouts Tobias as he has just fallen down in front of Roland and got trapped in a netting. Like a flash, there was a spaceship that came in fast from above, undid the netting that had Tobias captured. It grabbed him as Tobias looked weak. He had used most of his energy to escape. He looked up and saw Nixo-Stain-Dexun "my best friend" and dropped to the ground.

Nixo picks up Tobias, takes a moment and says, "Boy, you are heavy, what do you eat?" as he places him on the table to regain his powers. "Don't worry about Tobias he is only charging." At the same time Lunarnise has a call from Stimpultonnes, "Could you be helpful and go to Tobias's aid?" Lunarnise asks, "What happened to my brother?"

Lunarnise was really worried about her brother, and rushed to get him well again after the attack that happened. Lunarnise used her wings for the first time so she was flying around and bumping into objects. Lunarnise finally figured out how to use them and flew to the spacecraft, "Where is my brother?" Nixo motioned, "Come this way, my dear friend." They both went to the room where Tobias was and she started to put her hands on Tobias's face and body. He started to wake up, looked up at her and said, "Thank you, my dear sister, you have helped me once again." "Right, Tobias, you wait here," says Lunarnise. "We will go to rescue everyone from underneath, so you can regain your strength for what lies ahead."

Off go Nixo and Lunarnise. As they leave the ship Tobias is left in an unknown ship, that no one knows where it's currently from or who might be lurking on it. Lunarnise decides to take the lead through the side door to retrieve her friends from down underneath, and continue to the murkiest activity ever at play. She turns to Nixo, "Follow me this way, I see a secret room." (Just like that from nowhere Narrator shouts out "hello" and it echoes.)

There is a tiny roar and in seconds everyone starts laughing and saying, "What is this supposed to be, what a big baby!" "Oh, come on," says Lunarnise, "that's not helping my brother. You wait till he hears you." Helena says from above, "He is a mighty warrior." At that point Tobias lets out the biggest roar that rocks the walls of buildings beneath. Lunarnise, "Oh my Lord, there's no way this could have happened, we can't get past to save the people." What Lunarnise doesn't realise is that it was her brother who shook beneath, as Tobias continues to roar, then stops slowly.

Lunarnise makes her way through the room that was trapped beneath, before the mighty roar had opened up the passage. As they walked down the burrow even further into the night, they find themselves trapped inside. Helena is with Lunarnise and she sees an eagle-eyed torch, picks it up and turns it on. It shines brightly all around them. "Okay, boys and girls, this way, follow me as the light is shining, it's lighted up the tunnel for miles," says Helena. "Yeah you're just trying to impress my brother with your ways," Lunarnise says. "Oh, lighten up sister, it's the new age." "Thank you for your words Helena, now let's all go. Follow me folks, to the rescue," says Lunarnise.

It seems calm and quiet. Just then Lunarnise gets a SMS message from above saying 'is everything alright down there, or do you require more assistance?' from Stimpultonnes. 'I'm guessing we'll get more support from people above that it would be interesting to hear from them.' Within seconds there was a huge explosion. Lunarnise says, "That sounds closer than we thought. Let's go to help people escape." There was crying from the other side as someone shouted, "Hello is anyone there? We're trapped here inside an unusual room." "I should let you know, Lunarnise, remember to trust in each other's abilities," says Claudia.

The crowd gets louder. As Helena and Lunarnise are both walking towards where the noise is coming from, they hear a chanting. "Hold on," says Lunarnise, "I know whose voices those are – Jake, and wait, my dad Noah." "Dad, I'm here to save you," shouts Lunarnise. A voice then says, "Ladies, they know they're here," replies Marilyn, disguised still as the swamp woman.

On the other hand, just around the corner Jake says, "Oh my goodness this is so close and Lunarnise has no idea, wait when will she find out the truth?" Lunarnise, "Jake, dad where are you guys? Oh, by the way Jake, I heard everything you said, and who else knows this?" (Narrator, "Girl, I'm sorry you found out about this. She has known all along, but please don't be upset about it. I'm telling you it was done for a good reason by all of the bad clan who want you dead.")

Lunarnise, "So where is she now? Have I met her before since I thought she was dead? It looks like I have got it wrong again, oh man." Jake, "Just before you try and release me from this situation I have to tell you that you've got to play the tune on the floor first. And Marilyn is closer than you think and will always be there, and yes, you have met her three times since." Lunarnise gets ahead and uses the power she never knew existed, and she makes the locks on the doors burn to dust. "Way to go," Helena says as she takes her sword out, ready to fight. With no one around Jake turns to Lunarnise and says, "Quickly, it's a trap, let's all run." With all the mighty power where people teamed up to get those doors open, everyone gets up to run out of the room as it fell on the floor.

Stimpultonnes, "Hold on everyone." There's nobody around as he stands close by to keep a look out. Lunarnise shouts back up to him, "It looks like it's been abandoned, this will be an ideal place for a few people. Stimpultonnes, "Oh yeah, that's right, I know what I can do with a place like this. There's plenty of room and I have a few troops here with me." Roland, "Do you know, Sir, I'm also the high priest of this town, I can grant you permission as requested, your honour?" Stimpultonnes, "There's also one other person we are missing." There is an almighty roar from above, "Yes," in a high tone. Stimpultonnes, "Well, there I have it now I am a proud owner of this place with many people who will live here in different rooms. There you go, lads, pick out a room to put your heads down, and plus it's next to the school when the season starts. Fronk and Kulumbush will share a room and Helena and Poppals, Roland and Tobias will have their own rooms nearest to the top to keep an eye on everyone." Just as everyone was getting into their rooms, a wise old lady walked up and asked, "Are you going to be able to do me a favour? This will also test your patience. First you need to help me find a shelter for the night for myself, I shall return the favour and give you whatever you need." Tobias, "I am going to go with my instincts and let you rest in the first room on your left, as it's a penthouse and the best place in here."

The wise old lady, "Thank you, young man, you're so kind as to help someone like myself, now travel to the light in the dark and collect what shines the brightest." As she looked up towards him, 'if only you knew who I was.' Tobias accepts the challenge and sets out on the quest. The wise old lady shouts, "You won't need to use your wings." Noah runs to the front of the building and stares into darkness as he puts his head down.

The wise old lady, "Don't worry about your son he goes on this journey in peace, you will see he'll be back before you know it." She disappears, leaving Noah looking for her and all puzzled, "How do you know that Tobias is my son?" From the distance, "I can see the love between a father and his kids, what lies beneath is the true fact of the journey of the untold."

Kulta, the cat, started to walk around the house to try and get someone's attention, whilst Lunarnise was still sleeping. She turned round and looked at Lunarnise and made her sleep on the ceiling, "Oh my goodness what just happened?" she says. Lunarnise looks at Kulta in disgust, "Get me down from here," as she throws her teddy at the cat and laughs.

As Tobias was slowly walking down the stairs he had seen something like a black box with a sticker on it that says 'to who picks up, this cherish it'. Then he noticed it more clearly and opened it. Out came a gecko, jumped up to his back and fell asleep. Tobias continued on his journey in finding the brightest light, in the distance a light shined, 'I'm guessing it's this way,' Tobias says to himself. There seem to be shadows all around him as he gets closer to the light. Tobias is calm and relaxed as he continues his search for the missing global treasure as well as the light. As he travels day and night in search of the missing treasure, the gecko was woken by a strange sound. Sudden sounds in the background seemed to be coming from behind in the forest, with animals and birds chirping. Tobias and the gecko were approached by short bears dressed in Indian wear, with spears of all shapes and sizes.

They started to talk in another language, as they all surrounded themselves around Tobias and the gecko. The next thing was that one walked out with a crown as he or she must be King or Queen. Then spoke in a low voice, "I am the queen of my people, how may I help you?" Tobias explained how he has been told to look for something that shines so bright, just then he notices it coming from the tree huts.

Queen, "I think I know what you are looking for. A wise old lady once came to me, and said that you would come here one day for it as she gave it to me." As she explained to the people around her, "So you see you may have to do a little something for me in return, can you please go with the best of my troops and locate the Golden Eagle from the evil one?" says the Queen. Tobias, "Me and my people have already thought of him, now he's in a cage and we don't remember seeing the Eagle." Queen, "He's not in the cage anymore, he had most of you fooled, he keeps it in an unexpected place, go now before sunrise. Well I'm guessing it's what he does to many people who have never heard of him, and you'll never know where he's going to strike next." Tobias, "So just the thought of it makes me furious. I wonder what he's thinking of doing next." "I'm guessing that we have to be prepared." "Yes, Your Majesty."

That's the point where Tobias and his pet friend go deep into the woods. "Don't worry little one I'll keep you safe," Tobias says. As Tobias continued his search for the golden Eagle he discovered a whole new world within Tiger Warth. Miniature people roaming around and going about their business, when gecko saw something through the corner of his eyes. 'No, it can't be, it looks like Sir John in the distance.' Tense music was playing and it was getting louder. Tobias, "No way, it can't be happening how did he get here?"

Tobias, 'Remember to hide, his powers are unstoppable you need to find a way to stop him completely. Uphold your power and dodge him with what you have been taught, be careful not to take your eyes away from Sir John, he's crafty.' So as Tobias looks on to battling Sir John once and for all, he gets prepared. "I've been told how Sir John influences people, I need to be on my guard." As Tobias looks increasingly concerned about the situation he tries not to think about it, and rages in to battle. He puts all his energy into the fight, and finally turns around and is face to face with Sir John. "You are mine," Tobias shouts, "it's time for you to leave and never return." "That is exactly what your sister said to me when she disappeared, and her mother. I have all the power and not even you can stop me," Sir John replied. "That's it, enough of the baby talk, I'm taking you out now," Tobias says, then he goes in to battle with him. There is fighting and rolling around the floor, fists in all directions, hitting parts of each other's bodies.

(Designer rushes over to explain to Tobias stop, "He is too powerful, it's going to need all of us to destroy him." Narrator, "My boy turn around, duck your head.") That point something happens to Tobias. Sir John takes a strike and defeats Tobias as he slowly falls to the ground. (Designer rushes to his side and says, "Tobias are you okay?" Tobias replies in a softer voice as he struggles to get his words out, "I'm sorry, just please look out for my sister." (Narrator shouts out to the highest level, "Noooooo!")

Tobias closes his eyes, "My friend, my dear friend what are we going to do now?" Just as Sam is about to leave, Sir John looks at him with a smile. Sam gets angry and takes his sword out, swings it at Sir John and takes off one of his arms. Sir John vanishes into thin air with smoke that forms from nowhere. Just as Sam turned back to pick up his friend, he is gone, left behind was just a gecko. The gecko looks up to Sam and says, "tweep tweep". Sam replies, "Oh what the heck, yeah buddy, stick around here." (Narrator, "Well, I guess I should be heading back to the group now, what am I supposed to say to everyone else?")

By the looks of it, Sam is starting to get anxious about what just happened, and the thought of losing his best buddy. He doesn't look happy as he's got his head down to the ground. Sam says, "I'm not looking forward to seeing Lunarnise." As Sam started back to camp in the middle of the woods, he saw a bright light shining through the other end of the forest. 'I wonder what that could be?' Getting closer, there in front of his eyes was a unicorn white with purple and green stripes, hair long and shining. 'I wonder if this is what Tobias was talking about? Well my brother I found it.' He then walked straight to the unicorn as it ran off.

(Narrator, "Right then gecko, here goes nothing, I believe it is this way back.") Calm and quiet music playing in memory of Tobias, the wind is strong. It is dark and cold. As Sam is going through the woods he continued to search for the light that Tobias was looking for. Out of nowhere something shone. A unicorn came close to Sam. "Oh I remember you," said Sam, "you must be the brightest light Tobias was looking for all along, let's go girl." The unicorn turned her head back and forth in the breeze of the wind, and put her head down for Sam to climb up on her back. And she started to gallop back up the path with Sam and gecko on, gecko shouts, "gim gim". Panics. Sam says, "Go left."

They go to a clear path and build up their speed. In the background they can hear people talking and screaming. Sam says, "We're nearly home. I know that voice sounds like my wife's." He hears Claudia, saying to Lunarnise, "I wonder where Sam is hiding?" They just go round the next corner and the unicorn says, "We're here now," in a polite and gentle voice. They arrived at the camp and Sam was worried about how he would tell Lunarnise about Tobias.

Lunarnise, "Did I hear anyone say my brother's name? What's going on with him? I hope he's okay." Jake, "Well my love, I think you should sit down, there's something I need to tell you about Tobias." Lunarnise, "Don't tell me you're going to jump right to how you have lost him, because you took your eyes off Tobias."

Jake explains the whole story to Lunarnise in a few hours, after which she looks at Sam and explodes into tears, shouting out, "No, no, no, this can't be happening to me again, now I have no family. What do I do? Now I have the wand, could I bring Tobias back to life?" A voice then spoke, "Remember you can't bring anyone back from the dead." "Oh, okay is that how it doesn't work, right? What am I supposed to do now?" Lunarnise whispers to herself, 'I hope one day I'll get the chance to see my brother here on earth.' Claudia looks at Lunarnise and says, "That poor girl has had it rough, she shouldn't worry, there is a prize at the end of the road."

Lunarnise, "I wonder what surprises are coming along the way and if I'll meet someone famous?" Kulta, "me meow" as she surrounds herself around Lunarnise and purrs heavily. "Oh no, something's not right, what is it girl?" says Stimpultonnes. Everyone is surrounded by shadows. Roland is demanding answers and puts his guard up. Voice speaks out that remains ominous, "We have come for Lunarnise to take it back to where it all began." Lunarnise didn't realise that she had to leave her friends behind so she went straight to Claudia and Kulta. "I'm going to miss you guys more." Her pet came over, running around her legs. Lunarnise said, "Don't worry, I will be back before you know it." Just then a door opens, and she walks inside with many people. As she went through, her pet ran into the hole with Lunarnise, at least she didn't notice her.

Chapter 8

Lunarnise Visits Unfamiliar Grounds!

Lunarnise didn't realise the loophole existed until she finally found herself back where she was only a few years old. 'There's something unusual going on with this particular place, I wonder what I have to do here? I'm guessing it's got something to do with a close connection? Could it possibly be that Tobias is still alive? Wait, no it can't be true, can it?' The Queen of the clan makes her way over towards Lunarnise and says, "Hello there, you are much appreciated here in our time of the world, please feel free to join me on this quest and make it your second home whilst you're here."

"Thank you," says Lunarnise. "Do I get a personal assistant while I'm here?" "Of course," replies the Queen. "Gimme, gimme." Fluffy comes out of nowhere. Lunarnise just looks, "How did you follow me here?" "Wait, am I missing something here, how do you know our secret agent?" "I found him when I was in the house," says Lunarnise. The Queen says, "He was on a mission when he got lost, and that's when he found you, and his assigned name is Flobber."

The Queen then said, "There is that guy again who keeps on annoying me. Every day he rolls around my flowers in the garden." Lunarnise, "Your Majesty, do you mind if I go over to speak with him?" Queen, "Of course why not? My people have tried but they haven't succeeded yet." Lunarnise looked around and saw something unusual, as she continued to make her way over to the unknown man. She got closer and began asking him what he was doing. The gentleman turned around to look at her and said, "Do I know you from somewhere, you look familiar, my dear?" It was said that she had a history back in her younger years but didn't remember anything.

"Yes, my lady, we all knew you were alive so I remained a secret to find out where you were, but now I found you we need your help." The gentleman continued talking about what happened since she grew up, "Your father is the one who is causing the trouble with her majesty that is why you have been brought back from the future."

As the man gets to his feet he shows his true identity. Lunarnise looks and says, "Unbelievably happy to see you again, Thomas." Thomas, "So, Lunarnise, how did you manage to keep my name all these years, oh and Your Majesty I'm sorry for rolling around, that was part of the plan. Thank you," as he lifts his arm to do a thumbs up. Queen "Oh my, I think I like him, and how do you know that man again, Lunarnise?" Lunarnise, "Don't worry ma'am," as she walks to her palace to explain everything, "you're right, I shall tell you everything he is my .... !!!"

As they both walk in the hallway of the palace Lunarnise tells the Queen over a hot drink and a cake. After a short period of silence, the Queen tells Lunarnise what she needs to know about the journey. Flobber walks into the room with Lunarnise and the Queen, stops by Lunarnise and lies down on his back. Lunarnise, "I know what you want, you require your tummy rubbed, don't you?" He lies down, feet in the air, laughing, as tummies were being rubbed. "That's it, boy, I need to get back to work and find out what is happening, and why things aren't going good." Just then a young man comes running into the palace, "Hold on, Your Majesty, I do apologise for my actions recently." "Oh, come on, Thomas, you did have me worried," replied the Queen. "Great! Lunarnise I got your attention, now that we have decided to go for that walk, it's taken over ten years to happen," says Thomas.

Lunarnise, "Wait a minute," stops in the middle of the road and says, "that was you!" as she goes red in the face, "I thought you were the other guy on the right." Thomas, "Girl, do you remember our youngest lives? Since then it's made me think, I never knew where we would've been now if I had taken the marriage. I left because you once told me to go with your heart, she was a nice woman but I wasn't ready, there was something about her."

Lunarnise looked as she thought, 'you know what, you could have been happy, you need to love someone who knows how you feel.' Thomas, "Are you happy now where you are and live?" Lunarnise, "I feel like I have just lost everything within a few years, recently my long lost and newly found brother."

"Wait, you mean Tobias, right?" says Thomas, "We need to get ready and start to prepare ourselves for what is coming. Can I ask you a question? Would I be able to join you going forward, lass?" Lunarnise answers in surprise, "Oh please do, oh bye ee, hey, don't forget about me again." Thomas looks over at her with surprise and smiles, "At least you're the sister I never knew or had," and begins walking.

Lunarnise gets broken up interference on a device that she thought she never had that seems to be coming from Stimpultonnes. "Oh no," says Lunarnise, "what could possibly be wrong?" The device reads, 'get the ball' then goes off. Lunarnise shouts out to Thomas who is just ahead of her, "What could this be?" Thomas responds, "Don't fear my lady, all is well, it means we need to prepare to go to a secret Ball tonight. I knew this day would come, I have the perfect dress for you."

Lunarnise, 'I wonder what he is planning, why is he so nice after all these years?' Lunarnise is thinking. As they both wander down the path, they see a young girl who is looking lost. Same hairstyle as Lunarnise and smile. Thomas asks the young girl, "Where's your mother and what's your name?" The girl responds, "My mother is just leaving and my name is Lunarnise Pestra."

Older Lunarnise looks at her with a different kind of expression and says that she remembers this day and walks away from both of them and stands next to the river. Younger Lunarnise, "Have I said anything to upset her? Who is that person? She looks like someone I know." Thomas, "This is beyond ridiculous to me, honestly how is it possible? Love yourself through all your phases, learn something new every day. Most of all be yourself and surround yourself with good people, enjoy life, last of all learn to love."

Older Lunarnise looks back and walks over as if she was in shock. "You explaining the ways of life, my dear!" "By explaining how the ways of living are, we may even help the people of this world to understand how things are different." Flobber is trying to refer them down to the right path as they are not looking while they are talking. Before you know it, they are entering the wrong direction and Flobber is starting to panic. Thomas gets wind of Flobber in the corner of his eye. "My lady, something's wrong we were busy talking whilst Flobber tried warning us about this, look ahead, girl." In an instant Lunarnise realises in the distance someone coming towards them, rushing halfway in the ground and half above. They looked at each other and Flobber stopped time with only the three of them still able to move. "How did you do that? You remind me of someone." Lunarnise started to cry as she looked around and said to herself, "How did I get into this situation and the fact I didn't expect that to happen?" as she pulled out tissue from her pocket. Flobber said, "The thing coming towards us is known to be very scary, no one wants to be around him."

Lunarnise, "Fluffy, you've just spoken, what a beautiful surprise!" Thomas, "I wouldn't get your hopes up, girl, it could be a glitch, I have seen it happen before." Lunarnise, "Are you ready for the creature that's coming towards us because Flobber is losing power?" They were both struggling to keep themselves from falling, with the whole situation. Thomas shouts out, "He's starting to move his body." "So that makes sense now, oh yeah RUN," says Lunarnise as she kicks her speed up. Thomas shouts out, "Leg it!" Flobber gets in front of both as he's yelping, with the sky getting darker really quickly and as the moon rises to shine brighter than before. It's as if werewolves could roam around in the middle of the night which is not that long away.

That makes the creature stop instantly in front of Lunarnise and then look scary with a statement that shocks both sides. "I actually have an acknowledgement to give to you from your big brother, be aware of the unknown and people you trust. They may not be the people you think they are. Keep your eyes open. Just call 'pops' three times and I will be there by your side to help you. Good luck!" "I wonder what happened there, he was ready to come and fight and he was cool, Tobias must have been a great guy, poor Lunarnise though." Lunarnise sweetheart, I don't know who you are, but do you know I can hear you? I am sure you will hear from me but I'm just a person who's been pulled over to tell you the story of the growth of a little girl called Lunarnise Pestra." Lunarnise, "Hey lady, you are looking at her," as Lunarnise stands tall and elegant. Unknown Woman, "Now let's see, I'm not sure, I'm looking at a woman who has lost her dignity to be able to be who she really is. It is not wrong about me, but she has lots to learn about her body and power, plus there's a spy within the team put together. I want to give you a key to an unknown city, which you should have from Roland." "Can I get a glance of it?" The woman, in disguise, puts it across to her. "It's lost." "May I ask where it could be?" Lunarnise speaks up, "Tobias and Kulumbush went to look for it before his.." Unknown woman, young Marilyn, "Unfortunately I can't proceed to the next level without the lost key, go to retrieve the key and return through the same door I'll be waiting." At the time of the unknown woman mentioning this to Lunarnise, there was another whisk of wind appearing in front of both so Lunarnise and Thomas Greg enter.

Thomas, "I'm getting an unexpected feeling about this one, are we entering the right way?" Lunarnise, "Open your eyes, my dear friend, it's such a beautiful picture, I can see a flying shadow in the background but it's blurry as if it was my brother." Thomas, "My lady, you are getting delusional sightings of unexplained things within this hole."

Noah is galloping around shouting out for Lunarnise, and Tobias and keeps putting his head down while tears of magic appear all over the floor. Stimpultonnes takes a jar and puts the tears inside the bottle and screws it up. Everyone turns to look at Lunarnise and says, "We all are sorry, what can we do for you?" Lunarnise says, "I'm going to need a team that I can trust to be able to go to battle when I say."

Everyone laughs and says, of course they will, with a serious face. (Narrator, "Oh my, did I just see you all agreeing with the princess, what a wonderful surprise, it's great to see you back my lady." Everyone gathered to hear her story, of how she went through a circular door. Lunarnise remembered Fluffy. "Oh dear, what must have happened to Fluffy, oh I do miss him, it would make my night so happy to see him again." Lunarnise looked up at the stars and said, "I'll name this one as it is the brightest, 'Fluffy'." There was a big gathering in the courtyard for a meal before Lunarnise's findings, I mean, her journey.

A man came shouting “nee aaw, nee aaw” and screaming. Lunarnise was ready for anything that came her way. The man was holding a brown envelope with money inside, a currency never heard of called yak aaw. And a message that reads ‘open me when you hold the lost golden key’. “So, I’m supposed to find the key that my younger self was supposed to hold. Oh, I get it, I did have it but my father had taken it off me when I wasn’t looking, that means I will have to pay him a visit especially with only one arm now, and shrunken.”

Lunarnise, “I’m sure I can do something for retrieving what is ours.” Kulumbush, “I’m supposed to be going to show you the way, now that our brother... it’s here at present.” Noah, “Son, what’s that supposed to mean? Do you know something we don’t? Talk to us.” As Noah draws out an unknown object, ready to charge at Kulumbush, “Oh no,” replies Kulumbush, “what I mean is that he’s not dead to me.”

Lunarnise, “Who’s coming with me and Thomas, to bring back the golden key that unlocks a secret place?” Right after, Lunarnise gathers a small team to take on the journey they head towards the southern border. Which means it’s spelt for trouble, there are troops who hold spears and bow and arrows. With the dark of the sky closed in there are unusual shadows in the background that appear in a form similar to those previously lost. “Ladies and gentlemen, boys and girls, partners of those unseen can we get your attention? We all need to watch each other’s backs.”

“Oh my, a strange book bus is coming towards you, Lunarnise,” shouts out Roland, it’s a mixture between a bug and an alien. Fronk thinks, “I’m guessing that we are supposed to be taking this cab.” Lunarnise wonders, ‘what is he doing?’ and goes on to say, “Everyone get inside, and inspired by the gadgets that it holds I found it out for myself, be aware of the sinking floor,” when a voice calls out, “What are you going to do about this problem? How are we supposed to find him?” Lunarnise says, “Show your face, where are you from and who sent you?” Voice, “Steady on, girl, I’m not here to harm anyone but we have met before, look deep into your heart to find me. Bye for now.”

Then the wise old lady disappeared even though Lunarnise couldn’t see her, as the team continued within the vehicle. Vehicle, “Flie bie, flie bie.” Lunarnise, “Flaba dabba dabba, right, and team fasten your seatbelts, and enjoy the ride." Not everyone has their seatbelts on as people are roaming around inside and banging into each other. Nixo-Stain-Dexun, "Can this vehicle go any faster as we need to go and find my friend, he is trapped in a building?"

Lunarnise says, "I believe it's my brother, I'm so sorry but please be strong, he would want that." Nixo, "I'm off on a hunt." "No, stay with me," says Lunarnise. "You will learn to become a better warrior," said Roland.

Stimpultonnes offers the best advice to anyone who wants to learn, "Be the best person you can be, and look out for each other."

(Narrator, "Cut to the chase, old boy, I'm sure they will be just fine, with everyone willing to set sail on the next adventure and continue their quest. Oh, hold on, we're entering a promising land. But with bad intentions lurking around every corner remember not to let the flowers on the floor let you fall asleep.") Roland, "Right then troops, we're coming to the end of the road with our dear friend, get your gears together anything may happen now." Lunarnise, "Yes, as our leadership, what he's trying to say is, it's not too late to back out, are you all ready for this war?"

Everyone looks confused, "Oh well, let's go," shout all. Fronk, "What's the worst that can happen? Let's go and claim what is ours."

Lunarnise looked straight ahead at Stimpultonnes and smiled as she walked off the bus and into the crowd. "Let us know what we all are supposed to do and march forward. Helena, you're up front with me, girl." Helena, "Sure thing, princess, let's do this together, I mean all of us, gang, everyone drink your water up and let us march. Oh, if only Tobias was here he would know what to do." Helena was thinking, 'anyway I'm doing this for you, babe.'

There was the shadow in the sky again, but nobody notices this. Could it be possible for the mighty Lord to be revealed? Wait what am I thinking, can you imagine if it was true though? Just as it was happening an army of men was already heading towards them with long sticks and shouting out. And all the women of Roland's group head out running and screaming, "Come on, come on, we will mess you up."

With heads and arms rolling around it's hard to see what's going on. "Hold up, Lunarnise's group, there's a few scratches and bleeding." As they continue on their journey through the gates, "Ladies, we got through the gate, now the door in front." Right behind Lunarnise there was a tall one-armed guard standing and staring down at her. "It can't be," says Noah. Lunarnise gets her left fist up with her right hand flat against her left and steps back with one leg ready. The tall, unknown guard looks and shucks his eyes and lays a punch, that misses her as she rolls over to the other side. He grabs Lunarnise by her hand and swings her around, then pulls herself out spinning to the ground.

He looks up and his headband falls to the back, and she notices it's Sir John, "Oh no, he's back, why?" Lunarnise says. Sir John jumps up and goes to the ground with his elbow to her head, she looks at him and moves to the side, he falls to the floor. On the left side of the door there is a cage, just the top is open. As he was about to fall inside, Lunarnise grabs his feet stopping him from being eaten. He just looks at her and runs away. "I'll be right around the corner there's no running from me." Helena, "You do know that he'll be back to get you, girl."

Lunarnise, "Yes, but not for a while, mate, we will be ready." (Narrator looks over, "My lady I think I know why you did what you did, but it's reasonable for who you think he is." Lunarnise, "You mean that he isn't the same person who was there for me when I was born? Narrator begins to tell a story, "You see, when you were younger you weren't the only child in the household, you were the only child that was born differently. But no one else understood what happened with you so you were given up for adoption and that is where you were raised, in a nun's house so you were introduced to me. Ever since then I have been along your side with everyone being introduced to you and your father had to disappear from Sir John. Before you ask me, not many people have ever heard of his whereabouts but there's one who may know of his existence, and the name is Posteonski.")

Roland, "This again, how could I never want to hear that story. So sad, girl, he's known to be around the mountains and lives in the third cave in the middle house the last I heard of him." Lunarnise, "I'm guessing that it may be of interest to me when I go around that area later. I got a few things I need to take care of first." What Lunarnise doesn't realise is that Posteonski is being held back from his past and family, with spooky chains. There was a squawk coming from the basement, "I wonder what it could be? What happened to the key?" asked Lunarnise.

A voice says, "Look within to find the key." Lunarnise says, "Wait, who are you? I can hear that." The voice says as it's fading away, "You know. Stop kidding yourself." Lunarnise looks around and says, "I wonder where the stairs are?" A secret staircase opens right in front of them. Kulumbush says, "Are you supposed to be telling me that we need to follow it down there?" Stimpultonnes, "Get in there, girl." Fronk laughs, "Come on, girlfriend."

[Man's voice sings this] *Oh, 'cause move your own legs, come on, come on, and let's open up your eyes babe!* Lunarnise, "Hey guys, where has this came from? You know that it sounded awesome." Lunarnise looked straight ahead at Stimpultonnes, confused. Everyone says that it came from a guy's voice. Stimpultonnes, "You know what? I was amazed by the song, do you know that it's in the charts ready to see where it goes 0/100? I wonder who the artist is and why they did the song now, is this world changing every single time? It's just so beautiful to hear it live from a distance and suddenly, that makes it even funnier. We're going through a whole new era." As everyone continues on down the staircase there's different patterns on the walls. Lunarnise, "Are we genuinely getting lost or something else is coming out to prevent us from achieving the key? It seems to be a bit of a problem to notice what is coming our direction, there's something long and silvery with a few heads."

At last, Lunarnise was able to see the creature and managed to make sure it wasn't able to get them. Felixstowe, "Let me introduce ourselves, we have been sent to distract a young woman called Lunarnise." "Lunch," says second head. First head, "No." "I'm supposed to say you're not going to get the key but if I let you, can we follow you?" Lunarnise, "Sure, come on girls."

Then Felixstowe grabs Lunarnise and throws her into a secret room. As Lunarnise goes through the air she finds an opening to grab the key. And swings round to hold it and gets out quickly. Felixstowe pulls her out in time as the room disappears. Lunarnise, "Yes, we have the key," and puts it in a safe place as they start to travel back. Everyone leaves including Felixstowe. “Well ladies, I have to return through a door to go back and open a door.”

When they arrive back to the gate of the camping area the wind pole appears to collect Lunarnise just before it closes. Felixstowe follows through. As they are going back through the hole, they see the colourful lighting outside of the carriage and finally arrive. The unknown woman was waiting for her at the entrance and says, “Well then, young lady, I’m guessing you’ve retrieved the key.” Lunarnise, “Yes, my lady, I have it with me and here it is.” She shows the unknown woman who looks in surprise.

“Let us go towards the back of the palace where you find a secret door,” so both Lunarnise and unknown woman head in front of Felixstowe. “Oh, hello there, where did you come from?” said unknown woman. “They are with me,” Lunarnise replied. Unknown woman, “They, oh yeah, I didn’t realise. Sorry ladies, how are you both?” Felixstowe, ‘Ma’am we both love how you showed us your support, me and my sister are well.” Second head, “Thank you, we have something for you in return, it’s a gift of knowledge and strength.” Unknown woman, “Thank you both, I will treasure this gift for the rest of my life and use it well.”

Lunarnise just looks up and smiles. (Narrator, “I’m wondering if Lunarnise has recognised the unknown woman, I don’t think she has ever but it’s good that she’s there for her own child. And she has been through a lot of trauma so there’s a good reason to believe it may be the unknown woman or I could be wrong.”) Unknown woman, “Lunarnise, this is the only way to get to the point where the key needs connecting and unlock a hidden connection.”

“Okay so what is that thing called ahead?” asks Felixstowe. Both Lunarnise and the unknown woman, look and are amazed. “Where did they come from and who let the rabbits out?” both ladies said. “Where are we supposed to be going? This path is going on for miles.” Lunarnise, “There’s no lighting around here, oh hold on,” and pulled out a stick and shook it, and lights appear. Lunarnise, “Oh my goodness, I didn’t even notice that I could do this, and it’s going to be fun. Unknown woman, “We’re almost there now, have you got the key ready for us to insert it into the lever? Myself and Felixstowe have to go to the other two to direct them the other way."

At that point of arrival all three of them have to climb up the stairs to be able to get to the gate and then go through. Unknown woman says, "Excuse me ladies, are we all ready to grab hold of the levers?" Lunarnise gets the centre one as it has to be pushed down, from a standing position. Whilst the other two have to be moved up in an awkward angle, one on the left to a 60 degrees angle position and the other to a 90 degrees angle. Lunarnise moves into place and shouts out, "Are you both ready for me to go ahead with the lever? 1,2,3 go." "That sounds good, but hold on tight for this to happen," says Fluffy as he tugs at the bottom for a few seconds, before the floor rises up with a secret world to emerging from underneath, from nowhere.

Lunarnise looks at the unknown woman who is there with her and smiles at her as she walks away and begins to cry, as she says, "My work is done, see you soon." Lunarnise shouts out, "But I still need you." "I think you have got all the help you need, honey." Lunarnise starts with the procedure to unlock the hidden village, "I am strong and courageous enough to get through this." With some help from Felixstowe the village rises up and screams come from beneath, laughter and some crying. Someone shouts out, "Freedom, we're set free from the noise of the goblin he is mean, short and armless."

Lunarnise, "Oh my goodness, I just realised it can't be, could it? Felixstowe, what do you think we should do with the goblin?"

The goblin runs through Lunarnise and Felixstowe, and starts grinning as he moves farther away from them. Just as Sir John ran away, Stimpultonnes walked over to Lunarnise and took the stick out of his pocket and said, "Do you know what you have left behind in the house?" "No," replied Lunarnise "Your magical stick, my lady."

Lunarnise reached out to grab the stick and thanked Stimpultonnes. "I didn't know where it was, thank you, my Lord." Just as the goblin went around the corner Lunarnise managed to grab him with her stick and put him on the highest roof. Felixstowe said, "You do know that he is going to be angry when he comes down." "I know," replied Lunarnise, "so let's enjoy the moment before he gets down."

Kulta comes from behind them and looks up at Sir John and says, "Does he know how much he looks silly, lol?"

Lunarnise, "Wait till he finds us later and see what he will try, but we will be there when he comes back." Lunarnise took out a photo of Tobias and said, 'if only you were here!' Then there was a low voice in the background that she heard but couldn't understand because of the sounds of nature. As soon as the unknown village finished rising up there was a huge explosion and everyone turned to see the supernatural creatures. A pig was seen running around with a goose face and human arms on two legs wearing jeans and a black shirt. Then many others jumped out of the village doors and they all were different animal species of mixed creatures.

Lunarnise said, "Welcome friends, are we ready for class to be brought together and to be taught by the best teachers?" Everyone started to gather round Roland and Stimpultonnes to get a vehicle to travel to the school. So, it was, if they all were on the desert and they all passed the camera, they pulled a different face. As each one passed the camera they soon got to where the entrance to the school is and waited for the others. They were visited by the Head of School who was inside the school who said, "Hello everyone, and welcome to the Central Whisper of Grats School, I hope your stay with us will be interesting."

Chapter 9

The Central Whisper of Grats School!

It's the only school where the students know the truth, universally acknowledged, that is why people may feel compelled by the magic. Unbelievable things that happen and can't be explained, the castle itself moves in such an odd way to make it seem like it has no meaning.

As time moves on with its own development it will eventually become more interesting for individuals to explore the underground of the walls within. Without any doubt this will become our best year yet regardless, explain the rock and the knight who came from the walls itself. "Oh, come on, what do you expect from the kids this year? HOS mentioned to me that it's about the best we have to get out of them. My dear friends of the book or even whoever is reading, oh you, yes you, the one who has stopped by to pick this book up. What do you think of it so far?" "Why are you speaking to the other side? It's not like they can hear you," said Pinto the pig, goat guy.

Head of School was standing in the middle of the yard, greeting everyone as they arrived at school. People were saying all kinds of things to him and that he had a great school, he said under his breath, 'if only you people know what you're getting yourself into.' Lunarnise, "Hello, good morning, pleased to meet you, how are you doing today?" "And you're looking well," as she stood up tall and elegant, smiling to everyone. Then walks over the headmistress looking gracious in a long summer dress, speaks in a gentle and soft voice. Clariot (Headmistress), "Welcome back some of you, but for those who are starting this year, good luck and be positive about yourself. Am I missing anyone?"

In the meantime, the rock and knight are getting excited, "Oh, do you remember last year a well-known popular student eventually beat us at our own games? Quick my friend, they are coming back."

"Sam, where are you gone to these days? Hey, have you heard of the swamp woman? She's been helping people, and a boy nearly died but she took him in under her wings." Lunarnise walked through the door. Even though she didn't hear the conversation, she heard something and she caught the eye of something moving upstairs. Lunarnise said to herself, 'There's something about this castle, it's like I know this place, even though I haven't stepped foot in until now.' Fluffy came running up to Lunarnise and continued with his barking and running up to the stairs and back.

Lunarnise, "What boy, do you know something that we are unaware about?" Sometimes I wish you could talk." Noah, "Where is my daughter?" As he says it out of breath with galloping too fast, 'hold on let me catch my breath'. Clariot, 'Oh hello, Noah my finest student, you were a spontaneous person and unique in your own way and everybody loved you, and an inspiration for the school, thank you. How are you anyway? Oh, and your daughter, she's gone up those stairs." And says under her breath, 'hope his daughter will be good like Noah'. Noah, "Thank you, Miss. By the way, I love your hair," as he went up the stairs.

Head of school, "Good morning, all right if you're new, follow me for an introduction. The others go to your class of last year and they will advise you where to go." Stimpultonnes, "Your honour, we have to try and make it exciting and fun for the students this year. I have got a few ideas. I will run them by you after everyone's in the class." Head of School, "That sounds good, I will definitely look forward to hearing about that in my office right after my first class at 10.30am." Kulumbush, "Oh my goodness, look at this amazing place, I think I'm going to enjoy school here."

Rock and knight were moving around which made Kulumbush jump, they both couldn't stop laughing. Fronk came through the room to see Kulumbush in shock as he was standing talking with someone who wasn't even there. "Hey man, are you feeling fine?" asks Fronk. Kulumbush says, "Do I know you?" "No, no, he's lost his bloody mind," says Fronk. In the meantime, Lunarnise is about to go to her class when Kulta ran to her to see where she was going, and meowed. There was a voice that said, "Oh good luck girl, you can run the show and shine for the trophies."

Everyone in the school laughed nervously and went quiet. "Well done to you guys, for being able to make it to school safely this morning," said Roland. He added, "You wouldn't believe what I just saw on the way to school today, a unicorn crossed with a chicken!" "Oh my, that looked remarkably similar to what I had seen in the past," says Kulumbush. "Who is this person?" said Helena. Fox girl, "Well, hello there, Helena, my name is Tyra. Pleased to make your acquaintance," peeking at the camera. The fox girl is wearing a short medieval dress. Helena, "Lunarnise, where are you?" She shouted to her loudly. Oh my, she looked lost and confused. Stimpultonnes, "This is the new age of unity for all people around you, you need to learn quickly to be able to get along with all, so welcome everyone into this world and make sure that they are happy all the time."

Lunarnise comes running and says as she's just catching her breath, "Are you okay? Thank you, sir, I'm going back to class now." Fox girl, "Could I possibly follow you? I would love to go to school and learn a trade and you look lovely girl!" Lunarnise, "I don't see why not. I can speak to the teacher, let's go." Stimpultonnes, "Well look at you all grown up, Lunarnise, you did great today. That's how we encourage intelligence to come into the school. Have a nice day, love."

Professor Ponsternose, "Well, hello class, come in come in sit down." (I won't bite), he says under his breath, (oh, but you don't know that for sure). Lunarnise, welcome to my first class of this term. Right then, everyone, can you please get out your books?"

Meanwhile in the castle the walls were moving around and singing. Out of nowhere Ponsternose was just sitting there and clicked the button to get Sir John's attention, (we're aficionados). Head of School talks through the microphone to tell all the students to be aware of the second floor, it's out of bounds. Fronk goes to Lunarnise, "Should we go to check it out?" Kulumbush comes running, "Don't forget your noble friend. Guess what I heard? That other day a great song was being sung, only trouble with it, was no one was there."

Teacher 1, "Good morning everyone, and welcome back from holiday season, did you have a great time and what did you all do?" Then it happened again as they were all split into three groups around the school, teachers two and three are upstairs, and listen to each person's number. Head of school speaks over the microphone and calls each person and gives them a number 1-3 to let all know what class to go to.

Lunarnise says, "Is Fluffy in the castle?" Fronk responds with, "No, he's at the bottom of the lake," but there's no lake around here. "Oh, hold on a minute, is that not Fluffy who's going through the door? Wait, is that a rock from the top of the castle?" Somebody is having a laugh as Fronk and Lunarnise look at him, "Okay he's having fun, Fronk," says Lunarnise, "he's still my friend even though he's an important person." "Huh," replies Fronk.

Kulumbush, "Me and Fox girl are both waiting, let's go and see if we can figure out what's beneath the school." "Okay, down to the basement," imaginary friend says to Lunarnise. "Well, hello there, I haven't seen you for a while now, so tell me all about the wedding." Imaginary friend, "Hold on love, how do you know, girl, I was married? First so much to tell you then you can tell me."

So, the imaginary friend started to tell Lunarnise all about his story, how he ended up with the love of his life. (Narrator, "But wait children, let's be honest is anyone tormenting you? Know your rights, get up and face your fears with the right help. Thanks for listening, let's continue. Sam, where are you? Come from your tea break to tell us what happens next." Sam finishes with the coffee and coughs.) Well as the imaginary friend explains to Lunarnise, she and her friends go towards the end of the castle. And then find a ramp that says, "Please don't enter. For your safety, be aware of the......"

"Well guys, do you know what could be worse than being dragged off by trolls?" "Kulumbush," shouts everyone. "That's not cool, man," says Kulta. "Lunarnise, did you know that she could talk relentlessly?" says imaginary friend. "No, I didn't," Lunarnise replies. "Kulta, say something." She started purring and walked around Lunarnise's feet. "Okay girl, I heard you, no guys she didn't talk."

Kulta looks at Lunarnise and walks away with a smirk, 'at least she hasn't worked it out yet, he he'. Lunarnise to herself, 'Oh my what just happened, am I supposed to know something or is it true?' While she was saying it quietly, ("Guess what, girl? I can hear it," says Sam. "Oh hello, Narrator, I guess I didn't see you there, how are you and your wife? Haven't seen her today." Jake, "Yes, well, she's not feeling well at the moment, its nothing serious and stop calling me Narrator, we are family.")

Lunarnise says, "Yes sir," and walks back to her class, closing the door behind her. Just as she goes in the door an unknown person comes running out of the basement and disappears. (Designer says, "Well, I don't think that was anything to do with me, I haven't seen this behaviour before since we found this world." Narrator looked over at him and smiled, "Thought you were lost in the sand," walks towards the door.) The unknown person ran away, laughing, "You were lost in your own eyes, just 'cause Claudia is p..p..p.." Sam quickly, "Don't say it, wait what?" Jake, "What? How do you know about this situation that I know nothing more of?")

(Designer, "Yes indeed I am sure you will find out shortly, like n..n..n, hello my dear, how are you?") Claudia, "I am grateful for your concern, where is Jake?" Her husband came running back, 'sounds like I'm in trouble,' he says to himself. Claudia looks and says to herself, 'you don't think I can hear you?' Jake as he grins, "I'm here my love, I thought you were under the weather, and I haven't seen Designer too." Claudia, "I have some wonderful news for you today as you are going to be a.....

Claudia vanished in a hole by hands that came out of the sky and pulled her inside. Just then Lunarnise came out of class and saw, so she flew in too. Lunarnise was struggling with the flying as it was only her first time using her wings. ("Oh my," says Narrator, "she's just crashed but managed to get in the hole where Claudia was pulled in." Narrator looked up to where his wife and new friend were pulled in, 'as I was thinking I didn't know what was happening around me. I think it's time for me to call the long-lost cousin and, yes, Tobias I know you told me, not again, because he's a little crazy but he gets the job done.')

Not long after there was an unexpected something in the sky as it ran through the night and stopped suddenly and then went on the back two feet from four and neighed. It was as beautiful as the night itself. Someone shouted, "Is that a Pegasus?" Noah looked up at him and said, "Wow that's really nice," walked away with his head down as he trotted farther out. Even though he missed the hole he knew where he had to go and flew away calmly as dust flew behind him leaving a trail that spells something entirely different each time. This time it is a riddle!

'What can run but never walk, talk, has a head but never weeps, has a bed but never sleeps?' Noah "Umm, I know this one is it a nose?" "Wait the answer is, where you can follow me if you'd like to help rescue the pregnant woman and her daughter. Oh, did you know that she was pregnant with your baby?" Sam, "Right here, that Pegasus is good. Wait he's gone."

Lunchtime bell rings. And people are running around like a bunch of idiots, who? The dinner ladies appear from all sides to help serve them food from the kitchen. How about that? Everyone is literally lining up one side to get their own food, there's a lot of them shouting and screaming. There's an argument between two of the groups, who should go and help after lunch to rescue the pregnant woman and child? So, between them it's a solution that both parties are going to work together and fight for their freedom. Once lunch is done everyone cleans up quickly and rushes out to grab an animal of their choice and runs into the night, with Noah galloping behind them. He shouts out, "I know the riddle now, it's River," as they're approaching the river on the other side.

"I'm guessing we all should follow that river and go uphill to get where we're supposed to go, and then there will probably be challenges on the way. But I'm pretty confident that we can figure out how to deal with any problem, hold up another riddle. Are you ready guys? As you approach the end of the river you will find a gallon jug, you need to empty 3 gallons first. Everyone will spend the next few hours trying to figure it out." In the end Stimpultonnes arrived. It took him a few minutes, by which time he had a piece of wood to put behind the jug. Roland had to take time out at the side of the river that reminded him of Tobias when they were younger and shouted, "Go on, I'll catch up with you later."

So, everyone else continued to go forward in the same direction. Just as they were about to get around the bridge there was a huge group of people standing ready for battle. Helena jumped out of nowhere to the front and said, "My friend, stand aside, unless you want to meet the other side, girls and boys let's finish this." There were hands and legs going up and down, fists moving in, oh no someone hit the cameraman to the ground head on. Despite that happening, Designer stepped in to take care of the camera. "Hey up, what a catch, I'm filming right now, oops that's the fish pond, lol. Poppals, step on it please, help this young gentleman who has fallen on the floor from the camera."

Meanwhile Lunarnise managed to get into the hole where Claudia was pulled through, flew like she had never flown before and held onto her hand. Thought of something in her head, and they both fell to the floor in a busy town full of people and traffic. "Oh no goodness!" exclaimed Claudia, "I think we're in England, London." They both looked at each other and laughed, then screamed.

Lunarnise got off the floor and started looking around. "Wow!" she replied. "So wonderful!" A lady bumped into them knocking Claudia down. As she fell her water broke. "Oh no," Claudia says, "I'm having a baby." The kind and concerned lady helped them both out and took them to the hospital.

On the other side the team was getting ready for their battle with the skyline, the fight was overwhelmingly fought. They were fighting at a losing position for their survival. The animal people came up to give Helena's team a hand. After a long battle they won, thanks to both parties, but they had lost Lunarnise's master to a second thrilling defeat.

Oh no, what happened! What about Lunarnise, we have to make sure that he is remembered forever. Little do they know that when he vanished he made it look like he died, but truthfully he had no obligation to rush to his master. On his way to her he ran into a few obstacles along the way, first was a young woman with the same red shirt. That was weird. Perhaps she was pushing a bin, which was probably carrying an unknown object that had been thrown into the street. Second was a small black car that had fallen off a tree and tried burying itself in the road. Last being a small house that was just behind him so he reached out to speak to it and asked, "Why do you seem so lost and lonely?"

House just looked at him and said he had travelled far and wide to find his true self and that he may look small on the outside but was a magical place to live in. "Well, may I say people have probably never settled down because of their own personal life."

House, "Wow, master, thanks for that information, would it be possible to offer you peace in my shed?" Sterito, "Of course you can, but I know just the right person who will love you and your home, and her name is Lunarnise, my master." House, "Thank you very much, master, so we both have a purpose, please look inside." Sterito walked in the door and he was shocked and lost for words. After a few hours he finally came out of Lunarnise's new house, someone shouts, "It's a treehouse."

Sterito, "Oh my goodness unbelievable! that was amazing, it's like a dream come true better than a castle." Jake, "What have we got here, Sterito? Will you introduce me to your new friend, oh do I know you from somewhere else? Well I guess you better get going now, the bridge won't hold forever." Jake pushes them both through the door made of cloud.

Sterito shouts as they go through. He's lost. Lunarnise's new home, "leased to meee.." House fades out, they both arrive at Buckingham Palace. "Where are we?" says House. "London, oh no, how did we miss the turning point?" replies Sterito. The guards noticed a small white cloud of dust in the middle of the courtyard, but saw nothing suspicious so they continued their duties. That way it gave them enough time to sneak into Buckingham Palace. "This way," Sterito said. "There's a gap in the corner of the ground. Do you see the mouse that's just gone in?" "Huh, so are you suggesting we get in there?" Sterito hands over a piece of bread to House. "Here eat, don't worry it's just temporary."

On another side of London the young woman continues to help both Lunarnise and Claudia to the hospital. They finally reach the hospital where a wise old lady greeted them and told the young woman she would get a chance at one thing close to her heart and then left. The young woman watched the wise old lady leave and tells herself, "She seems familiar," and proceeds to get a nurse to help deliver the child. At the hospital reception there was no one around so she looks over to Lunarnise. "Are you ready to be my assistant?"

Lunarnise takes a look and says, "Let's do this together, girl." They make it to the next room which was free and prepared for the birth of the child. After a short while twins were born - a boy and a girl. The young woman says, "Congratulations, Lunarnise, you have delivered not just one child but twins. How do you feel Godmother?" The young woman cleans up and leaves. "I have to go now." Claudia was overwhelmed by all the news. "I'm a mother of two, not just one, thank you for this blessing of joy, and thank you Godmother, how do you find it, being my children's protector?" "Wow, Claudia, thank you so much!" Lunarnise responded.

There is loud shouting and banging from the outside, both children looked straight at each other and were worried as they must have known what was about to happen. The outside noises started to rise up, with footsteps coming in their direction. Lunarnise began screaming, just as she was about to get louder, both children opened their arms to make a big invisible cover for all four of them. They had seen Sir John and two other men walking into the room. He looked straight to the circle but didn't realise. Lunarnise whispered in the hole, "I see what my father looks like now." The Pegasus came running up from behind and charged at Sir John, grabbed the half man, half goat and threw him off the ground. And turning around quickly to catch him, he threw John out of the hospital window. Lunarnise picked him after he fell and jumped him to Atlantic. Then she returned. After the Pegasus helped her get back out of the cold, Lunarnise dropped to the ground in front of Claudia. "Please, sir, she needs warmth." Pegasus sets a fire up in a fire place and leaves. Says as he flies out, "She will be fine now and bye, guys."

Both children released themselves from the circle that was formed and started giggling at one another. They then began to speak in a different language as they looked at their Godmother who was warming up. And while she was warming, her Godchildren were looking a lot happier. They turned to look at their mother and Claudia says, "I know what both you guys want, come on, here." Claudia pulls the blanket over her shoulder to cover herself.

Back at Buckingham Palace, Sterito and House get in behind the mouse. "Hey, I wonder what he knows of this particular Palace?" So, the mouse looks pretty much like a cat and says, "Yes I know what you are thinking: 'why don't that mouse show me the way to the Queen'?" The mouse has understood what they were here for, as he replies,

"Follow me this way, and watch your feet." Just as they were following the mouse the back of the walls started moving up and down, the floor would become the ceiling and vice versa.

Sterito, "Oh my, what a great way of looking at this as both floor and ceiling mix." Mouse says, "Now eat this and shrink down temporarily to make it through the other side and get back to normal again on the other side." Finally, they both reached the other side and squeezed into the wall, went back to their usual size and continued their journey to find the queen.

When they became their usual height they were both so fascinated with the fact they had been able to get to Buckingham Palace. Mouse took them as far as he could, "This is the end of the line for me, good luck," and leaves. "Right then," Sterito says, "we're on our own now." "That means so much to me Your Majesty, thank you." "Wait a minute, House, what just happened? Who were you talking to?" says Sterito. The House replied, "Oh that, that I was just talking to the Queen, oh my!" then falls to the ground.

Moments later, Sterito is shouting, "House, wake up." Finally, House gets up from the floor and looks at the Queen again but this time, fear in his eyes, and softly says, "Are we in trouble Your Majesty?" Queen of England, "No my child, you are both welcome here and you will be guests of mine today, I believe you are trying to find your master, Sterito." Sterito, "Yes, wait, how do you know of such things Your Majesty?" Queen, "Well, I have had a visit from someone who's very important in your world and a highly respected wise old lady."

Sterito looks at the Queen with a smile and refers to her as a well-known but secret lady, "Yes, your highness, my master's mother but it had to be kept secret for now because of her father and I refer to my master, Lunarnise." Queen, "I'm guessing she has been through some kind of incident and she is not sure whom she can trust. Thank you for your assistance both of you, please do give this to Lunarnise." The Queen hands over a bag to Sterito to give her.

Sterito and House get up and leave the castle with bodyguards all around them as the Queen suggests. They finally reach the exit of the castle and the bodyguards who have been appointed to them, watch both Sterito and House as they go but look sad. One of the guards says they were good people and respected by everyone who met them on the way, this is what is expected from the Buckingham Palace. "Right, it's time to go and find Lunarnise, your master." "Hold on," says Jake, "my wife, she's at the hospital, quick, let's go.

An unexpected surprise, as a vehicle pulls up near the castle to pick them up and take them to the hospital. They arrive at the hospital with the young woman who was kind enough to help Lunarnise and Claudia. Jake thanked her for her help, and again she went on her way. They went into the hospital and approached the reception desk. To find out where they were. A nurse came over and said they were in the next room. Jake and Sterito went to find out but when they got there the room was empty. Jake said, "What do we do now, where have they gone?"

House came back with some information about their disappearance, "Guys, I have been told they were met by a few people who arrived in a strange ship and took them back to Tiger Warth, so we should find our own way back home." Just then the Pegasus came with a trailer to take them home. Everyone looked up at the sky and saw the beautiful black flying horse. Slowly he continued to land on the ground and they got into the trailer while Pegasus was secretly watching, happy as he flew away into the night.

There was a huge explosion and a massive hole appeared. He galloped faster before it disappeared. They came through into their world. Pegasus dropped the trailer off on top of the treehouse and left back into the night. Sterito and House watched the Pegasus climb into the sky as Jake got up to find out what happened to his children and wife. Sterito then turned to the House and said, "Let's go locate where our master is now."

Both Sterito and the House climbed down from the treehouse and started looking for Lunarnise. As they approached the campsite the two of them started singing to themselves and all animals began dancing to their songs. "There's no way they could hear the sound coming from our mouth, how could this be happening?" House saw something in the background so he says to Sterito, "What do you call a headless man?" Sterito said, "Who?" House responds, "A blemmyes, and don't look behind you." Sterito says, "Is that not Sir John? But wait, how did he get back from Atlantic time? No, it's not him, oh no we're in trouble."

The unknown man who is yet to introduce himself is walking up slowly, saying that he's Gratiol. "For people who don't know anything about me, please, I'm a good person, well I would like to believe that. I would like to welcome myself back to this country if it's possible and one person knows me. He goes by the name of Tobias, do you know him?"

As Lunarnise heard him speak, she started crying, then ran away. Gratiol turned around to see the woman who was in distress. Gratiol, "Please do accept my apology for the fact I have upset the Princess, oh no have I come at a wrong time, my friend called me only a week ago, said that he had a job for me."

"Oh well then, I'll have to pass you over to Stimpultonnes who will be able to assist you," says Noah. "Yes, I am sure he has called you in to help with the issue of Sir John, he needs to be dismantled immediately and you were the only person to do it." "Okay cool, that is for me so we will start training for a good team in the morning after breakfast," Gratiol said. "But before we rest and get up, forget the 'mona', so far so good let's feast together and 'poo oww' we learn to walk and pow." Sam, "It's been a long time, where have dee been I haven't heard of you since first grade." "Wait, how do you know Designer? How do you know he was around all of us?" says Kulumbush. Gratiol then mentioned, "He reached out to draw a chair for me. Come and join us for grub." Sam climbed out of the skyline to greet him, "Now look at you my dear friend, you dee change."

As both Sam and Gratiol started to dance around and did a silly move with their hands and feet, while music was being played in the background, House listens to the music, jumps up to his feet, runs into the forest, and finds himself a nice spot, gets comfortable and sleeps. Seconds after, a small but fearless little creature comes out and makes a noise, dressed in armour. A voice from above shouts out, "Where did you come from?" Moments later, he replies, "Oh sorry Sam, I am Rubicon I am AKA House."

Designer, "Nice to meet you, Rubicon, hope your stay with us will be a good one. I see you're Lunarnise's acquaintance, am I right?"

Rubicon speaks in a different language, "Yes, yes sir, she's my master." "Gratiol, where are you, you've got a little task to do," calls Noah, "I need you to go with Lunarnise and take care of a situation for me." Gratiol decided to go and look for her as she wasn't anywhere near him. "Okay I hear you loud and clear, I've been told that Lunarnise is in a class and I have to wait in the lobby for her."

Bell rings so suddenly, Lunarnise shouts, "Kulumbush, where are you headed to? Me and Fronk, we're wondering if you want to hang out with us." Just as Lunarnise starts walking down the stairs she hears a voice that sounds familiar then shakes her head, it can't be. "I know you from my brother Tobias, your voice, we have spoken on the phone." "Indeed, we did, your highness," replied Gratiol. As they were recreating themselves there was movement in the castle which was a distraction as Pegasus was above in the sky looking down. They went back down to the end of the castle to check this out. Kulumbush, "This looks scary." "Come on, you, big girl," Fronk said as he was laughing. Lunarnise says, "Come on, you big girls," and goes in front to lead the way in and find where the noise came from. She then says, "There's something fishy about this, guys."

Everyone else ran off, playing a trick on Lunarnise. Lunarnise, "This isn't funny anymore, I'll find you," she says quietly, "wait, I will surprise you all." She tries to recall the last place she can remember when she was here and proceeds to jump. She disappears into a bubbly hole, and makes it through to the other side still in the darkness of the castle behind everyone and shouts loudly. Kulumbush replies with, "Ahh, who goes there, oh it's only Lunarnise. Who, wait, what did you do? I was scared." The others shouted, "You got us, good girl. Where did you come from?" Fronk was looking a bit confused.

"I'm not too sure," as Sterito found Lunarnise and winked at her. Kulumbush nodded, "Why am I nodding? Did anyone else see that eye trick?" "No brother we didn't notice that you're being ridiculous." Lunarnise looked at some of them and said, "Oh, I didn't know what I did but it seemed to be fun, wow!" What a head rush that stage had turned as she began to look pale in the face!

Stimpultonnes, "Okay, everybody, show is over, get back to work. You need to take it easy the first few times then you will start to feel like yourself again." As Stimpultonnes was explaining to Lunarnise, there was an interesting situation where Pegasus had to come out of nowhere to break up a fight against the Mountainterus and the Gruwpertorious, as he challenged the opponents. He released a thunderous loud noise that made him shiny. There was a lot of shouting and screaming in the background of the fight as if something else was happening at the same time. Suddenly there was a tall dark man standing and shouting, "ne Yaa oh ja, ne Yaa oh ja," and he handed something to Pegasus who looked upset and angry before he left in the dust.

Pegasus says, "Wow, I like that guy," Voice, "The boy who has been given the parcel by the unknown man, please take care of the item as it's needed later in your journey." Pegasus looks around sees nobody else nearby, so then he flew away, really fast, just as others were watching him go farther away.

Clariot, "As you are aware the other day when the games were going ahead, we have made a decision to go with the Gruwpertorious to challenge for the title. The results are not yet known but should arrive soon and when we know it will be announced. Oh wait, we've got a singing bird on its way to announce the winner." A knock on the window happened, then a roll of paper flew into the room. Clariot, "Everyone, the winner of the contest will go to…." There was a big silence as each person became nervous. "the winner is Tobias." There was some laughter and Lunarnise had a tear, suddenly there was a big explosion in the room where all sat down, and all three groups disappeared into the darkness.

Chapter 10

A Quest of Knowledge!

In the beginning there was a question of rights from the past, and the present goes far back to a great grandfather of a great man who lived and served well. And was a prophet born to help guide the people of the future by making a new generation to excel his own life. He was born in the early years of our ancestors, one of the most influential and respected individuals of all time and loved by many. Known as the greatest of orphans and heroes in history, he died at a level of power that was lost in battle and still remains untouched today.

The question that holds a truth out there which today is held in dark woods, as an orphan place brought to light, teaches all creatures. An old professor who was raised by the very school before your own eyes, but with extremely high expectations and poverty levels. It's known to be a great school of wonders. At the age of two years he already had the ability of a ten-year old. At the age of ten years he was forced into battle as he had talents that were not available for years before. His parents were not able to get him into school because of the high expectations and unknown powers that they knew nothing about yet. Shakahi was devoted to training as hard as he could to reach a higher level, he then became a hero of the world. At the age of 15 years he had become a teacher of magic, and training people who were interested in battle. That's why today you see great powers among all nations standing before others in harmony. My friends, there is a challenge before our eyes.

There was an explosion in the past and Shakahi had been put to trial for his crimes and he had been prosecuted over the uncreated person. No other than this own enemy not known to the world, John, had started to make things worse by his actions. But even though Shakahi had been put to test, it is still unclear, his knowledge of the

Mountainterus, Villgarious and the Gruwpertorious. As far as I can remember these three groups have been involved in challenges to championship to try and achieve the cup. For many years we have seen getting to the finals and an unknown challenger always has picked it up, but this time it seems different. He saved his way through the enormous tournament in the first match as they were never in any games. This is how he was able to get all our teams out there to make it happen, but John, a lost boy, became an enemy of the tournament. Making any chance for us difficult to win, as John started growing stronger than ever before, getting people behind him all the way.

Shakahi's knowledge is not only what we know, but what you may benefit from and a time to learn about the future. It is also known that the Designer Sam has been working on a good relationship between the artist and the people who are involved in the story. Throughout this journey you will learn about the Designer and the different aspects of each story. It is also recorded that Shakahi brought as many people together to create a unique experience.

As it's all known that the three groups were brought together through the same time line of the same events. With it being the same year that Shakahi challenged for the first championship, immediately they got underway with the traditional training.

Noah said, "We need to challenge ourselves to the max. if are to compete against the toughest teams. Prepare yourselves for the most fearless of battles yet to happen now and in the future. As you were chosen, Lunarnise, learn to take them all forward. Through the help of Stimpultonnes with the group behind you, I am sure you'll find a way to figure it all out." "Well listen," says Fronk, "at least we get a chance at a proper fight." "What do you mean?" asks Kulumbush.

Helena, "Isn't it funny how the girls are trying to tease one another?" Lunarnise looks at Helena and laughs. Kulumbush, "Oh chicken, you think that is funny? Wait until you get mine," he pulls out a large watering can from his hand and proceeds, chasing them.

"Good morning class," an unrecognisable creature says, "I shall be teaching you how to use your mind and skills, good luck to you all. Hope you have all eaten well and have had lots of rest. Right, let's get ready." With the kindness of the host in place and it's as if he knows the ground like the back of his hand. "But sit, just before we play fight with one another as if we're going to battle, I want you all to notice the qualities in your opponent. You need to brace yourself with fierce determination - I want to win this show." As the host embarked on his journey, there was a new person on skates who ran inside of the two fearless groups who were going to fight.

"It's believed that the more we learn the better you realise what we don't know about ourselves especially when in training. Though this can often become a yearning to learn how our bodies react in battle, which may be a quest to understanding what we have visible. Right here I am, I have been sent by the Queen of Tiger Warth from the future. I have been told to believe in each and everyone's capabilities and learn to love yourself so you can forgive your enemies. But wait a second, a member of your royal family is missing from the list. I shall have a conversation with Stimpultonnes on that matter. Secondly, if I may, I would like to introduce you to a new move, it's called the way of the tiger and Roland is going to train you. Over and out." Then vanishes.

Roland, "Okay then, everyone, how are you doing today and are you ready to take it to the next level? Start out by stretching yourself." "I think they should learn a new technique for the upcoming battles ahead, be ready to stick your head in your mouth, hahaha. You should be more focused than the words being spoken, come on you blues, how about you learn to go invisible?" All three groups are in the courtyard of the castle, starting to get prepared and working up their sweat.

"That's it, you'll see it will be worth the effort in the long run, come on, Kulumbush, put your back into it. Push yourselves to the limit for a bigger battle is yet to happen. Sam, are you there? I need some obstacles to help with this training. It looks like we have got extra help from these guys. I believe some of you may have already introduced yourself to them, rock and knight. Right then, guys, where do you want to begin? Choose your opponent to the right of you and then pick up your weapon. And off you go, you see if that wasn't so hard." There was a tall dark knight who was advising with the moves of a twisted wonder. "You have to stretch to the left and to the sky, and then bring it back down and repeat it with the other side. Let's go back to the beginning of your moves as we go through the foxtail glass like we have done before.

"Let's start with this process of moving around and making sure that you don't miss anything else in the future. Because there have been a few changes over the years that haven't benefitted us. Hey you, with the odd-looking cap can you please show yourself?" "Yes, your honour, it is me, Shy horse. I'm sure you could do with the help of an intellectual young man that's a black belt in fighting." "Oh hi, Shy horse, do I know you from somewhere else?" "No, my friend, I'm new around town. I overheard someone say that there's going to be a battle." "I heard that there's a new whisper in the area and I would hurry to catch up with them and he's one of the best. He is supposed to be an old friend of Tobias."

"Not this again, it's becoming too much for me," Lunarnise says as she walks away into the dark night. She gets discovered by the unicorn, "Hi girl, where are you going in a rush? Please come along let's go, you look like you need company." Lunarnise, "Okay girl, come on let's get going, I need to finish my brother's mission and find the egg as it was lost." Unicorn, "Right, I understand, you are very distracted now but I can assure you the best years are ahead of you." Unicorn says to herself as only she hears, 'if only you knew the truth about your situation.'

Lunarnise looks up to the sky and says, "Why did you have to leave me so soon, go, uni to the left side of the bridge." She came up with an idea of how to get to the top of the waterfall at the opposite side. "I wonder if it would be possible to cross over to the bottom of the waterfall as there are some stories about how the cave people hid something valuable." "How is this possible and how are others going to believe me?" Gratiol, "Lunarnise wait up for me, I've been told I have to be by your side, oh I see they must have gone that way."

Gratiol picked up speed as he travels towards where unicorn and Lunarnise went. As Gratiol gets closer to where they are he suddenly becomes weak and falls to the ground and says, "What just happened?" Pegasus happens to be nearby and goes to Gratiol's rescue, "I noticed you flew into the spikes." Gratiol responds, "Oh, is that what they were?" Gratiol jumped up on Pegasus's back and he flew up to the tree above. "You'll be fine here. Rest and I'll take you to the others."

Meanwhile on the other side of the tree Lunarnise and unicorn were just going down the waterfall. Moments later they found the room and there was something shiny in the bottom left corner of the cabinet. Unfortunately, it looked like there is a lock on the door where it is shining from. Lunarnise said, "How can we find the key for this door? Oh, I remember where it was. Roland held it once before."

Sterito came to Lunarnise, looked at her sadness as she spoke. Sterito, "You called for me, master? I have been told that you want the key. I know where you can find it." Lunarnise, "Where is it? How can we find out, if it's true." Sterito vanished into thin air. Lunarnise, "Why has he not mentioned it to me, hey you, yes you, I know that you're reading this book do you know where he went?"

Unicorn, "Why are you worrying the readers, are you expecting a response from them lol? At least they don't know what they're going to expect next. Sam, where are you? Can we make it fun for them?" "Hey, you down there? "Who summons me from the castle in the sky?" "Oh yeah, hi Jake, I didn't know it was you." "What can I do for you?" says Sam the Designer. He then takes out his stick and puts water in the room to make it harder for them to get to the cabinet.

Sterito laughs as he returns with the key, singing and dancing around trying to make people smile, and talking. Sterito, "What happened here, Lunarnise? Where are you girl?" "We're over here in the middle of the floor with water all around us," shouted Lunarnise. Unicorn starts screaming as something is trying to pull her underneath the water. "Quickly," says Sterito as he shouts out for help. Guess who was the first person in line to save unicorn? That's right folks - Pegasus.

"Yes, hey you with the camera, I'm down here as I go under with a splash," and pulls up unicorn out to safety. As the unicorn lay on the dry ground she looked weak and was breathing slowly. She looked at him and said she had seen something. Unicorn, "There were three arms stretched out to grab me from the top, but I only saw one figure like a fish troll."

Lunarnise just looked towards uni and became sad. Pegasus said in his head, 'Don't worry, little sis, I've got your back and will protect you.' "My training will be over soon and I will return home," Sterito told Lunarnise she shouldn't worry too much as she will go on different trials. And there's plenty of room for improvement, and she will have a lot of time to prepare herself to be the person she would become. "As long as you, Lunarnise don't follow the same path as your ancestors and fall into any traps. Watch out for the con man." Lunarnise looks surprised when she heard the news, then says, "You haven't got no problem with me, I'm not like my family."

"Likewise today, as we see problems of knowledge in understanding needs to be addressed as intelligence to the way we live. Maybe due to the lack of awareness in our society, make yourself aware of the dangers that come your way. Lunarnise, my girl, bring yourself into light as you will push forward any opportunities to fulfil your needs in order for us to improve and resolve." Lunarnise quickly, "Uni, Sterito, this way, we need to get the golden egg, and then get back to the rest of the group, let's go."

The fish tail troll notices that they are leaving through the gate below and tries stopping them. Sterito has been found on the back of uni, unconscious. I'm guessing the fish troll knocked him out as they were passing through. Lunarnise decides to take the second key from him to get to where the golden egg lies at the very bottom of the waterfall. Just as Lunarnise was about to take the egg from the container a fish monkey came by and grabbed it and gave a cheeky kiss to Sterito. Moments later he woke up. As the river of the waterfall began to rise and came to life, woken by a huge scream, which would work to an advantage for some people.

Meanwhile back at the school, there was training getting underway. Roland stepped up in front of the whole school and began to speak, "We have a new talent that is going to be introduced sooner or later, but first we need to rescue a talented student from the river of secrets, her name is Lunarnise."

That might've made everyone feel powerful enough to train harder than ever before. Kulumbush, Fronk, Helena, Poppals, were missing talent. Sam, "Okay, yes I heard it but I may regret it later. Pegasus, where are you? If you can hear me can you please help us out?" Noah hears the voice of a young man as he makes a big noise then starts galloping towards them high up in the sky, sticks his head up straight. Stimpultonnes, "I'm going to send you out to bring home our daughter to us in one piece, you all be there for each other and find out your own talent, so go now."

The group assigned to take up the next quest slowly leaves the room, while the rest of the teams stay behind. Noah trots up and down the stairs, seen with his head down, Fluffy comes running up and comforts him, then Noah smiles. I wonder what Fluffy mentioned to Noah. Judging by the way Fluffy has mentioned, we're guessing he had special information about something that is going to happen. Fluffy has a little run around and he then vanishes into thin air, or maybe he's just gone for a walk and will return. Noah laughs and looks confused, "Jake, how do we know he was genuine or just plain evil?" "There's something about him that doesn't seem right," says Stimpultonnes.

"There's something wrong, I don't think Fluffy would do anything like that because of Sir John's track record. But if he was the one who was involved how do we stop him from getting the egg? He has been trying to get the egg ever since he was aware it existed." Roland, "Stimpultonnes please explain why he has been chasing you." Stimpultonnes, "Well my child, grab a chair and come closer and listen, it goes as far back before Lunarnise and Tobias were born. He never did like what I done in school as I was the top of the class in every class we were together, so one day he tried to teach us a lesson and burned our clothes. But we got him in trouble with the teacher in front of everyone and he was so angry that he bullied us using a little bit of glue, as he glued us in a small room." Roland, "Sir, how did you manage to free yourself?" as he looked puzzled by the way things were heading. Stimpultonnes, "Well we were aware of his weakness and worked it out between ourselves."

Back at the waterfall there seemed to be something fishy going on. Sterito thought the fish monkey had gone with the egg, but it only wanted to help so she swam along towards where Lunarnise was. Then squirted the fish water into where she was standing and it turned into jelly so it could help them out safely. Lunarnise had a good mind set as she helped the fish monkey to make lunch for her tribe and waved at them as she swam out of sight. They were able to swim out and under to catch the air, which was very good for Lunarnise, and the gang somehow managed to get her to the beach in time.

Just as she gave Lunarnise the egg it accidentally got stuck in the water and Lunarnise gets to it in time by swimming fast and grabs the egg and swims to safety yet again. Kulumbush runs over to Lunarnise and says, "Are you okay girl? We're here now to help out. What should we do, have you guys eaten?" Lunarnise, "Kulumbush, please slow down I am fine but hungry," everyone else begins to laugh. Before they knew it, Pegasus flew over to drop food for everyone to eat, and water to drink.

They all gathered together to feast as Pegasus looked down to make sure that they were safe and well. After food and drink, a few sodas later Pegasus began his journey back into the distance. As he flew off into the mountains Lunarnise looked up and wondered where he had come from and where he went. Not long after, she disappeared into the forest and continued her quest in search of the golden eagle and said, "I will conquer all." Sterito came running behind her. "Do remember this, there will be challenges on the way. Kulta told me about her experience with the forest fire." "Wait," Kulta, "is it that you don't believe the stories that come out from hiding?" She appeared from behind the trees and said, "Me meow, wait up girl, my paws are getting tired." As the fish monkey swam past, Kulta licked her lips.

Lunarnise, "No, Kulta, please don't lick your lips or stamp your feet or even wag the tail." Kulta continues to waggle her tail. Lunarnise was then in a bit of a bother as there was another unknown person who grabbed the golden egg yet again and flung away quickly. "Oh, come on, how did you get that from me? Unbelievable!" Lunarnise cried, "what do I need to do to get this egg home safely?" Voice, "Well, there is something else that will be requested for you to achieve, gain the knowledge of a well-known person."

Lunarnise and the crew were ready to go on to meet with the one troubling them in a way which was not possible for her to understand. "You will have to undertake a knowledge of the most difficult challenge to overcome your deepest fears in order to release the egg." Voice, "In relation to this, child, I am going to send you down the stairs in front of you." "What stairs?" Lunarnise asks as she's thinking of no assistance. Designer looks over towards the waterfall, takes out his pencil and starts drawing.

Moments later stairs appear from nowhere, "Please could someone kindly let me know what's happening?" Someone continues to mutter. That was it, everyone ran towards them as they were walking around the spiral, an unknown object or person it looked from far, but appeared with a question. Unknown person, "You will come into three circles of the world, first one you will come face to face with your past and challenge your worst nightmare. Second, you are yet to meet a well-known woman to uncover a secret. Third will come out towards the end of this book. Watch out, your friends can become your enemy."

Lunarnise maybe a clever and powerful young lady, but she will embrace different forms of love, regardless when she is caring for others. As you the reader will get to know her in a different light through the upcoming books. Lunarnise and her small group are set to find out what appears at the end of the stairs as she says, "This seems to be forever, I'm getting so tired of walking." There was a brief moment where the dragon Lunarnise befriended earlier in the story seemed to be possessed and was coming towards them. Helena shouts out, "What do we do? I know, run."

Everyone who was there starts yelling and screaming, then runs. Gratiol, "Wait for me to come to your rescue. And wait, what's happening?" as he starts speaking in a high voice and his eyes become red. Lunarnise, "Quick, everybody this way, I don't want to hurt him. He was just with me, it's like something took over the dragon." Gratiol, "Lunarnise move now." Then his voice gets bigger and starts shouting at everyone around him. Lunarnise, "No, I won't leave you, as you are one of us now and I'm going to help you," as she stood to look at him.

Lunarnise flies up towards him, and shouts out to Helena, "I know what to do, cover me, girl." Helena, "She's insane or she's crazy or has a plan, I'm behind you."

Helena jumps up in front of the dragon to make sure he doesn't breathe fire at Lunarnise. Lunarnise looks for something else around Gratiol's body. He swings his tail at Lunarnise and knocks her out. As she is falling down something amazing happens, somehow her chest shines, she's just had a third eye appear and it helps her heal from her injuries. She manages to get to safety but out of breath as she heals herself.

Pegasus flew in quickly at the same time, ready to grab Lunarnise yet again. ('Oh my, if she only knew who I really am!') As Lunarnise gets closer to Gratiol she notices a third eye on his tail and it looks to have a slight damage to the skin with something else looming around it. She starts removing the object from around his eye. Within seconds it was done. That was it, his main eyes changed from red to yellow so he was normal and yet calm, thanks to Lunarnise and Helena. Lunarnise, "I'm so glad that he is back to normal now." Helena, "Thank you for your help."

Zanura, "Come with me and I only need three of you - I think Lunarnise, Fronk and Helena, you will learn a valuable lesson." Lunarnise, Helena and Fronk followed Zanura to the edge of the field to make their way into the clear glass. It took several hours to complete this journey but it was worth the effort with Fronk being the only player who had brought food to the table. They ate and drank together in memory of the first Lord, Pepino who died and, was the father of Stimpultonnes. Moments later music started playing in the background. Zanura, "Right now, people, capture this moment, with all of us in together now, we have to go through this glass door ahead." Gratiol,"I know where you're going, so see you there, Lunarnise."

Chapter 11

The Return of Prince Tobias!

As with all the other previous chapters this one will focus more heavily upon the story of Prince Tobias's return. We'll now we see how Lunarnise is about to embark on her second challenge and a chance to make a difference to the unknown woman that she will meet. Lunarnise decided to take the opportunity and took her scooter out instead of flying. She thought it would be easier as she knew it would be tricky so the scooter went to the right direction as she was going downhill a road in Tiger Warth called Taritijan. Where the land was named after a famous horse and indigenous tribe where unknown creatures lived.

Lunarise, "Before I knew it, the scooter had changed into a wooden brown cart as I decided to go slowly. I then saw a pirate's treasure chest. I was cautious about my sightseeing and my safety at the same time, but something happened. The chest moved around so I had to stop the cart. And I needed to take a look, got out of the cart walked over towards it and I got the courage and determination to take a look inside. To my shock I saw a young woman looking at me. As she looked wet, I said, 'Who are you? And why are you in the chest?' I helped her to her feet. She said that she is a mermaid and her name is Shelby. I realised that I had heard her name somewhere else. I noticed that she was the kind mermaid who helps the needy. I just had to help her. I whispered her name so nobody would hear me.

'I took a few leaves from the garden nearby and waved my hands quickly to form a dress. Here you go, take this dress, as she did lie naked, only a blanket to cover her. I'm ready to embark on my second quest out of three, I was told that I would meet a well-known woman who would reveal a secret to me."

Shelby, "Well girl, I think you know that yourself, but I shall be at your service and help find this wise lady."

Oh, my goodness, does anyone know where Lunarnise is? She's all the way out there from home without her friends. And all the way in the middle of the desert must be hundreds of miles away from anywhere. "I maybe hundreds of kilometres away but at least I'm happy as it must be something special." This whole situation has given Lunarnise a princess look with the air, as she took a stylish scarf from her bag and wrapped it around her neck.

"I remember just standing in one place and thinking what a mystery this was, like how would I ever get myself out of it? Even though I knew I could jump from place to place. What, what's the point of doing that now? I want to do it naturally. Then the wind blows down houses right before my eyes in the distance.

"I understood that I couldn't make it from here on. Just then I noticed something flying towards us. At first, I didn't know what to expect until it got closer, only then I realised that it was Gratiol who seemed to be struggling as he came down pretty quickly and rolled over. I understood straight away that I couldn't leave him alone all defenceless in this place without food or water. Even though nothing about his appearance seemed to be life threatening, I was certain I had to be careful before approaching the weak. The fact that Gratiol didn't wake up seemed to be so obvious to me as he must have been hurt. I looked quickly and put his wings at his back."

He then opened his eyes and looked at Lunarnise as he was still lying there in pain. "I looked over and couldn't do nothing but smile and feed him food and water. He slowly started to feel better and over a period of time recovered and was healthy again." Lunarnise started to look at Gratiol and said, "I am thirsty." He got up to his feet again, began to fly to collect water. He immediately came back to present her with some. As Lunarnise began to drink the water she realised that there was a soft voice calling her, "That is strange," Lunarnise said. "Just imagine we're on a long journey, it could take several days to locate the lady." Lunarnise calls out to Shelby, "Where are you?" Shelby responds, "I'm here, girl, I slipped behind you. I'll just get in front of you now." Lunarnise took out a beef and tomato sandwich from nowhere and gave it to Shelby. She grabbed it out of her hand and finished it off in seconds.

Meanwhile Lunarnise stood against what appeared to be a broken window and fell inside. Shelby looked around to see where she had gone. She saw the broken window and pushed it, and also went into it. Lunarnise said, "It's strange to see people living out here with limited access to places." When Shelby looked over to where Lunarnise was lying she saw something at the door as it vanished outside, "Did you see that?"

"See what?" replies Lunarnise. "Oh, never mind, it's nothing," says Shelby, "Well, this place looks like someone or something else is living here." Lunarnise, "Come on, girl you don't believe in ghost stories do you, who else could be here?" Shelby, "Lunarnise, come here, look at this for me please, in a back room there's a skin like a sheep has been skinned."

Lunarnise walked up to Shelby to the room where she stood. To her surprise Lunarnise was absorbed in thoughts as she mentioned that she had seen this somewhere before. Lunarnise looked around and noticed a strange object on the floor. It was a necklace that had been given by her mother. She leaned forward to pick it up from the floor, and turned to Shelby, "What do you suggest I do? Shall I put it on my neck?"

The moment Lunarnise placed it on her head she remembered when it was originally given to her. "Someone came to collect a box that I didn't know what it was, everyone else was laughing and smashing drinks together in another room." After a while they saw a couple of random rabbits. One of whom looked sharp and caught her attention, and decided to come right up to her. He said, "I can help you out with the journey as we know why you are here." As the dark and scruffy rabbit began his way, "Well come on, are you sure you'd like to hang around here or be protected from pain?"

Lunarnise, "I have a problem with my friend who is stuck at the bottom of the hill." Scruffy rabbit, "What problem may I ask? Your pain is our pain, consider it solved." He then speaks in rabbit language to the others. Other rabbits run away down the hill, moments later they return with the dragon. Lunarnise, "How, what, how did you do that?" Scruffy rabbit, "Well, my love, with a little bit of persuasion and a magic touch we were sent to you, and you're protected. Let me tell you something, girl, you are the most special person of this land."

Rabbit shouts, "Go," in their language and music plays moments later, someone shouts, "Stop. Big problem," and there's a figure running towards them. Lunarnise starts racking her brain to the point where definition becomes meaningless, which of course means the unknown figure becomes irrelevant. But gets closer to reality by who it possibly may be, as it became more clear. Lunarnise, "Oh my, no it can't be happening, Levi is that you? You've not changed a bit since school. How have you been? I was worried what happened to you at the fall."

Levi, "Enough of this chitchat, we can catch up later, we need to get going quickly." Lunarnise looks at him confused and goes to him. Levi, "Quickly, trust me all of you, this way." Scruffy rabbit also asks, "Who sent you over here?" Levi, "My lady, and I think I could look after her better than you, what about you, wabbit?"

Scruffy rabbit, "My master sent me here, yes, with no purpose whatsoever." Levi tells Lunarnise of the unknown possibilities, saying the truth will be revealed in the coming months. This part will be interesting for sure, as there's a third key hidden in the unwillingness of the two parties involved. That key will also unlock a gate to the Secret passage which allows the door to open for a new era, and reveal that truth.

Well, Sir John is on the move again as he is trying until he gets an opportunity to get rid of his own children. But he doesn't even know that Tobias is his, yet if he's still alive he will be the only person who may stop him. Shelby gets up to say she can't sit around and watch him take advantage, "I'll give it my best shot to take that pain away forever." They all decide to start walking away. Gratiol says, "Where are we going?" "I don't know, anywhere else, far from here," replies Lunarnise. Levi and Lunarnise start to blame each other for the lack of love they both had for one another in the past. "You guys please stop threatening each other's feelings. Take it from me as you both were young and stupid," Shelby responded. "Work on it now and let it just happen, the longer you leave your feelings hidden the more complicated it will become."

"What do I need to do when I find the key?" she went on not giving Levi a chance to get a word in. It seemed Lunarnise wasn't going to apologise to him for what was wrong, but all he did was, look at her face and smile, and said nothing. He got up to his feet and said, "Let's go, we need to locate certain objects along the road." Levi, "I remember that one of my first trips was when we were in town together and you said that I could go farther than I thought." (Narrator, "Hey you, down there I'm suggesting that you require a bridge up the top of the road to get across the mainstream." Without a doubt Sam gets out his pencil, "I will draw two logs together and tie them up." Sam draws them together, a rope to hold them firmly and laughs, "This should do it.")

Lunarnise pretends that she doesn't hear Narrator and Designer talking but when nobody is around she winks at them. They get on their way to the mainstream and for some reason there's an audience, a crowd also. There's shouting and screaming, as the crowd is looming over an unusual object, then they all approach the bridge. "I'm guessing this is where we're supposed to go over, right?" "Why are you saying it like you are scared of something, Gratiol?" Gratiol, "It's not that deep is it? The water I mean. What if it's cold? I don't want to freeze." Levi, "Oh come on, how about you stroll in our middle if it makes you feel better?"

Lunarnise flies out over to Gratiol and lands on his back, then grabs him firmly and tightly. "How about that?" as she puts her arms around him. That was it - he was up to his feet and Gratiol says, "I'm ready, I can do this, my bestie will come for me if I don't make it." "Lunarnise, I know that you were discouraged from a young age by certain people, but I can assure that your heart is secure with us," says Levi. Shelby decides to swim over the mainstream, whilst Levi hops over. Lunarnise flies through, then everyone shouts out to Gratiol, "Come on, you can make it." At that point there was a young woman who was walking up to the entrance of the bridge, and she looked up at Lunarnise in surprise. She leaned over to ask, "I can help with this young man who seems to be scared of the water. Oh, by the way, my name is Rosetta."

"Rosetta, right then, love, I am here to reassure you that I will be there for you if you're going to work with me." "I would also like you to be patient to start with getting to know one another on this wonderful journey. And if I may show you something that will amaze each other, stay pure in the heart so you can make a difference." Lunarnise, "Wow, she is good. Actually, I love meeting up with new people, I always say, treat others how you would like to be treated."

Stimpultonnes comes running up to Lunarnise, tries to speak but it doesn't come out properly. Stimpultonnes, "Look at you, all grown up, I would like to say that I am proud of you. You're constantly improving every single day and you have shown yourself to be a great warrior." Well, as they approach towards the end of the day, Rosetta continues to make a difference when she gets started with Gratiol and the effect that she has with everyone around her. She makes every single person feel good about themselves. "I really haven't seen anything like this since Lunarnise was born. So calm and energetic with so much love to give, do we see the dragon crossing over the mainstream?" Amazing picture after several attempts. With a lot to say about her, Gratiol has a smile upon his face and makes it over the river to celebrate his victory.

Now that everyone has crossed over, they decide that it's late so where each one is, a campsite was created. There was some laughter and screaming, birds singing. After some singing and dancing everyone settled down to sleep in the region of their happiness. Suddenly there were footsteps approaching really quickly. It was known Stimpultonnes was still there to help with demands for the people's successor. He began by asking, what is their purpose of this journey to them at this hour?

Horse Man, "My Lord, we have travelled from far beyond the mountains of Flimpustone town and I am looking for another kingdom so we can join them together. I have a young and beautiful daughter who can marry, and I believe that there's a prince within your world." Roland, "I'm wondering who this maybe?" Horse Man, "Well, I wish to give you some knowledge about this person, but I am not allowed to say his name. I shall begin, he is strong enough to take on Sir John. Only three have the qualities by which he will be defeated. He also has a heart of gold and the eyes of an eagle. Oh dear, I have said too much already, and has unique powers, good night, Sir."

Stimpultonnes, "Oh, remember who the other two people are, as they galloped away into the night and the last is yet to be found." Jake,

"Wait, who's the second I know. The first one I believe it..ssss Noah's son, right? Oh yes, silly me. First is Lord Pepino and Kulumbush." Lunarnise wakes from her sleep, "It can't be, my brother is dead, and there's a story behind Lord Pepino, it's not known how but he lives within the high trees of the mountains. Where he watches over at night. His magic is a mystery. People have gone to seek for the truth then they don't come back."

Lunarnise looks around, sees something unclear in the darkness, and she turns back and sees Stimpultonnes and falls back asleep. Stimpultonnes notices what she was looking at and picks up his stick to go towards it. The unknown object that was in the darkness looked straight at Stimpultonnes and went head straight, kicking his feet and flew away, leaving a sparkling light behind him.

Stimpultonnes was wondering, "I have seen this somewhere else. What could it possibly be? And the way he looked at me that used to make me warm inside. Every time I held him, oh well, I'm sure that it will come back to me when I least expect it."

During the night, while everyone was getting some rest a problem arose in the area where they were sleeping. A few people were talking outside. A big bird had landed on someone's bed and by the look it was injured. "Oh my, it is an overgrown monster, I haven't seen anything like this before. Where could have it come from?" "Well you have seen a hole in the middle of the star up above on the top right of the sun." Lunarnise comes up to the bird, "Please guys, take it easy on the poor fella, let them be. After all, how do you know if they're sensitive?"

Kulumbush looks at Lunarnise and says, "You are right my lady, I'll be more careful in the future." He walks off, mumbling. Kulta passes by but pretends to not hear him as he says quietly, "If only Lunarnise gets to find out what she is going to do. Just around the corner is a trap," and laughs evilly. Kulta looks up at him in amazement, "I got to go and warn her." Just then she's grabbed and put in a bag, carried away, oh my, what happened? Kulta has been kidnapped.

Lunarnise, "Oh no, my bestie has been taken so I am going to appoint Helena for this quest as I need to find out who's taken Kulta. She will be my second choice when I am called off for another job, and will lead the people of this world." Helena says, "Thank you, your highness, I am proud to be serving you," and she continues to speak to her group. "I believe that we need to be heading towards the right path for the safety of the key. Then we can start to look for the golden eagle. Wait there's something else out here and I think I know who it may be."

On the other side of the mainstream Lunarnise is waiting patiently to see if Helena can lead. And it seems that she will become something more important in the eyes of sisterhood. As Lunarnise was about to leave to search for Kulta she was stopped by her father, Noah. He was gasping for breath as he had galloped as fast as he could to explain something special. "Not now, papa," Lunarnise replied. "I have to go and bring back my bestie, love you, we will continue with this conversation when I return." Noah, "Oh my, she will be so excited like I was as someone spotted Tobias. I know it was him because of the mole and where it is."

"Noah, we need you back at the school it's under attack, I know you are strong enough for that, we all are counting on you, quick." Noah gallops to the school, when he finally gets back he sees a black horse with wings. As he looks towards it, it stares back. Noah notices that he has seen this before through the eyes of someone special and proceeds with the battle. At this point Zanura comes back to help as there's lots of damage done by the enemy. Zanura rages at the enemy to end the conflict.

With the fight coming to an end at the other side of the world, Lunarnise is able to get to the place where Kulta is being held. She checks around to make sure that nobody else has followed her, then enters the room. As she tries to get inside there's a small window in the floor of the room from which a siren enters and looks at Lunarnise as if she was lunch.

The siren screams out loud, comes forth and opens her mouth with sharp teeth, but luckily Lunarnise doesn't spare any time to move around to the back of the siren. Grabs her and drags her down to the ground, then Lunarnise's third eye wakes and shines a light on the siren. The siren begins to turn around and flops down as she goes back into the window, the cage opens up by the siren's tail. Just before Kulta jumps out of the hidden cage, runs up to Lunarnise, starts purring, and says, "Let's go home."

On the way back home, Kulta says to Lunarnise, "What just happened? I don't know how I was taken." Lunarnise, "At least you are out of there and free and you don't need to worry about anything else. I'm here for you if you need me too, bestie." Kulta, "No your highness, I promise you that I will always serve you in every aspect of my life."

"Well done, you. I hope you get to enjoy the experience as a sidekick of Lunarnise, and keep her from any kind of trouble." "Hey there, Jake, I heard that, I have just the person who can help with it, hahaha." "Lunarnise, I'm sure you will, but I also wish to let you know Claudia would like you to choose a name for our baby girl."

Lunarnise, "I'm happy for you both and more to place my mark in the world with a name for your first born. How about if we go with a new name that will make the little girl a first to change the way she sees the future, what would you say to 'Beatrice'?" Jake,"Well, that name has a good ring to it, so we will call her 'Beatrice' thank you, your highness." Beatrice starts crying and Jake mentions that he has to go and feed her breast milk from the bag as he taken it out. Lunarnise warmed it with her third eye. Lunarnise, "The princess of time is calling, I'll try to get a moment and go over to see them later."

Lunarnise said to Kulta, "Let's go and help Helena locate the golden eagle, I'm sure we will find out the truth." Kulta responds, "What do you mean by the truth?" Lunarnise literally looks superior as she said, "I am sure I will find the outcome if it's the last thing I do." As Lunarnise says this to Kulta, a man appears in front of them. Kulta looks in shock. "Where'd you arrive from, sir?"

The man who was wearing a shirt and tie responds with a smile and a polite voice saying, "Follow the caveman." Just like that a caveman apparently walks through the front and goes in a different direction than what they were about to walk. Right before their eyes the caveman takes the first corner and says "Remember to follow the young man," then disappears. The caveman while passing, looking scruffy but proud and speaking in another language, picks up a banana from the tree. (Narrator, "I don't think we will be seeing the caveman again, and I'm sure with the look on his face he had a lot to say. Wait, did he just take a banana, and got away with it? Hey mister that's ours.")

Lunarnise, "I've a rough idea what it could be, but at the moment I don't wanna get too much into this because it would just make me sad." Kulta, "We're not that far away from Helena. Lunarnise, quickly duck, watch your head." Lunarnise quickly moves to the side as the falling trap misses them both. Lunarnise, "Wow, that was a tight miss. I didn't expect that, come on, let's go, let's catch up with Helena and the gang."

They were walking and talking when another unexpected incident occurred. Unicorn was sitting there and looking straight at Lunarnise with tears in her eyes. "Hold on," Lunarnise said to unicorn, "what happened to you? And wait, didn't you go to achieve the golden eagle in return for Tobias to help you, wait, what did I say? Where's the golden eagle now? And what happened to your back legs?" Unicorn, "Can you imagine, I had eagle with me and I was running to hide it, when I got ambushed. They attacked and hit me to the ground. I didn't know what was happening and a kind lady helped, and now they've gone away with the eagle."

Lunarnise starts the healing process of the unicorn, as her third eye wakes up and sparkles. The eye responds to Lunarnise by the mind, saying, 'Girl, you are now in body lock down, please be free from any sharp objects. Stay positioned where you are but be conscious and comfortable with your surroundings.' Lunarnise starts with the procedure of healing. As the eye opens and moves forward, up in front there is Helena and the others who are heading towards the dark of the night. Helena looks ahead and sees a big red flag. "I wonder what that means, it's something that we need to do to pass the next level." Just as they got closer to the flag, there was a box on the ground that contains food. A dark shadow jumped up to his front legs in the air and left a riddle that read: 'Riddle that tells a story by saying – what may be touched, and not seen. A loving heart that has never shined before.' As Pegasus rides off into the night through the clouds, Lunarnise sees this and wonders. She gets a recall of the moment. "What! Wait, I've seen this before no, no," as she finally finishes healing Kulta and collapses on the floor, weak.

Kulta looks down at her and says, "Please girl, wake up, don't leave me alone, I'm too young for you to go." Helena looks over at Lunarnise and starts crying but she goes beyond the red flag to find a secret place. Just before she goes into the secret room she notices above, something else that appeared, the Pegasus had vanished into thin air. There in the darkness of the night stood straight above was Tobias. Helena's eyes shone with love as she smiled over. She turned to Tobias and asked him what happened and why he didn't say anything to her and his family.

Tobias looked at her helplessly and said that he had no choice but to keep someone's identity secret. Now Tobias had taken his true identity, to show Helena who he really is. "I had to protect the people I love so it was hard for me." But as Tobias was talking he went back to the form of a Gryphon. "I have a question, does anyone know where my senses are kept? Does anybody know where my sister is now?" Kulta looks up at Tobias and does a curtsey. "Good day your highness, lovely afternoon for a stroll. Wait, it can't be. Hello Prince Tobias, your sister is in this tent as she's recovering from healing me, as she keeps on going in and out of sand to a cat."

Prince Tobias proceeds to the tent and enters it. Lunarnise wakes up and looks up at him and lets out the biggest scream, for all around to hear. All the animals from far beyond start to form a wall around the camp area. Lunarnise, "Am I dreaming? How can this be possible? Please explain it to me." She hugs him but won't let go. Prince Tobias, "No problem at all, sis, you can let go now, I am here, little sister. I've been there for you and protected you, as I will always. I'm here to stay and help make this our home, watch me." Just as Tobias talks to Lunarnise he changes to his original form. Lunarnise looks overwhelmed by this information. "I never knew that you were my true brother, I'm glad that you are here with me." Tobias takes the form of a Gryphon, "I think this is me." As they talk and laugh together, Lunarnise's third eye speaks in her mind, 'I love our brother.'

Kulta walks into the room and says, "Welcome back home, Prince Tobias." Lunarnise looks at her with surprise. "I have my doubts about where your golden eyes, our, I mean the golden eagle. It's known to us that they are safe, but in the long term we need to be careful about spies."

Chapter 12

The Battle of Two Princes!

Prince Tobias of Tiger Warth, and Prince Levi from the Kingdom of Freetown will go head to head with a new generation of young men to challenge their leaderships. As they are not aware of each other, they have to learn the ropes of time and form a relationship between themselves.

Ever since Levi was a child he was a spontaneous person who was always spoiled by his parents. Anything he did had to be blamed on the other person, he used to question time and again, and had to grow up without knowing many things. What I mean by this is, he found out that he was living a secret life as he didn't find out until he was older that he was royal. Whereas Tobias was born to an unknown family, but what we do know is that pretty much of his younger age will be exposed when a spin off story will be revealed all around him.

But I can share with you what he has learned throughout this process of a becoming a young man and the only two people that he cared about, first being his mother, Marilyn and the other Lunarnise, sister. Marilyn, Tobias's mother had to give birth to him in a barn just like Jesus Christ, who for this storyline through the journey will be a saviour. Marilyn, has anyone else seen her or know of her existence? (Narrator, "No, but I'm sure she isn't far. I know that Tobias is a great guy, and he has time for people, someone who cares for all before his own desires. So, what happened to him that got the poor kid adopted, which has a lot to do with Sir John being the evil father of an innocent child?")

Kulta looks at Prince Tobias and meows at him, Tobias responds with, "Okay, I guess you can come," as he stands straight. Lunarnise, "My dear brother, I'm not letting you slip away from me this time that is why I'm sending my second with you. Lunarnise calls out to Helena.

Helena, "Yes, your highness." Lunarnise, "I need you to go with Kulta and Prince Tobias to retrieve the golden eagle for me, please."

Kulta and Helena agree and they both start to make their way with him, as Lunarnise looks on slowly returning to her normal self. Kulta looks back at both, Prince Tobias and Helena, "I know a short cut, it's this side, but watch out for the spikes." They go through a dark room where the light comes on when there's movement on the floor. Roland, "I believe that there is an unknown secret behind Levi."

Helena looks straight ahead at Roland and asks, "I wonder what it would be?" A voice is heard but not seen, "Well, we believe that he may be a secret pirate, take a look at the way he acts." A screen monitor comes up from nowhere and starts playing. "See this video for yourself, what do you think?" "Oh okay, it looks like the younger self of a man who also likes the attention," says Poppals. Helena, "Oh my girl, what have you got that men have offended you?" Poppals just looks overwhelmed and confused by this and continues to walk and is quiet all the way.

Lunarnise is amazed by how it was acknowledged that she thought of stepping in to help Poppals in the process of believing once more. Lunarnise, "Let's look into this situation, and if I may say, sorry, how you feel, I know how heartbroken you felt at the time. Let me start by asking, is it a past love or something else? What it's telling me is that something has hit you deeply. I don't know the reason why but let them know that you have forgiven, plus they will be the ones who may miss out. Let me remind you that you're special and are always loyal to others."

Poppals, "Thank you for your kindness and support in the midst of all this pain, I appreciate everything you guys have done for me." Prince Tobias, "Are you all ready for an incredible journey? I have done this several times. Follow me in this tunnel to nowhere, I'm sure Kulta would agree that it's on the way. There is screaming and laughter in the tunnel of love. Oh my, Lunarnise, can you see what I'm saying here?" "My Prince what on earth is going on?"

Helena, "Show some respect." "Oh dear, did you both get married?" as Jake was saying this Helena looks up to him and laughs. "And say, don't be ridiculous how could we get married?" Jake turns to Helena, and says, "Well, look at the tattoo on your back." Tobias thinks that he should take a look. To his amazement he notices the tattoo which states 'my amazing husband, Tobias' - how could this have happened? Helena had rolled over where Tobias was standing and her armour had fallen off, or could it have been pulled off?

Both Prince Tobias and Helena exchange a kiss, thinking that nobody else would notice. Prince Tobias then realises that he has seen the loveliest woman, stands up straight and says, "What an honour to be on this quest with you my lady, indeed I'm happy!" Then, "Oh look at that," as he looks up to the sky and notices a flying goat with spikes on the back and small wings flapping. "It's looking quite ravenous." You wouldn't believe what happened next, it was as if a collision occurred from out of nowhere but the unexpected appears. Right before their eyes they saw a small object flying overhead in front of them, "I wonder what it could possibly be?" says Tobias. There was a bump in the middle of the tunnel, which made the vehicle spin around and end upside down along the streamline.

Voice, from I don't know where, shouted, "Are we landed yet?" Fluffy appears to be out and about running around the sky, "My name is Damian." "Oh, my goodness, is that you Fluffy?" says Lunarnise. "Where have you been since the last time I saw you? Damian, do you happen to know what happened with Prince Tobias's eagle?" Damian, "Wait, I thought I saw your golden eagle only the other day, but I'll be honest, she was struggling so I made her comfortable to rest."

They make their way to the top of the highest point in the town. Damian started to lead them to where he had left the eagle, "Wait," he recalls, "this isn't the same place that I made a straw bed." Poppals shouts out to Damian, "Duck your head now." As soon as she mentioned it Damian put his head down, a spear swung over him. "Wow, where did that come from?" says Damian. There's an unexpected thing flying around here too, something's going on in this mysterious place. Helena runs towards Tobias and jumps on his back as he is in the air and takes a shot with her arrow. Hits the unknown creature shouting, "Ha ha ha, got it." Prince Tobias, "Indeed but you have only wounded it, wait till it wakes up, it's going to be angry."

In the distance Lunarnise is fighting someone. Fronk comes up to help her escape but first confuses it, then it makes a sharp turn and grabs Lunarnise and flies away. Damian rushes out to get Lunarnise but is far too slow and they all vanish from the scene where Fronk is the only one still there. "Oh my, what happened and how can I explain this to my dear friend Lunarnise?" "You can start with going on the search for a spy within." Fronk, "Well, it looks like I have my eyes closed, so I have a new quest," a green axolotl with a leaf on its tail comes up to him from outside of the barn.

"Oh, would you look at that? She looks so cute and adorable I want to squeeze." Without question she looks at Fronk and walks straight to him. She may seem adorable but she's always on guard of her own tail, if anyone wants to try and touch it. Meanwhile back to where Lunarnise has vanished.

Damian rolls over and struggles to get his wings out and lands on his head. Oh, what a joke, as big as that, how did he manage to make the recovery? "Ouch that hurt," Damian said as he looked around to see how the city looked from down there as he's not used to seeing it in the skies. In the distance he could see two unknown things in the sky, but couldn't make it out properly. He was unable to see as he was hit over the head and knocked out. "Oh, yeah it looks like the shadow of a horse or flying dragon. I think that I should go and follow them slowly so they don't see me. This is Dangerous," as he calls through. "Yes, Dangerous, we have your location where are you heading now?" "I see a dragon carrying Lunarnise away. Are you in the range of shooting the arrow at it?" "No ma'am," responds Damian, "hold on tight." Moments later an arrow is fired from the nearest field.

The arrow shoots out of the field, looks like something else is out there as tense music plays, then a voice, "Shall we put it in a bucket?" Hits the dragon in the left wing and at first it carries on flying for a while but then it goes downhill and with Lunarnise tied up. It was to act quickly as Damian flew out as fast as possible to try and save Lunarnise. Instead he decided to help the dragon as he was hit by a tranquilliser, which meant he was not able to move. As he managed to make it easier for the dragon to be able to breathe freely without being trapped by a rope, he was able to get Lunarnise free. "Hold on," says Lunarnise, "where did the rope come from? That wasn't Felixio."

Damian, "Who's Felixio?" "Did I not tell you, it's the half horse and half dragon?"

Damian, "Wait, what is that supposed to be in the background? Are they goblins that can run as quick as rabbits?" Lunarnise, "See what I mean? There's more to this world than just being me," as she was searching for her stick. "I've lost my stick, the naughty boy has got it." Goblin boy looks back at Lunarnise and cries in fun, "Chase me if you can, babies should be fed with a bottle, he he," and disappears. Lunarnise, "Oh is that what he said? That I'm a baby and should be bottle fed, can you believe it? I need to go and find my stick." Damian on the other hand was still a little bit confused as he finally got off the floor, "Here I go," and Lunarnise is just ahead of me. "Howdy girl? Wait for me, I'm sure I don't want to lose you again," as Damian came from behind the door. Lunarnise was so excited to see him, his tail started wagging, "Oh my, that's not happened in a while."

"Oh, hello Rosetta, your dress looks lovely, how are you today?" says Lunarnise, "What a splendid lady she is!" Rosetta, "Hey hi," as she paused for a moment. Enough time, so Lunarnise could see her smile. "Girl, if I could tell you that I have seen a small and lovely village. Well, if I do say there's a lot of work needs to be done, but I'm sure that we can make it a good place to live. And what would you say about if we call it Picnilow Bay? Yes, that's where I live at the moment, but I know Lunarnise can make it a home. Come let me show you around and there's plenty of plans, there's already many different malls inside." Lunarnise, "Great, I think a western style restaurant would be nice and a nice stylish look for the village. Picnilow Bay has a nice rhythm, especially being close to the river."

Jake, "Good afternoon, Rosetta. You have been introduced to the wonderful Lunarnise, she will look after you as her own daughter. Be true and humble as the people you are but remember not to get trapped by wicked minded individuals. It's good to see both of you as I've known you from childhood to see you grown into young women.

"I need to contact the local building individuals who are very nice people to make a wonderful village by the sea. Levi has been seen in an unknown location where he looks like a pirate 🏴‍☠️, if only Prince Tobias would see. I'm guessing that it would be interesting for the two men who are going to fight, I believe, for a unique and interesting empire that's set out to be in the west coast."

Prince Tobias looks over at Jake and says, "You do know I can hear you. Remember when me and Roland were kids?" Jake is amazed by his ability and smiles. Prince Tobias secretly takes himself out to fly into the sky and sees in the distance that Levi is living a happy life with many pirates around him. "Oh my, Prince with a touch of pirate, how interesting! This is going to be fun. Right now, I'm getting a signal from somebody out there."

As Prince Tobias flies towards the signal, "I wonder what it is calling my assistance in this situation that the signal is coming from the clouds. Is there such thing as giants?" As he is going through the clouds there's a strong storm coming from above. Prince Tobias gets knocked over by lightning and lands on a cloud. Just as there was a patrol of giants passing by, when one stopped to look down directly at him. To realise this was no coincidence, but the giant remembered her friend from the forest once told her that she had a brother. So, the giant decided to pick Prince Tobias up, not noticing he is royalty and took him back to where she was staying in the cloud castle.

Meanwhile Lunarnise and Rosetta walked around Picnilow Bay to see what they could build. Rosetta calls out to Lunarnise, "Hey girl, have you seen your friend yet? He was here one minute then flew off." Lunarnise, "No, I didn't even notice that until you mentioned it to me now. Thanks for the advice though, he is my brother and it's unlikely of him not to be around."

Lunarnise was getting anxious about whether he was in a good place. What can I do? A tear drop started rolling down her face. Her third eye then opened and spoke, "Don't worry he is safe with Aviana." Lunarnise asked herself, 'Who is that?'

Lunarnise, "Wait I know her, she's my bestie giant girl." She stands straight up and smiles, on the other side in the clouds someone starts singing – *On the top side, I don't know what's on your mind.* Prince Tobias wakes up immediately, he responds with, "Where am I, and what happened?" He tries to get up then falls down. "Why have I fallen, am I broken?" The friendly giant replied, "No sir, you were knocked over by some kind of lightning, I saw something do that as they were holding a stick." "Was it Lunarnise's?" "No way." Prince Tobias, 'Calm down first of all. Do you think we can get it back?"

The friendly giant, "I'm sure we will retrieve the stick from the goblin, then find your golden eagle and if you want I can come and help with the goblin." Prince Tobias, "Oh yes, I do recall that. Okay are we ready for a recovery?"

Music is playing. Well, as Prince Tobias and Aviana start to go on an impossible journey Prince Tobias starts getting the same signal from over the top of the trees. "Oh my, I wonder what this could be about again?" as he explains it to Aviana. She looks surprised at the fact that it has happened before. She replies, "Don't worry your highness, we will get to a solution, if you don't mind me saying." Music fades out.

They come up to the trees, on their own the trees gently move towards both Prince Tobias and Aviana, look at each other and say, "We need to avoid any collusion." Both of them were trying much to not let the trees catch up with each other. Sam saw what was happening and drew up a secret passage. Prince Tobias quickly grabbed Aviana and pulled them both through the passage. "Wow, that was close, boy," says Aviana. "Oh my God, this tunnel is taking a toll as it's been a while since entering," Aviana said, "this is not the end yet as we have to jump in the next lane soon."

Within the next couple of minutes Aviana picks Prince Tobias to the second line quickly, "Your Majesty, I do apologise for the inconvenience caused by this situation but hope that you enjoyed the experience." (Narrator: "Well done to both of you and you showed how to work together in such a short period of time.") As Prince Tobias strolled past the crowd something unexpected happened. He saw a bright light that sparked like the golden eagle so he stepped into the door. He started to fall down a cliff and shouted out to Aviana right before she saw him, and was completely oblivious to the sudden explosion.

That took Aviana from her feet to the ground, by which she was unable to get to Prince Tobias. He was tumbling into a tree where there was something amazing. There happened to be a love riffle who was hidden behind the tree and happened to quickly drop a net for Prince Tobias and saved him. "Hello there, what are you doing here? I thought I wouldn't see you again." Tobias, "Who have you been told to spy on this time?" Takari,"Oh really, so how have you been and did you miss me whilst I was away?"

Romantic music plays in the background. Takari, "Well my friend, it has been two years since we last encountered Prince Tobias." "How indeed did you know it was me? I wasn't a Gryphon last time." Takari, "How can I forget you? You stand up tall with a grin that I see your mole on the back of your head that nobody else has."

Prince Tobias looks up at Takari and makes a slight nod as he says, "Umm, I bet you don't remember both of us, my dear. What is that thing over there? Could it possibly be the golden eagle?" As Prince Tobias looks it lets out a big squawk then flies off. "Sir, you have missed your chance to get her but remember you have to befriend her first." "I suppose that shouldn't be too hard, I'm sure we will get on just fine." Prince Tobias thinks he should put her to the test. But the fact is golden eagle has a trick up her sleeve. As she makes the most dangerous move, Prince Tobias takes a chance on grabbing her. On the spur of the moment she moves quickly into a looping ball and sparkles him with fairy dust.

Prince Tobias becomes moisturised with the magic as he transforms to his original form. Prince Tobias, "What happened, why am I the fairy now? Indeed, please change me back, love, I promise to take care of you as if you were my daughter." The golden eagle transforms Prince Tobias back to the form taken, which is the Gryphon. Within a flash Prince Tobias changes into the Gryphon, magical music in the background as she stands still to look at him ("Umm, I see what's happening, says Narrator.) Prince Tobias was happy with his achievement even though he may be far away from befriending the eagle.

Golden Eagle, "Why are you not happy within your soul? When I took a look there was sadness that would happen later on. That is why I am here to help you and your sister and future children, I can help you and be your extra eyes before you go out to battle. So, you will know where to go and fight like a king. Who is your wife?" Prince Tobias, "Thank you for your support and love towards me and my sister, and may I take the honour of knowing you?"

Stimpultonnes came over to see Prince Tobias, "Oh you have finally found her and I am glad you both have worked out your differences. She will work as your mind and soul, your vision for you to carry out the journey you deserve." The golden eagle squarks. Stimpultonnes leaves to go home, as he goes he says, "Remember to bring the unexpected to life as Goldie will show you."

Meanwhile, Lunarnise was preparing to go on and find Levi, it's expected she knows nothing of him. Fronk came running to warn Lunarnise about Kulumbush as he has his suspicions that he is not the person who he says he is. But as he reaches the scene Lunarnise has already taken off, so Fronk finds himself with Sterito. "How are you, sir?" Sterito just looks at Fronk and says, "How can I be of assistance?" Fronk, "Well I ...." as Fronk carries on with his story Prince Tobias sees Goldie leaving and squarks.

Prince Tobias has been ready for this all his life and stood up high, ready to fly in the same direction but then waited patiently for the report to come through his mind. He sees Lunarnise was leaving in the woods without a word to anyone. Prince Tobias says to himself, "I wonder where she is going? I think I can guess," as he watches her leaving. "I need to see Levi, if it's true if he's a pirate, oh my what am I thinking?" Lunarnise. She hears footsteps from behind. She creeps into the long grass and hides herself behind the tree only to find Kulumbush walking around as if he's up to no good. Lunarnise, "I wonder what he is up to and where is he going in a rush?" He stops just ahead of Lunarnise but then disappears. "That was strange, I thought he would at least acknowledge me. Could he be up to something or just planning a surprise for me?"

Lunarnise decided not to think about it and carried on with her journey to find Levi, "I wonder what all the fuss is about, what different people are saying?" As Lunarnise continued to walk along the road she began to see something strange in the distance ahead. "It seems to be a little calf, doesn't it look cute!" The closer she walks to the calf, it looks at her with its head down, then cranks its front leg backwards and forwards. Lunarnise stands quietly and looks terrified as its coming towards her, as it gets nearer Lunarnise begins to panic. Right before she thinks of being attacked by the calf it pauses and speaks to Lunarnise, "I do apologise for the little show. I had to protect myself as I don't know who you are, my family was slaughtered by an evil rabbit."

Lunarnise, "I know who it was that did this to you, the same person tried it to my own family, so if you want, join me in the hunt for the truth." The calf looks scared as Damian was passing by behind Lunarnise without her noticing and pulls a funny expression on his face. Lunarnise was looking at the calf, as she started to look scared and ran away, took a look around and saw Damian's tail behind the other tree. "Damian or Fluffy, what have you done, you know that you scared her off, right?" Damian looked sad and said, "I know what I did was wrong, but you can never tell because of Sir John." Lunarnise, "I thought you knew better than that boy, remember how I found you and was always there for others. And they're looking to brighten up our family, please go and track her down."

Damian responds with, "Yes, your honour," but comes running back to Lunarnise as there was a big squark in the sky; a big golden bird flew by. Lunarnise looks up at the sky and says, "Don't worry, you will understand soon, don't be afraid of her." Moments later she sees Prince Tobias flying over in the same direction as the bird. Prince Tobias, "Lunarnise is that you, guess you we're going in the same direction?"

Lunarnise sees Damian going the same way as the rest of them, and he finds the calf, "Hello my dear, I am sorry forgive me and follow us." The calf was surprised to see her new friends were not horrible, so she was delighted to be able to have a family again. Damian pursued, "I can hear people shouting like pirates on the sea." "Where?" Lunarnise asked. "Just over the trees, my dear. Oh my, they are singing and dancing, your highness, what do we do?" says Sterito. "We take a lead through the trees to get to the other side," responds Lunarnise.

Upbeat drums are playing, and screaming, as Lunarnise goes through the trees and discovers that Levi is present, dressed up as a pirate. Holding a sword and shouting, "Batten down the hatches!" Prince Tobias says as he jumps to the ground, "I think what he's trying to say is - hold everything down a storm's coming." Goldie is flying around in the sky, squawking. Lunarnise, "Brother, sorry how do you know that? Oh, by the way, I love your scent. Have you changed your perfume recently?"

Prince Tobias, "Indeed I have, and I was taught 'pirate' when I was younger, our mummy was a great teacher throughout, growing up. Well the little that she was able to teach me, wait, I have seen her recently, oh my I didn't realise it was her."

Just like a flash of light the eagle came out of nowhere and squawked out from the sky at Levi. Prince Tobias was there before anyone could even say anything. Levi looked around and saw Lunarnise and said, "You look rather good in that dress, what's happening here?" Lunarnise said, "I'm unsure of the matter but thank you for your compliment on my outfit," and blushed. "Oh no," says Fluffy "he's seen your response to Levi." Lunarnise "Who?" She then noticed Prince Tobias, "Please brother don't, he's not worth it." "I have been given specific orders to attack him because he is a Prince and therefore we need to fight to save the kingdom, as it is not known who will take charge."

Prince Tobias makes a loud noise like a lion as he stands in front of Levi. "Hold on, is this a challenge?" Drums start to play, Roland comes to the battlefield, "May the best soldier win, you may begin after the third whistle." Roland blows the whistle for the final time and the battle begins. "Look at these two grown up men battling for their lives, as they struggle to survive by throwing punches and kicking each other. They seem as talented as my grandmother as Princes of Justice should not be subject of any whims, their destinies have been chained until the end." People in the background who are watching this fight are singing their own song.

Everyone sings – *Glory days are coming soon! Beginning of a great empire is about to happen! Then we will live to witness a great future warrior of time!....* Beating of the song begins to fade away. Darkness rises from nowhere. "Damn those black coats why are they looking over here, bro?" Prince Tobias challenges his enemy with a sword fight and rapping contest together. "Wait, how is this possible? They can barely stand straight. Prince Tobias, you remember what happened before, you know that we don't like it, but it's a joke right?" They both ignored Stimpultonnes' orders and carried on fighting with the swords. As Prince Tobias was rapping he lost control and hit Levi in his shoulder. Levi had no choice but to bang Prince Tobias in the face with his foot and they both fell to the ground.

'Oh my, who is the winner of the unknown palace to take charge? Once one wakes up and talks about it, is when we can choose." Stimpultonnes tells everyone, "Quick! Now that Prince Tobias is unconscious we need to catch Genium." "Who?" everyone shouted, "Goldie?" So, everybody gets ready. As Goldie was falling down quickly, Takari comes running to grab her, "I got you, girl. Rest. Your bed has never moved." From a distance Helena was spying on Takari, and says, "Who is that charming woman? She caught the eagle just before I could. Where did she come from? Does she know that my man is unconscious? Wait is that a horse and cart? Now she's placed the bird on her lap and riding off."

Helena, "Wait, where's my man, I thought he was in a battle and passed out. And the other guy?" "Hello my friend, how are you today? The lady who was just here has taken all three of them to a safe place, there's no need to worry about it now. So, if you are a friend or a relative you can go ahead and go home. Thank you everyone. Shows over, there's nothing else to see." "No wait," says Roland, "you are speaking with Prince Tobias's wife. You see they were sitting under a magical tree that can cast shadows on people's lives." Helena, "Wait, so what you are saying is that Prince Tobias is not my husband in the eyes of the God?"

"If that's what you are saying, then yes, and just before you say anything if he also knows, well the answer is 'yes'. Probably Prince Tobias was playing along to make you feel good about yourself. After all, he did plan for the end of store manager to pretend to be the vicar. Anyway, enough of the small talk. If you're comfortable, let's go."

As Takari took all three of them to a secret cave underground on the outskirts of a waterfall, and says to herself, 'Does Prince Tobias know it's his place, from little I just modified it.' Soon as she came to the waterfall she pressed the remote and it moved to the side and the electric gate started to open. Takari was amazed by the way that it looked inside, "Wow, this is posh, open space and an open fire. Let's go and see what the kitchen looks like. Oh my, this is the future of settings and a big remote control, this must control everything." Takari hears a big noise coming from outside and it says, "Your house is closing, please be aware not to hang around, you may get hurt. Or there's something else that says don't worry, what we say inside doesn't have an effect outside." "That's good to know, must only be for the first time I'm sure."

Takari walks to the carriage to pick up all three of the injured people and takes them indoors to make them feel comfortable, but all are in the same room. Then there was an unexpected scene where Goldie was rolling around the room as well as squawking at the window. Takari took a look at Goldie and turned to see if she could hear anything, "What is it girl? Could it be? Wait..." Sterito comes into the living room from nowhere as smoke formed. Sterito, "Oh my, what's happening, have I come to the right place?" Takari, "No, I'm guessing you could have missed the location, your house is in the same place it's always been in the front yard in the tree." Sterito, "Oh I do apologise for the inconvenience, but whilst I'm here I could go and check out the injury report that came through. Oh, look my dear friend is this Prince Tobias, it can't be, what happened to them all?" Takari explained about the fight that happened, because of an unclaimed kingdom. "And Prince Tobias saw pirate Levi flirting with Lunarnise, so the battle began after the instructions were written to Goldie." Prince Tobias had gotten onto his feet after a struggle and Levi sat on the floor.

There was a moment of silence for Prince Tobias and Levi, so it was Sterito who asked about the kingdom unknown. Levi looked up at Prince Tobias. Then Prince Tobias said, "Levi, what do you think about that unforgettable kingdom? I would like you to come back with me and check out the kingdom and you could take it over and I don't mind helping you." Levi, "Okay, but you have to know that I am not going to be doing this for you, only for Lunarnise as I have known her since she was in school. And you can be my knight. If anything happens I will send it over to your senses for her to see and you to battle with your team that you will create to join me there."

Prince Tobias turns to him and says, "Okay, I agree but I have the right team for the future of the kingdom." He makes a few phone calls. First to be called and on his way is Nixo-Stain-Dexun. Second person who has answered but will arrive later is Dillon. Helena and Poppals have been on guard for the kingdom secretly. Levi, "Well, Your Majesty, this is a celebration that we cannot forget. Let's go and invite all those whom we know." Aviana, "Finally your highness, your ride is here to take you to the kingdom where it's magical in its own way."

Both Princes board and are taken to the palace.

Chapter 13

Levi's Challenge!

Levi had to let Prince Tobias know that he was to go and look for Helena and the rest of the team. He was about to go when Goldie finally woke up from her nap. Prince Tobias stood up straight in the middle of the room where they were resting, and saw Goldie had taken a knock back slightly. Prince Tobias, "Hold on, there's a message coming through." Sterito heard a voice and in an instant some dust appeared from nowhere and he walked into it and vanished. Takari, who had brought them to this place only a couple of days before, "Well, you three seem to be getting along with each other, at least that's what Lunarnise would want."

Back in the next room where Goldie and Prince Tobias were, the message had come from a high school. Prince Tobias had been thinking about going out to look for his mother but then thought, 'Could this possibly be something to do with her?' "Don't rush out there too quick, wait for me to get there first," says Goldie inside Prince Tobias's mind. "You are right about that," says Prince Tobias, slowly, but in his mind so Goldie hears. Within a few minutes Goldie gets to her feet and flies off towards the mountains. "Oh well, I guess I'll have to get ready to leave and find out what I'm supposed to do."

Meanwhile Lunarnise was on the other side of the mountains with Kulta. Could that be why Goldie has been called? Kulta had fallen off the cliff and was stuck in a hole. Lunarnise was above, trying to climb down to rescue her. There were baby rabbits lying there on the ground, and as they were sleeping Kulta was trapped by a rock that was covered in a substance of unknown liquid. There were two unidentified people lying on top of the tree upside down, sleeping - one dressed in black leather pants and jacket with sunglasses, and the other in brown pants and a dark shirt and tie. Lunarnise stopped shouting for Kulta as she didn't want to wake them up. As she looked down at them she saw one of them open one eye.

"Who on earth are you?" said Dimitri, who is siblings with the most diabolical vampire. "And you wouldn't want to wake him up, hope you haven't disturbed our breakfast lying there." He mumbled about how they got in there, as well of going back to sleep. "Quick," Lunarnise says, "I need to try and set you free before they have you on toast." Lunarnise struggles with the rope climbing in front of the diabolical man. Kulta turns to look at her, "I would be careful not to wake him up." Lunarnise gets caught in the rope as she's climbing down, so she came eye to eye with the vampires. It wasn't until Lunarnise had to breathe that a loud breath came through her nose, after holding it in for such a long time. There it was! Zyran had woken up. "I see that we have visitors here now and seem to be a bigger snack than what we already have." He looks up at Lunarnise and smirks, Lunarnise is worried that she has become someone's dinner. Dimitri, "I wouldn't worry about it, he was just joking." They all start laughing but at the same time Lunarnise was looking for a way to escape.

Before long Goldie flies into the cave from above and gives a big squark, and flaps around the vampires. Just as Zyran gets his fangs out, Prince Tobias comes in. Zyran mentions to Dimitri that it would be unpleasant for the Prince to see this and puts his fangs away. Zyran, "Your Majesty," as he jumps down, and on his way, he hits Dimitri on the head who also falls down. Right before Prince Tobias's eyes. He sees him and starts kissing his feet. "How dare you do such a thing!" Prince Tobias says as he is holding a stick with garlic on the end. The small and weak vampire starts crying. Zyran, "What are you doing over there so quickly?" Dimitri, "Well, it's like this, there was garlic." Zyran, "And how would you have guessed that, there's no such thing?" Dimitri looks disappointed by the fact he had seen it, Prince Tobias had looked at him with a sudden grin. Dimitri, "See, did you see that? I was right."

(Narrator, "I think that someone is playing a little trick on these guys, and you know what the sacrifice is if you're caught.") Prince Tobias, "Oh, I know it was silly but it was funny to see their reaction plus I thought they were hurting." As he was about to finish off his sentence Zyran looked at him with disgust but didn't show he was upset. Zyran says under his breath, 'I'll be watching you, I won't forgive you," as both of them flew away. Shouts from above, "I'll see you around. Watch out, there's always something else out for you."

Goldie, "What should I do, sir? That sounds serious." Prince Tobias, "Oh, I wouldn't worry about it, they will forget, come tomorrow, after a night out and a good feast." Goldie, "Let's hope it's true. We wouldn't want to be caught up in another act like last time. Anyway, I'm going back home to rest. See you later." Prince Tobias, "Right yeah, indeed, as you look tired. See you soon, I just got something to take care of first." As he was finishing his sentence, Goldie flew off. Prince Tobias, "I'm sure we have to go through this together, sis. Sis, where has she gone, I can't see her anywhere?"

Prince Tobias was scared, nothing like it was before but little does he know she can defend herself. He looked like he was frowning, with no obligation. Prince Tobias had to carry on the journey as he stood up tall, head up straight. Prince Tobias, "I wonder where this leads to, and is this a cave?" An unknown voice replied, "Certainly, and if you follow my voice, I will lead you when you need to go." It was the voice of a young woman and sounded sweet like blossom. But little did he know it was his own mother in disguise, yet again there to make sure that her children were safe.

Prince Tobias, "I hear, mother, but I can't see your face." The young woman responds, "Are you looking after yourself, how is your sister?" Prince Tobias, "Indeed we are." "But there's something you are not telling meee...." as she falls into a trap, then shouts, "Run, my child." Prince Tobias, "I won't leave you alone, I'm coming to help you, then we will go to look for Lunarnise." Young woman, "That's right I thought you may have forgotten, keep her close to your heart as there's things about her that you don't understand. Even she is not aware of it yet, you need to guide her through." Prince Tobias, "I'm here where are you? Which dip did you fall in?" Young woman, "Well, there are three tunnels and one dip without me," shouting. "There is a croak like a frog and a soft sound within all around you, choose wisely." Prince Tobias had to crouch down to go past deadly plants on the path. There were free tunnels, like the young woman had mentioned, he didn't see the whole, until a while later he decided to go down the hole. There as he climbed down he saw the Beautifullest woman, Prince Tobias claimed as he finally reached the ground, "Wow! mother where did you get your beauty from? You look amazing, just as beautiful as Lunarnise." Young woman, "Well, let me tell you that this was me when I was a little girl, you are yet to meet my true self later on." "Umm, I wonder what you look like now and how I look forward to that day." The young woman who was trapped looks over as if she had just heard. He then genially grabs her foot and pulls it from the back of the rock to set her free. She, in turn, grabs him by his hand and shows him through her mind. Prince Tobias pulls away from her hand to realise he has seen enough and says, "I need to get going now, until the next time, mother." The young woman tells him, "I know where you are going, to have fun." Prince Tobias, "Indeed."

He starts flying towards the abandoned plane in the deserted area. As he flew in, an automated voice said, "Welcome to the scouting travina cabin, please go to the airplane to sign in." Prince Tobias, "Good evening, Felicity, how are you this fine night?" as made his way to the plane. "Oh hi, Toby!" says Felicity. "You are a naughty girl, ma'am," responds Prince Tobias, (this actually makes her happy every time I come to do my training). Others wish him, "Good evening sir, how was your journey today?" Little does anyone know that Felicity is only a robot that has a memory of an attractive young woman. And if some people are not careful they can be mistaken as she has already grown fond of Prince Tobias. Lovely as she may seem even as a robot looking at Prince Tobias and then blushing, ("Oh my, this is the first time, I have seen this," says Jake who had to catch his breath.) "Oh my, sir, you are in a predicament, aren't you?" he smirks when walking away, then tells Prince Tobias, "Don't forget our meeting later." Jake smiles and says that he hasn't forgotten his favourite cup cake from Claudia. Prince Tobias, "Oh that, I can't wait, they are delicious too and I better make my way to my sensei." Prince Tobias finally reaches the table and gives Felicity a hug and a nice compliment, and goes to his sensei in the biggest part of the plane and starts his training.

Whilst Prince Tobias was doing his training he had a message on the messenger. A big bird came up to the open window and said that Lunarnise had been captured. His sensei said, "Well, you know what you need to do to bring her home safely," then mentioned underneath his breath, "bringing my daughter home is my dream, son." Prince

Tobias looked at his sensei and bowed with his wings to his side, went towards the door and flew into the night. As he was far away in the sky his sensei said, "Bringing my daughter to us is my dream, my son." Jake then mentioned to him, "You do know that it's hard keeping this from them both, you do know they are like our own children to my family. But as it has not been mentioned to Prince Tobias and Lunarnise it will get told later on in one of the series of books that would give them both a surprise." The sensei looks at the sky and continues with the training session, "That will help Prince Tobias as it is released from his sensei's body to follow him." Prince Tobias calls out to Goldie, whistling. She starts singing above him, "How did you know?" "Goldie, well, you do know the answer to this one my dear friend, let me go so you can follow and have some understanding." Then she flies off. With it being dark and the middle of the night she locates the place and speeds up, Prince Tobias gets ready for the information to be delivered to save his sister.

Within minutes he receives the information to where he needs to go so he can prepare for the journey of his life. As he's about to begin he looks back, then flies up into the clouds. It's as if he knows who was inside of the deserted plane. Prince Tobias says going through the planes and birds, "It's like I know who my sensei is, does he actually know me, how he looks at me?" So, to cover it up Prince Tobias starts rapping whilst flying and it goes like this:

I wake up in the morning,
But my girlfriend was boring,
Felt like a dragon hoarding a pile of gold.
The night's freezing cold,
I'm growing old,
And I'll never succeed in life I'm told.

After Prince Tobias finishes singing he catches up as there's not much distance between himself and Goldie. She locates where Lunarnise is. Goldie, "This is quite unusual, as she seems to be fine with no more than King Levi." "What, you got to be kidding me! She had scared me," Prince Tobias responded. "Well, I guess I should pop in and say 'hi' to him. Now come on, love, let's fly into the clouds," Prince Tobias jokes while he's back flipping. Goldie, "Show off." Someone looks over in a passing by plane and catches their eye. They both finally reach the castle and are greeted by Poppals and Helena, "Hello, Your Majesty, welcome, how was your trip?" Prince Tobias, "Indeed, it was interesting especially when you get attacked by a swamp of creatures. Have a lovely day, ladies." He walks into the castle. To be greeted by Lunarnise, "Greetings brother, I was waiting for you." Prince Tobias turned to look over at his only sister and was immediately worried about what she would say. A few moments later she looked at him with a tear on one cheek and said that King Levi had been taken away. Immediately Prince Tobias ordered King Levi's guards to bring Helena. She came in from the front of the castle to hear what was to be said. Prince Tobias, "Helena, I'm going to have to go and find King Levi, regardless of our relationship." "Oh brother, please," says Lunarnise. She mentions to Helena on her brother's behalf, "My brother is going to need you to step in and hold this castle and take charge." Prince Tobias, "Helena, your first order is to find out where my vision is, and Takari too, all four of us will meet up with the others on dry land."

Helena, "Yes sir, I'm on it, I shall locate them in no time. Poppals, cover for me whilst I'm gone." Poppals, "Roger that, you can count on me." As Helena was about to leave she gently puts her hand to her mouth and whistles, Damian appears from nowhere, "Oh, Lunarnise said it was okay to call her pet." Lunarnise looks at everyone in the castle, "Oh yeah, I did mention that to her. Fluffy is a good friend, and he loves to get involved."

Helena then jumps up onto his back and they both fly into the clouds to go and look for Takari and Goldie, and bring them to the castle so that Goldie could go to locate the whereabouts of King Levi. The only thing is that Helena doesn't know where Prince Tobias's private mansion is located. Not long after she gets to homegrown land and she can see the school just over the bridge. Someone walks up to Helena and says, "May I be of assistance?" "Hello, my dear friend may I know who I'm speaking with?" said Helena. "I'm afraid it's classified information as she keeps her real identity hidden. I had a feeling that this would happen. How does Aelia get to know where Lunarnise is?" Jake was called back home before he could say anything else. Helena, "Lunarnise, is that you, how did you get here so quickly?" Aelia, "But, madam I have been here all day, maybe you have mistaken me for someone else." Out of nowhere Aelia was standing there looking elegant and her hair seemed glittering, as she saw something running through the woods towards her. She had no time to gather her thoughts. She charged in front and picked up the steps fast, but started to panic thinking she would be attacked. Out of the blue she began to feel strange as if strength had fallen from the sky, then leapt into the air as quickly as she could, jumping, flying through the sky and running fast at the same time. Helena, "Did you see that - how, who?" Helena was shocked to think Lunarnise could behave in such extreme heat. "I'm sure it's not her, but who? It had me convinced for a moment." Stimpultonnes, "Well, in all honesty, in the years I've known Lunarnise, this is not her and she has become one of the favourites in achieving gold. "It was," Helena heard a strong voice coming from over the other side of the trees. "Oh, what a lovely sound!" she cried, pretending not to worry.

A soft voice spoke, "Do you remember who you are supposed to be looking for or have you lost senses, my child?" "Wait, what is happening to me?" she said, "And why this delusion?" Sterito makes his way over to her as quickly as possible when he heard the Goblin. "Quickly, my child, come with me if you want to be alive." Fluffy immediately runs off into the sky and goes behind the clouds, and Helena readies to draw her sword but sees the Goblin get more angry. Quickly she decides to take her chance and grabs Sterito's hand, as he pulls her from behind him and vanishes into thin air.

Meanwhile back at the castle in the clouds, Lunarnise and Prince Tobias were both in the foyer, when they get a glimpse of Damian flying around outside. Prince Tobias receives a message from Goldie saying, 'Please read this tweet carefully, I am trapped here and need help but be careful of the dancing dragon.' Prince Tobias looks at Lunarnise and tells her the situation after he hears something else inside where Goldie is being held, then says I know that voice, "There's a spy in the house, no way it's your love interest." Lunarnise asks Prince Tobias, "Wait, no it can't be, could it be Prince Levi?" "Hold on let me see, no it's someone else."

"Kulumbush," Lunarnise called out. ('Oh, dear did I just say his name loudly, only because I caught him snooping around the forest some time ago?') "Okay, would you be able to show me where you saw him, again? But we must wait until Helena or Prince Levi return first, before we can go." "Yes brother, of course," responded Lunarnise as she looked up at him from over the other side of the table as they sat down to eat together.

Back at the school, Helena hid behind the rock that looked like part of the castle, as she had seen the Goblin leaving. He's laughing, "Nobody can catch me now." "Oh my, Jesus Christ, where did he come from? We have had trouble with him for many years now," says Stimpultonnes. Roland comes running up, "Sir, what is happening?" Stimpultonnes, "It's okay, you wouldn't believe who it is - Sir John," says Roland. "Hey there, Damian where are you going? Be careful with Sir John he is hovering around, we need to protect the children, we haven't lost a child yet." "Well, I am here. I heard that Goldie has been trapped. I am here to come and help rescue and get her out."

Well, at that point, the rock comes to life and at the same time makes Helena jump out of her skin and start screaming. Helena says, "Oh my, where did you come from? Are you for real now? And who are you supposed to be with or is it an illusion?" "No, your highness, I can promise you it is not an illusion. I was born in this castle where something happened to me and my brother, decades and decades ago. Well, nobody had ever noticed that or even heard of it before until now, they were so busy with their studies or adventures to have paid attention. Is that Damian in the background and what is he doing? Is that dancing? He is, oh it's funny."

"Oh, come on, seriously Damian, what are you doing? Why the break dancing in the skies? If only Lunarnise was to see this. Speaking of which, where is she?" says Rosetta. Fronk runs over to hear as he looks exhausted and out of breath. Fronk, "Helena, is that right? I'm here to help and assist with your needs." Helena looks at him with a smile on her face and taps his shoulder as she walks away. Fronk started to blush and he looked shy as he liked the attention. He thought, 'I wonder if she likes me or could be I'm getting teased. I think I'll play along with her too, she won't know.' Damian stops dancing and hears him whispering something so he decides to hover over to ask, "I heard you whisper something about the ladies, am I correct?" Fronk was very nervous and said, "Do you think she could like me?" Damian stopped and looked over to him, "Trust your gut instincts and follow the heart, and at the same time have no fear and follow what fate will bring." Well, it looks like Fronk has some sort of understanding so he takes his hand away from his head after scratching. For a moment he takes his eyes off Damian, so he starts giggling and wiggling his bum. Fronk, "This isn't funny anymore." Then they both start to wiggle their bums. Rosetta passes by and notices them, she starts laughing and gets their attention.

Helena receives a message from the police officer who was out and about when he came across a man who was walking his pig, that gave him information of Prince Levi's assistant. Police officer, "Hello ma'am, how are you today? My name is Nae Nae, are you still looking for a friend that is lost?" Helena, Your honour, my name is Helena, and I certainly would like you to accompany me on this occasion," as she toys with him for attention. Nae Nae, "Why are you rolling your eyes, do you have something inside them." "Oh dear, Helena, you are indictable. I can't believe, first Fronk, now a police officer, please, my child you need to relax." Helena walks away as she is blushing. Nae Nae comes running up, and says under his breath "Maybe I'll give you some company." "Nae Nae, where are we heading for and are we going the same direction as to where king Levi is?" That point of departure was when there was an appearance by a she-wolf, "Hello young man, I could be of assistance if you show me the unknown village." Nae Nae, "I do apologise, but I'm going in the opposite direction." She-wolf just looked at him, "It's a shame, you would have been a good snack on the way," as she shows her shiny teeth. Nae Nae and Helena managed to disappear from her and make their way to find their missing friends. Helena, "Oh my goodness, what a relief, thought I was going to be someone's dinner. Fronk, "She's scary," as he was about to leave really quickly. At that point, a kitsune, as the fox came quickly towards Fronk, and stood in front of him.

The she-wolf looked up at the kitsune and said, "Ow! him, Tyra, I didn't know if it was you, is he with you?" Tyra, "Yes, he's my friend's friend." Damian, "Is it, Tyra? I've an idea. Why don't you try to make her an ally of our family, in case we need her help any time?" Tyra,

"What you are saying is a good idea, give me a few minutes. Wait here for me." She rushes to the she-wolf and gets talking to her. They cry out, laugh and hug one another and part ways. Fronk, "I'm guessing by the way you look, you have achieved this." Tyra, "Yes, you can say that but now she's going home so when we need her all I have to do is blow this whistle." She pulls out a blue whistle to show everyone, as she stood up tall to see if anyone was lurking around.

Nixon-Stain-Dexun, "Well, if you are looking for me, yes, I'm here for the next lesson in getting the King released. Follow me, but you need to be quick." He decides to hop off to the front. "Aww, look at him, doesn't he have the cutest face?" Unknown creature, "Who is he and why is he leading us?" Tyra, "Never judge a person by their appearance. He is a childhood friend of Prince Tobias." She looks like she's confused as to who is Prince Tobias. She looked at Prince Tobias and said, "Right, are you ready for the ride of your life, like back at school?" At that precise moment they both looked at each other and held on tightly together, then within seconds it powered into the sky so fast. From a distance Helena looked at the mist of the night and saw what looked like a spaceship, "Oh my, is that the Prince?"

It flew to the left and vanished into a cloud and disappeared. "Oh no, I need to do something. Hold on, guys." Helena threw something heavy on the cloud which would help them. Nixo-Stain-Dexun picked up a sword from the ground and turned to face Kulumbush and said, "I know what you are up to, please stop whatever you are doing with your evil mind or regret the consequences." Nixo just drew the sword at Kulumbush, not knowing what he had done to him and put the sword away to walk off.

At least both Prince Tobias and Takari had made it through the star without crumbling. As they had gotten through they heard a loud voice coming from overhead. They both jumped down and went towards the noise together. They looked into each other's eyes and were about to... Well, let's leave it for the readers to decide whether they were to kiss. As something was about to happen they were distracted by a sudden burst of laughter right in front of them. It was none other than King Levi. Prince Tobias, "Your Majesty what happened to you? How did you get up here and where have you been? Do you know Lunarnise is going out of her mind worrying?"

With Prince Tobias taking a breath as he said it too quickly, Takari wasn't there. She had gone off and moments later she returned with a smile and a bottle of water. Takari, "Here you go sir, please drink some water." Prince Tobias just looked up at her and nodded his head as he took the water and drank. He felt much better. King Levi looked at the young couple and said, "You guys look amazing together I see it in your eyes. Anyway, come let's go. I have one more challenge to complete, then I'm free."

"As a fountain of honour in Tiger Warth the sovereign has the sole rights to the titles of past and present Kings and Queens. And it's no surprise to everyone who it is you need to find Zanura. Remember that he is not easy to track. As some of the additions are to be passed down to the present king or queen, a test of honour is to be made for King Levi. With the best warriors in the world who are in, to be ready to be announced as King or Queen of Tiger Warth. First, he needs to show his courage to see how he would protect his own people from harm. King Levi do you accept this challenge?" Roland speaks in Zanura's absence.

"Hurry up, as it's going to get dark soon and it will be harder for you to maintain but at the same time could be a first as it's never been achieved." They're all standing on a part of the world that's floating above the clouds, like a giant waterfall that is used for challenges such as this. Zanura comes to save the day. Well, nearly night, as he brings with him an army of beavers to pretend to be knights who can move around quickly. King Levi, "How am I supposed to challenge them? I can't do this." Prince Tobias walks over to help King Levi and says, "Your Majesty, remember whose heart you hold, you need to believe in yourself to concur with your dreams."

King Levi walks over to the centre of the waterfall and picks up his crown, everyone else stops and wonders why he has done such an outrageous act. King Levi, "Hey dear fellow people, friends and family, I am here to announce that a battle is coming and we must prepare for the worst. Let's join together." As he takes his top off, his true identity is revealed and everyone is shocked by this and kneel in front of him to say, "We will stand by you, Your Majesty, you can count on us." Zanura, "This is an act of a great warrior. I'm sure you have been trained well. Whoever your trainer is, they should be proud of you." A dragon shows herself as she lands in a clear view and transforms into a great wizard. I, Roslin, am his trainer and he is one of my favourite pupils please take care of him and my pleasure is all yours, I have a gift of honour." Roslin then presents Zanura with a box. "This maybe opened after the ceremony is complete." Zanura, "You can count on me, my lady, can I pass on a message to Stimpultonnes in his absence?" Roslin, "There is no need as I'm going to return to my world now. You can tell him I am getting ready." She transforms into the dragon and flies off into the sea. With a little bit of magic she dives into the ocean, and sparks fires from the inside out into the sky like fireworks.

Now King Levi gets ready to head back to the castle to present the new friends their first mission. Prince Tobias, "What happened to Goldie? I thought she was with you." King Levi looks over at Prince Tobias, "I'm so sorry, she's never been with me. Maybe you should ask Aviana, she is the one who has gone to look for her." Prince Tobias then stood up and asked King Levi where he could find Aviana. King Levi, "You should be aware she's gone to the other side of the mountain." Roland takes a breath of air and says, "Myself and Zanura will go back to the castle, you both go and rescue the two."

King Levi jumps on Prince Tobias's back and they fly off into the darkness. Zanura and Roland get ready to go back to the castle with the troops, to wait for the king's first assignment. They all gather together to wait for a ride when unicorn comes with a caterpillar coach. She lands carefully and the caterpillar opens its door. All the troops look around first, enter the caterpillar and put their seatbelts on, as the unicorn begins its journey towards the castle. Suddenly there was a large white cloud that made a huge bang on the side of the trailer and sucked everyone into it, even unicorn, and vanished into the sky. Out of the darkness came Roland. He looked terrified at what he had seen, as he managed to escape from the hands of Ponsternose.

On the other side of the mountain Prince Tobias and Takari continued to make their way through the valley of dangerous creatures, where they found a small fluffy little creature that had been attacked. Takari shouts out to Prince Tobias, "Please my dear, come and see this little girl." Prince Tobias rushed from the other side to see the little girl and then said, "She will be safe with us now, put her on my back." They continue their journey to find Aviana and Goldie. Just then he gets a message that reads, 'we're closer than you know, but be careful with the guy that is standing in front of you.' Prince Tobias turned around and noticed a small Man bird who was looking at him. Prince Tobias, "Please take Fleecy so I can find out who he is?"

When Prince Tobias started to walk towards him, the Man bird looked as if he meant no harm and spoke, "I come in peace. I have been sent to give you some advice and help you win over Sir John and he's not Lunarnise's father." Prince Tobias looked in relief as he didn't want to fight him, he felt like he was more than just a messenger, as he came to sit on a rock near him. Takari could only watch in distress what was going on. The Man bird noticed this so he mentioned to Prince Tobias if he could bring his wife and master to hear what he was going to say.

Prince Tobias was shocked by what he said so he called out to Takari for both of them to join him. Prince Tobias, "Please Takari it is safe for you to join and sit down on the stall." He got up and sat down next to her. Man bird greeted them and said, "Let's go straight to the point, I am from the future and a dear friend to you all. I have come to warn you of this Sir John and how he can be destroyed. And only two people will be able to get him if they work together." Takari says, "I wonder who that may be?" As she continued to wait for answers the Man bird says, "Only the love of two people who are willing, stand a chance of destroying him, as he will become weak but only if it's true love." Man bird blesses both with his hands over their heads, "Okay, I have to go back now, please combine your powers, first find your love." He vanished right in front of them.

As they both were to get off the floor they accidentally fell into each other's arms and shared a kiss. Straightaway they both said, "This won't happen again," at the same time were embarrassed by their actions and carried on walking. Each of them was trying to check the other out, when they thought the other was not noticing. ("How is it that no one else has noticed before? This must be a big relief for you guys." Narrator become more interested in Prince Tobias as he seemed surprised about the whole thing.)

"I believe we should go this way through that building you see over there straight in front," Prince Tobias stepped forward to say. King Levi was tagging behind. King Levi, "As my outlaw, I should bless you guys," walks through with Fleecy, as the little fur ball was now shaking more than usual. "I guess we must be getting closer now but I'm suggesting that something bad happened, take a look at your little girl." Prince Tobias came up to the King and picked up the shaking little girl and not long after she started to relax and stopped shaking. Takari turned to look at him and said, "Daddy Prince," smiling at both of them "as if you were meant to be."

("Oh my, what is starting to happen with Prince Tobias?" As Jake and Sam are talking, they come to where he is, glitching, going invisible and then normal. Fleecy, "I, Sir, I knew this would happen," as she looked up from a furry ball. She stood on both of her feet, even though he was glitching he still looked at Fleecy and bowed. That made Fleecy feel good and she remembered how Prince Tobias's glitching was dealt with back in the training camp, so immediately she held him down to relieve his pressure. That seemed to work. He was able to get some rest with Fleecy watching over him, Takari comes running over and says, "Where did you come from? Oh wait, Fleecy right? Wow, is that you? But you seemed to be scared and curled up in a ball." "Your man was there for me, even after training him I was able to find him. So, you see, Takari, I also got my home village, and other ninjas killed apart from two of us and others, but I went to the north whereas he decided to go to the south." (Narrator looked and said, "What a sad story, but at least Fleecy will be safe now with Prince Tobias and Goldie especially when she is finally found.")

At that precise moment King Levi gets an unexpected call from an unknown person who says, "I think you should meet me. I have something in my possession. Come to the river bridge." The phone was hung up. King Levi gets ready to go to meet the unknown person, but then realises it could be a trap and with Prince Tobias away he goes to Roland and mentions it to him. Roland says he should call Helena back to guard the castle so he can follow him at a distance. King Levi agrees with Roland and tells him to do the honour of calling her. "Helena, please you are wanted back at the castle, orders of the King." Helena receives his message and responds that she is making her way to the castle. As she whistles, the unicorn comes to collect her and they begin to climb up the clouds towards the castle.

King Levi sees Helena and unicorn just coming through the gates so he prepares the carriage and two shy horses and gets into the carriage for his rider to take him to the bridge. With the rider in disguise as the one and only Roland, so he can keep an eye on the King. At the same time on the lower ground of the mountain, Prince Tobias and Takari follow on their path. They come across a group of sirens that surrounded them both. There was a sound, and a tall lady who stood overlooking said, "I have something that belongs to you. Alarei is my name, I'm the leader of the group, I will fight to see if you can claim the golden eagle." Prince Tobias was ready to take her on, when he remembered what he was taught and his sensei had shown him. "My child, please don't lose yourself, don't take action straight away." Fleecy looked at him and understood. She said, "I shall challenge you for Goldie. If I win, I want Aviana released too." Another girl walked up towards them to say something, "My name is Pasilia and I'm the second child. I'm here to let you know about this fight between my leader cousin and the challenger."

Atarei gets ready as she has night vision and as it's late in the afternoon, she holds both her hands up and moves forward with the face and opens her mouth showing fangs as sharp as steel. And the other two start playing a beautiful song to try and lure Prince Tobias into the water. Fleecy notices and rolls around her as she attacks the siren. They are all trying to lure him so they can drink his blood and eat his flesh. Fleecy begins a dance of calm and then the curse begins to break away from him. Just like that Fleecy wins over her old pupil so then Oraney comes over to present a cage with an eagle inside." Prince Tobias looks and says in his mind, 'Wake up girl, dad is here now.'

Chapter 14

The Quest that tells no tales!

Kulumbush sneaks into the night to visit the village innkeeper, who tells him that he is about to become the talk of the past, at which he becomes depressed. Due to a recent verbal encounter he finds himself in a strange situation. "Go speak with the man who put a bounty on your head." Within seconds the man begins to fade away. Kulumbush, "I didn't think anyone was talking to me." An unpleasant feeling of cold air ran down his body. He looks around to see if there was anyone else out there but didn't notice movement in the area. He continues to walk and decides to brush off the pain of make believe, he thought that it meant nothing to him. Nobody knew Sir John was behind it all. He couldn't have a clue of where these messages come from, it is as if they self-destruct afterwards.

King Levi has already galloped out of the yard and is following the rainbow path that was there when unicorn had arrived. Where's he going now? He is supposed to be in the castle, but instead he's outside, enjoying himself - an unexpected surprise from the vampire family. As he decides to move through the castle gates he sees his teeth open at him from the floor so he bends over to pick them up and puts them back into his mouth. At the same moment a young man walks up and asks him if he can help in his situation that would make him noticeable. 'Ha, ha yeah, he doesn't even know what he's getting himself into!'

From out of nowhere it looked like there were a lot of miniature creatures let loose as if they were running from something, of all shapes and sizes, different colours too. Fronk then came up to check out what was going on with the little people, "Hold on, I think I have seen you before. Wait, no, it can't be. You guys, there's more of you now."

They started talking in their own language so he wouldn't understand what was being said, "wu yu mamama, du bat a bat." Then what seemed to be a leader comes forth with three surrounding him on piglets in armour. And he looks up at Fronk and says, "It is quite possible young man, we are here on business. Could you please lead me to your newly appointed King?" Fronk looks at the leader of the miniatures' team and responds, "Okay, let's go follow me," blows the whistle and within minutes unicorn comes. But this time Fronk looks up at the sky as he notices there's many of them and in different colours and sizes, and the rest of them which don't seem to have a ride get onto the unicorns.

They all reach the same colourful path that Prince Tobias once used, "Oh, oh, I know this path, doesn't it leave a riddle for you to remember?" Kulumbush looked as if he was a little more puzzled. The triplets hanging around look very respectful and friendly but at the same time as cold as ice. They were asking for directions to a friend's place. And when the triplets looked up as they were talking about their friend they made sure that any sign of Spanish supernatural activity would be kept secret. What they did not know is that two of the triplets were blood sucking vessels and the girl was only eating fruits but she was able to keep it from her brothers.

Then as the elder brother was calling her she snuck into the dark eyes of the night. "Oh, little sister, where have you ran to? Don't worry, I will find you," says Dimitri. Unknown to them there were mermaids all around this area. Shelby heard a young girl and got her brother to look for her. While Vera was running away from her brothers she came close to the edge of the river. One of the mermaids was seen but noticed two vampires not far behind shouting at her. Immediately he popped his head out of the water and said, "Do you trust me?" then grabbed her quietly and quickly went back into the sea.

The pale, young woman began to look and lean on the water gentleman who held her down, to escape from the pain of her own brothers. She was becoming breathless and as she began coughing he acted quickly and kissed her to keep her warm and awake. Just then Vera regained consciousness and said, "Where are you taking me? My brothers will become wary of my absence." Moments later he told her that there's something amazing she needs to see, "Come, it's just right there, open your eyes." As she opened her eyes she saw a fairy that was swimming in the ocean, "Wait, the fairy looks familiar, do I know them?" She became worried, thinking that it could be Lunarnise. The mermaid looked at Vera and said, "Please don't tell anyone about this, there's only one or two that come here and no it's not her. Everyone else had vanished from their homes, so they come back here for comfort and no, there's no resemblance to Lunarnise and Prince Tobias before you ask me."

Jake came rushing over and informed the triplet sister had been taken away from her brothers. They wanted to do something bad to her. Shelby swam up to him, also explaining how she got her brother to help and kept her alive from the twins. The next minute she jumped up out of the water and started to walk away from him, thinking how to handle her brothers. It seemed they must have moved on to the next place, at the same time hadn't noticed their sister was gone and Vera sighed with relief. She started to dance around the moonlight, "What am I going to do now?" She picked up her feet towards the way where everyone else was standing in the distance.

Suddenly there was the appearance of a woman who looked like she had been searching for something that was lost. She turned to Vera before saying something like, "I am the cause for this resonation," then walked away in the distance. 'What that was about?' wondered Vera, as she got closer to the group of people who were sitting there, chatting. Rosetta heard the sound and ran to Vera, "Let's go," she said, "today you are my guest and Lunarnise will be around shortly to welcome you."

Vera went with Rosetta and said that she was exhausted and wanted to rest a bit until Lunarnise came so Rosetta showed her where to go. Lunarnise quickly flew to the ground and saw Rosetta, "Oh, hi girl, how are you, there's a young woman here staying with you but has a disturbing family. Please don't let the twins take her. She will continue with us as family. Reassure her and point her in the right direction to me. See you soon." Lunarnise was ready to leave when she hears something screaming in the distance, then a voice shouts, "Careful sweetie." Lunarnise wonders, 'Who would say my name like this? What if it could be my mother? No this is insane, she probably doesn't even know me."

As Lunarnise was looking around and chatting to her friends she had noticed someone walking towards them from the distance. Prince Tobias came quickly behind her to see what was happening and noticed Vera had a small black cape on, so he asked, "Are you from the unknown world?" She looked around to see him. She was surprised to find herself hanging upside down in a tree and replied, "Yes, I was right there when my brothers forced me to be this way, now they bully me, Sir," and closed her eyes. 'Sleeping upside down in a tree, is this behaviour normal?' Prince Tobias thought. 'Anyway, my sensei has always told me to be there for people no matter what, so here I am again.'

He looks up at Vera, picks her up, thank goodness it's dark, and takes her to Lunarnise's treehouse and puts her down in the darkest room to carry on sleeping, says quietly, "You are now safe in our family, I'll protect you." She carries on sleeping, hanging from the ceiling, and hearing her saviour she smiles. Prince Tobias carries on his journey to Goldie. Stimpultonnes and the rest of the crew finally arrive and they get together for a festival, there's laughter and singing along with a delicious meal. Kulumbush comes running over. "I've been attacked by two people," then collapses to the ground. Lunarnise stood up and said, "Let's see what happened to him."

Jake looks at Kulumbush, "Oh man, he has been bitten wait there's more, look his body's changing and there's more, half vampire and half werewolf. So, what has happened, a werewolf and vampire have both hunted him at separate places, his chances are slim." Lunarnise plays a violin to try and wake him up. Right before everybody's eyes a big bird came out of nowhere, picked him up and disappeared into the night.

"Oh my gosh!" said Lunarnise, "I've never seen anything like that creature before, and where did it come out of?" There's a lot of people here, some not even seen before, as far away from them there's thunderstorms coming. Goldie comes at a speed and Lunarnise jumped in the air to grab her. They both fell to the floor as they were hurt by lightning. Damian rushed and picked up both of them and gave them a hug as magic was protecting closely. So, third eye had to open up on Lunarnise's chest to help with what it now looks like Fluffy, as he licked her, and a tear went down on Goldie. So she looked around and called out for Prince Tobias. Lunarnise gets an unexpected visit from Shelby and she tells her that she saw her own mother at a glance, she was tall and beautiful like an angel.

As Shelby continues with the conversation and discovers a small box shining in the background, Lunarnise tries not to take her eyes off it even when it appears and disappears several times. Sterito, "Your Highness, my friend and good master, what should we do with this one?" Lunarnise tells him to wait until it returns and then catch it. Sterito takes a deep breath, walks up slowly and takes a look around him to see if the area is safe. Everyone around him starts clapping and cheering for him as he moves in closer and counters the minutes between each appearance and disappearance. He asks Roland to blindfold him. "Are you sure about this?" asks Jake. "Yes," he replies. Lunarnise blindfolded him and stepped back. Sterito then counted one, two, three and, opened his mouth and reached out for the object. He caught it as he fell to the floor with a huge bang. Out came a small man with his arms around his head who looked like a common thief as he walked out of the shore looking wetter than a leaf.

He turned around to see a small crowd of people, "Howdy, partner? My name is Caspian, I bet you have heard of me. I'm on a journey to find a lost soul. I've come across the oceans of Tatina that is taking everything around us. I have heard he passed through here, can anyone help me?" Someone from the crowd shouted over to him, "What is his name?" "Thomas," he said. Lunarnise quickly stepped out of the crowd and said, "I know him, but I also know a person called King Levi." Caspian paused and said wait, "You are confusing me brain cells. Who are we looking for?" "Hold on, here young man, weren't you asking about Thomas?" Stimpultonnes was scratching his head, "And where did he come from?" Sam looked down, confused with this situation, says, "Do you want me to help him out to his own feet?" then laughs as he continues on his way.

Caspian says to Lunarnise, "May I ask who I am speaking with at least?" Fronk jumps in and asks if he knows the person who he is speaking of, and how did he get here? "Well it is quite obvious there is a mis-communication between the languages of sea and land," says Caspian as he walks around looking for something in the trees.

Roland was very surprised to see him and then says, "Please join us for food." "Splendid!" Caspian took a moment to look back at his own life as it was all of a mix-up. Within minutes the river began to freeze over from where they were as everyone was gathered round a table to eat. The dark skies were still. Lunarnise looks strangely like she had seen it somewhere else, but the truth that it's Odin is yet to be revealed as it's her father. He can turn into almost anything and make you freeze from inside so it only makes the heart melt, it will take just a few hours and you disappear into a million pieces.

"Well, I'm sure it's believed to be just a myth to scare people into thinking and getting rid of their own bodies. With the exception of those who are already living and working in poverty they should not worry about calling out people they shouldn't. But if you're going through this and you don't want to be seen by the Gods, then it's most likely not going to happen if you don't commit a crime. In fact, as we are talking there's another explosion beneath the horizon, as the world slowly shakes like a wave so powerful it blows you away from where you are."

Lunarnise was just flying around when she collapses into the darkest of the universe. This place hasn't been used in decades, what happened next is unbelievable. Takari was the only one around at the time so she did an unusual thing. Dropping the shining box was one thing but it all depended upon her so in seconds she jumped into the dark and started running fast. As she wanted to find Lunarnise and bring her back home. 'Which way was it again?' she whispered. At that precise moment, an unusual head appeared from nowhere.

Prince Tobias, felt something inside. He said, "Something isn't right but what could it be after an earthquake? My sister has disappeared."

Stimpultonnes turned up in a cart and looked at Prince Tobias and said as he though was speaking from the clouds, but was only in front of him. "I do apologise Your Highness, I wasn't aware my actions would drag someone in." Just then there was howling in the background and shouting all around, "I know who this is - Atchon and his werewolves." As he was saying it, the wolfs were howling in front and Atchon was nowhere to be seen. "I wonder what he's now at. He was seen dragging a body in the deep of the forest."

Fronk was screaming as he was being dragged away. "Oh no, what do I do now?" says Dillon. It was as if lightning got him. Something was helping him as he took the powers temporally and dived into the woods. He was seen by a group of men who were standing on a rock when he passed by and was elegant with the night shining bright like the stars. Fronk was being taken farther inside by the rock of a man as Atchon approached the rock through a secret passage. There was a small gust of wind blowing through in his direction as Dillon held up his arms and pulled Fronk from behind the stone, as Atchon went in without his accomplice.

Lucky for him, he could have been taken to the slaughter room to be made a new member of his team. "Oh, and how do I pay my gratitude to, oh hi buddy, how are you doing with your training?" says Fronk. "Who would think that anyone could forget about this, I'm imagining the next world's most important individual." As they both looked at each other in a different light and thought, "Hold up, who's this, oh wait, it's the Narrator of this story, how would you not know that?" He stood up straight and spoke with an electric field around his body, "Dillon is my name, playing is my game," in a deep voice and sighed. Even as Fronk had walked away from the door after being saved, he was still vulnerable to the forest's deep eye monster.

They weren't as lucky with the new ability that Dillon had acquired from an unknown source and there was someone else who could have his attention. Prince Tobias had been able to find out what was lurking behind the trees. It was only after there was someone else who was trying to claim Fronk, over the other side, where three doors appeared. They dropped out of the sky from nowhere and were coloured red, white and blue. "What do we do now?" Fronk stood to the side and cried out. A voice reached out to say, "Wait, I am on my way for them to get accessed by my pets," as Stimpultonnes got closer, along with three pigeons. "They will go in each door to see who shall survive. If it goes to plan we shall be able to make it through one of these three. Right pigeons, are you sure you want to do this?" They all nod. "Okay, in you go." So, they move in towards the doors, look at each other then one of them opens and out comes an unusual creepy looking creature. Suddenly looks up at Prince Tobias who was standing next to Fronk, shocked, when it spoke, "Père - oh my, dear brother you're a man now - what I mean is you're a father."

One disappeared into thin air from the middle, but it appears the remaining two are safe. "Is everybody ready?" shouted Sam. The two birds went into the other doors to see what would happen, but one flew out faster than you could say goodbye. And the remainder went farther away from his master so Prince Tobias went in to fetch him, but the farther he went the more inside he was. Prince, "Please come here. I am stuck in the dark side of the road and there's nothing here apart from buildings all around." Prince Tobias thought he was saving the bird. "Oh, Your Majesty, stop!" shouts egg as she pushed away the unknown man pretending to be bird. He looks up and grabs bird and throws her out to the skies as it looks many are above, but she was saved by a flying dragon.

"Wait, Damian where did you come from?" Lunarnise jumped out of the sky to grab her and then she went back through it again.

Chapter 15

The Capture of Sir John!

Narrator, "It all started when Damian was flying in the first light as there's nothing but silence in his presence so he was able to move to the vibes. As I stood in front of the waterfall and watched him fly away quickly as if something had happened, someone was shouting out, "Prince Tobias, Prince Tobias." My Lord have you heard? As a stream of fire was running down an old man's entire body, a young girl and her husband were taken away through the streets of the trees."

The old man stood about 50 yards from him. Anxious who it would be, as Prince Tobias was only 200 metres away he said, "Let's go." And while he was there the light from the fire was dazzling with bright blue eyes that were coming and going frequently. "That's strange," said Prince Tobias promptly. "I looked up and was astonished to see that we could have another journey into a new world to save our beloved ones. I am more egalitarian as to why I had been approached by the old flaming man out of nowhere." There was thunder and lightning in the background.

Fronk was in the background of the scene when he saw a young girl standing there all alone looking sad. A voice came from behind in the darkness which said, "Don't fall for the trap." He felt a little sorry for her but then moved on. As he was walking away from her, he saw Lunarnise and couldn't help thinking about the little girl, 'who is that person in a blue suit?' An old man who was in the middle of the road approached Roland with flames as bright as the sun, rose to the sky and back with a smile and a soft voice, "I am Sir John from the future." "Oh no," Stimpultonnes, "I think he is here to worry and confuse everyone, so why should we believe this man?"

Jake looks at his bag around the waist, as Sam pulls out his stick once again. He noticed that they were being hassled by the older Sir

John. The man turned back to the others and gave such a big grin and as he vanished into the crowd, never to be seen again as the water shook. Stimpultonnes then walked over, "He has just been seen planting a seed in the ground to make sure it doesn't fall, anyway I think it's time for a new challenge."

Unicorn came running down the rainbow from above with a message that says, 'Please come and find me and Lunarnise. We are somewhere you wouldn't have least thought.' And then it was that everyone else who was there gathered around, right before they were about to leave to get their friends and unexpected guest appearances. Standing there all elegant and beautiful was Shelby, "Well, hello everyone, you may be wondering how did I know, plus where did I come from? Well if you like to know, I am a..." As she was about to tell people that her identity is a mermaid, she was distracted by a girl who looked lost in the woods.

A distinguished blonde with dark skin was the only girl who was seen around, running and picking up flowers. "I am the Granddaughter of the greatest Medusa." Stimpultonnes stopped what he was doing and gazed down at her, wondering what he had heard, as she looked around and carried on walking away. Fronk had been traumatised by what he had seen, his body went into shock mode for a moment before he fell to the ground. He regained consciousness after a short while and said, "I have read the stories of Medusa, I just didn't know it existed. I'm shocked. What powers does she possess?"

Roland was very confused by what Fronk had said. "I believe it is just fictional, nothing to worry about, my friend." Fronk looked very much like he wanted to hug him but instead he just responded with, "Thank you for telling me this, I feel much better now," and reached out to grab Jake's hand to get to his feet, smiling at him afterwards.

As Prince Tobias was still flying in the sky on the lookout for Lunarnise and King Levi, there was a huge wave coming from the other direction. So, he stopped to take charge of the situation, and as he was about to stop time, a young woman came to him and asked for help. She looked up and saw it was Prince Tobias. She gave such an expression and said quietly, "I will get you this time, oh man, when I finish with you nobody else will have the time of day for you." Then gives out such a huge laugh and just like that, the wave was frozen in time just like Prince Tobias freezes everything. Something magical happened - Shelby swam up shining like a star. She wasn't the only one, there were others. A powerful voice rose from the water that Prince Tobias heard as he walked near to the edge. "What a wonderful voice!" he said. Something came up closer underneath the surface of the water and was looking at him, the way it looked was sad. "I'm sure there's a reason why the creature has been told to come to us," Prince Tobias said, as he looked down at the surface of the ocean. He started talking as if it understood. Then the creature sang and shined through the water and swam back to the bottom of the sea. Prince Tobias looked puzzled and said, "We need to help them."

As he was saying that, the creature swam down quickly as if he were going to strike it. It screamed loudly like a bird. Prince Tobias was standing there and was about to take to the skies in search for Lunarnise and King Levi when Goldie found him. She looked down at him, heard the noise from under the water and made a sound such that the creature went quiet. Prince Tobias looked at her, "What did you say, it went silent?" Goldie said that creature was in pain but, "I mentioned I needed to go and find someone first and would come back and help, so he agreed. I will be back shortly."

Prince Tobias then turns to his friend who goes to the next leaf of bedding and lies on it and speaks in a polite manner. "How do you know that?" As Goldie was about to let him know she starts getting interrupted and flies off quickly, shouting down to him on her way, "You need to follow me now, and I'll explain it to you later, this is impossible we're going to go for a ride, hold on to your hats." Goldie is then pulled into a whirlpool of water through the sky with it looking colourful at night as the sun continues to sleep. Goldie continues into the night as she has been tipped off with the whereabouts of Lunarnise and King Levi. Gliding through, there's a noise. It was as if someone had planned this, she was so peaceful as she was going towards looking for both her friends - what could it be? Goldie was trying to see where the noise was coming from as she was flying, it was if the noise was getting farther and farther away. (Narrator, "I think someone is playing a trick on Goldie. Sam, please try and keep an eye on her we wouldn't want anything to happen to the bird now. Let's not waste any time shall we?" Designer, "Hold on, Prince Tobias, good evening, watch out something else is out there, maybe it could be a trap.") As they were talking to each other there was something else, it was spying on both Goldie and Prince Tobias. Takari came up to see what was happening.

Fronk noticed that there was a creature lurking in the background, he decided to go closer and check it out. 'Oh my,' he said to himself, 'could it be the unicorn?' The unicorn had seen him, grabbed him and flew away. While flying away from the scene he hit his head on the tree making him unconscious, he doesn't know what is going on.

There was an explosion in the area which turned out to be a distraction for Lunarnise. She's still missing. An old man buried something and vanished. Stimpultonnes was standing there close by to see what had happened but didn't see any signs of digging in the area until after he disappeared as he noticed shining in the dark. But no one bothered to check it out as they thought it would be someone from the campsite that was just outside with a torch. Jake did mention to Stimpultonnes, "What ever happened to Kulumbush? I don't think nobody knows of his whereabouts. Do we know anything yet about Lunarnise or King Levi? I think Goldie is searching for them and I believe she may be closer than we think." While they were talking, Damian comes running in, having landed quickly, "Where's my little eagle, Goldie?" Again, he rushes off in the air. He was acting like a baby as he was dancing on his way, someone looked up and says, "Oh come on now, there's Fluffy." He was flying so fast that he nearly didn't notice Goldie, then he saw her and noticed that she was more cheerful. "I must be getting closer now."

Thunder and lightning hitting through the sky as though something was going to happen.

It was moments later they were firing lightning balls headed towards them. "What do we do now, Goldie?" cries out Fluffy. "I know, I've got a plan and it's being seen on TV." A second later, lasers were firing from the air. Fronk appears on the back of a unicorn and gets out a shield to protect them against the blasting lightning, then holds it up and shoots it back after a long wait. The blast stopped. It could've been a distraction or, it's something that Sir John is trying to do.

Kulta was walking around, purring, up and down and around different people, trying to find if Lunarnise was actually missing. Until she spotted something unusual. She couldn't believe her eyes as she thought Lunarnise was in the background. Then from out of nowhere she sees the light beneath the clouds so she ran into hiding. Stimpultonnes turned to Kulta, "Was that?...." he paused. He took a great look at the girl, that is Aelia, 'What's happened with her all these years?' he said quietly to himself. At that point he was so proud to have met her in a short period of time, even though not getting to say anything. She looked elegant, as she ran away.

Roland came up without a glimpse into the early morning as the sun was still rising from his sleep. He spoke to an unknown person who was casually walking through the garden. Everyone saw or heard the noise from in the woods, so they all came out to see what was coming down when a voice said, "It's okay you can go back to your rooms now, there's nothing else to see."

Without a doubt there's something lurking outside of the schoolyard and not far away from Lunarnise's treehouse. "Whoever it may seem to be can create a bad atmosphere, but I would like to get to the bottom of this, regardless," says Stimpultonnes, "as it's scaring people." With little of what they know, it's Sir John, as he is trying to lay a plan for the future so people wouldn't recognise. He has just been noticed standing at the back of the tree. He changes from a troll not thinking anyone is watching him. What he didn't know is that Fronk was watching him and he wasn't the only one looking. She-wolf walking around, noticed something unfamiliar. She wanted pounce on him there and then but Shelby came and said to her, "There will be a time and place, you can kill him, just be patient." She-wolf started to relax and sit back instead. "I shall set my boundaries till the day I can get him for what he did to my family," she said.

By the manner Prince Tobias looks over at the upcoming person from the distance it was like he had met him before. Prince wore a brown suit as he shape-shifted back to his normal appearance. From nowhere a golden egg fell to the floor out of the sky, it appears to be the same jewel as was lost long ago to the evil Klang. "This was not the time to be afraid," Fronk, as he stood watching him from a distant window. "What am I supposed to be doing by the way?" as he looked around for Stimpultonnes. As Prince Tobias went for the egg, Takari shouted out, "Don't go there, it's a trick," running fast like the wind to get to her lover. Jake, "Wait, how did she to know who she's here to look for, what if she gets the wrong person? This is Takari we are talking about here, don't forget that." He was only a short walk away, when an old man was standing in front of Takari.

Right in front of the old man Prince Tobias stood, after swinging down from the trees, and turned around as he noticed a she-wolf coming in. Soon as he turned back to the old man, old as he is, he immediately grabbed Prince Tobias around his neck, held him high, and threw as hard as he could before changing into the form of the Devil. Prince Tobias flew away in the air and bounced into a wall near a crowd of people. Sir John was getting ready to jump into the air to hit him with force. The she- wolf cries out loud as she races towards Sir John and knocks him away clearly. Prince Tobias manages to get to his feet in time as Sir John falls down just inches away, then grows big, turning red and looks at his opponent only to hit him on his left shoulder. Prince Tobias takes a stumble to the ground only to move his leg as he swipes at Sir John with his knee. When Prince Tobias takes a shot at his opponent in the head, he only moves to push the wall towards him trapping Prince Tobias. He takes a shot to jump over to him as he growls repeatedly, Prince Tobias manages to avoid him by pulling the ball over his opponent.

Just before Prince Tobias gets to his feet once again he turns to see she-wolf on the other side of the building ready to pounce. A little bit later Sir John comes back to charge again with a big growl leaping up to gain some speed, hitting Prince Tobias on his head. Knocking him off the wall and then picking him up and throwing his arms up and down on him. As he was doing this, the she-wolf growled and hit Sir John so hard that he fell to the ground with an almighty bang. The way it was done she allowed sometime before he got up again. Without her noticing something fell and nearly hit Prince Tobias. He had to move quickly so it didn't get to him. As Sir John got to his feet Prince Tobias grabbed a part of the wall and hit it at Sir John who was standing there, dazed. Hits him again with a broken window as Sir John hits through the glass, then Prince Tobias grips his arm and bends it at the same moment. Sir John grabs the window to hit him repeatedly. Sir John growled louder as he pushed him away to the side when Prince Tobias rolled over and tried to catch his breath.

Sir John turns around again only to try and hit him repeatedly once more with the broken window. He sees he is growling. Then turns to throw broken window at Prince Tobias but misses so Prince Tobias jumps through the air and uses it to climb up. Sir John comes running towards Prince Tobias. Prince Tobias gets all his energy with a little sparkle into his feet to double kick his opponent's head and knocks him into the ground. He jumps down, kicks him several times, grabbing his head and hitting it to the floor. Sir John growls and grabs him at his knees and hits him that sends Prince Tobias rolling over again.

Sir John comes up picking up the rock at his side, throwing it towards Prince Tobias. He misses as the Prince slivers out of the way. With Sir John jumping out of the sky to hit him, his opponent moves to the side grabbing him round the neck, double kicking him in his shin. Sir John throws him to the skies. As he is thrown she-wolf waits for Prince Tobias grab him so he doesn't fall and get hurt, as she makes sure they both fall hard and tumble over and over. Prince Tobias was on the floor as he looked up at her and nodded. This was a way of respecting both prides, at that point Sir John ran over just as he was about to grab Prince Tobias. She-wolf turns around quickly without thinking and bites Sir John's head off clean from his body, but within seconds his head relocated to his body. Both, she-wolf and Prince Tobias, look at one another in surprise, that instant Prince Tobias gets a plan and a sparkle in his eyes. Sir John is panting. "Quickly," shouts she-wolf, "he is losing energy. Move now before he recharges himself." Prince Tobias slides underneath him silently and uses his eyes to strike him. Instead of scaring him, it makes him split into half as blood is pouring out of every angle of his body. At that instant his eyes come back to normal and he drops to the ground. After that Stimpultonnes comes over and thanks Prince Tobias and she-wolf, "I'm happy for both of you, you've done it, you have unleashed the powers that were needed as Sir John took them from us."

Right after the big fight Lunarnise and King Levi came running off the carriage that just jolted down from the clouds to see what was happening. King Levi turned to she-wolf as she looked with her head down and her two paws spread out in front. With blood dripping down her face as she looked towards Prince Tobias, it was only then Lunarnise had noticed she must have saved her brother. Lunarnise turned to the she-wolf and thanked her for saving Prince Tobias and made her the king's pet right in front of King Levi. He turned to look and agreed. "Your Majesty, I do apologise for this as I have been hurting for a long time with how he attacked my family and slaughtered them. And then to see how he was going to get Prince Tobias I acted quickly, as no one's given me respect the way he treated me. Lunarnise come, I heard you can heal. He's resting over here out of sight, his paw's got something in it." Lunarnise agreed and followed her. Moments later she arrived where Prince Tobias was lying, she moved quickly and then her third eye woke up. Lunarnise started crying. As she cried, a tear dropped on his paw and her chest started to shine so brightly, without a doubt his paw started to look and feel like new.

And Lunarnise lay there to regain her strength as the eye slowly closed. King Levi sat on the chair and watched over her as Prince Tobias was called by Goldie. He said to King Levi, "I have to go but I'll be as quick as I possibly can." She-wolf says, "Your Majesty I want to go and return to help, it will be great for my training." The King agreed, "Prince Tobias will bring you back home when all is good." Prince Tobias changes back to his Gryphon form and says, "Are you ready? Jump on." Then they fly into the sky. Few minutes after they flew into the sky there was unpleasant noise coming from outside. "Hold on Prince Tobias, did you forget something?" King Levi started to get closer towards the crowd. Only to find it wasn't him, it was Atchon and his dogs and vampires, then there was an unusual voice, "I am here for the child." Kulumbush, "Is that you and what happened? You're half vampire and half werewolf," as Lunarnise, Takari and Takari came running.

Lunarnise's next Journey

The Reincarnation of Cynthia

Two years later after defeating Sir John, Lunarnise and her gang cruise out on another world warming adventure. A young free lady as she continues to meet all kinds of creatures along the way.

Meanwhile, a struggle between friendship, jealousy has been weakened dangerously by the curses of the wicked, gift of love is what keeps them alive with the mean losing control. Zyran, Eryx, Dimitri, Delythena and lastly Vera are the siblings that were stepped on and forgotten by Prince Tobias that come to revenge the triumph that had overthrown their village long ago now come to claim Tiger Warth.

Pegasus reappears and cannot be ignored as it was once Tobias, he's back to shine the light along with new friends, with Atchon to make a deal with the quintuplets to try and capture Prince Tobias. Lunarnise's strength grows even more as she gives everything in her power to save her sister, with the help of the King and Rosetta. From an old ally, Kulumbush, who has been controlled by an evil Cynthia. And learns that Lunarnise has a twin called Aelia who will have the power between them to defeat the Antagonists.

And there's an unwanted, retired God that appears as a Shepherd, who has been sent secretly by their own father to send Lunarnise and one good person, on an underwater adventure to look for a woman called Shelby to go and rescue a child from an evil clan. Later to find out that the child will become a powerful God that will live between good and evil.

Sally-Anne & Jovan Matthews are the authors of these upcoming novelties called Lunarnise Pestra. They were born in the United Kingdom, and are from Leicester. They both go to school and have been inspired by their Father, Paul Matthews, and JK Rowling.

The two of them are new authors, with faith that they will gain fans and become popular. They like to help different kinds of people, just a friendly smile goes an extra mile, so pass it on and be safe.

Please feel free to check the information on their website or Wikipedia.

https://sallyannematthews2.wixsite.com/my-site

Feel free to message them here:

Sallyannematthews23@gmail.com

LUNARNISE PESTRA SERIES

Lunarnise Pestra

Book 1 - Caged with the Sprits

Book 2 - Reincarnation of Cynthia Book1 - Into the Cave of the Arachne.

Book 3 - Prince of a Golden egg

Book 4 - Into the Cave of the Arachne.

Book 5 - Welcome to the unknown world

Book 6 - The Princess of time is Calling.

Book 7 - Spin off: Takari and the Tribe of Yeti's

Book 8 - The tale of two Statue Dragons

Book 9 - Powers of Kingdoms and War

Book 10 - The Last Straw

Milton Keynes UK
Ingram Content Group UK Ltd.
UKHW030947071224
452128UK00011B/533

9 781835 383230